A
PLAGUE
YEAR

A

PLAGUE

YEAR

Edward Bloor

Alfred A. Knopf
NEW YORK

THIS IS A BORZOI BOOK PUBLISHED BY ALFRED A. KNOPF

Visit us on the Web! www.randomhouse.com/teens

Educators and librarians, for a variety of teaching tools, visit us at
www.randomhouse.com/teachers

Library of Congress Cataloging-in-Publication Data
Bloor, Edward.
A plague year / Edward Bloor. — 1st ed.
p. cm.
Summary: A ninth-grader who works with his father in the local supermarket describes the plague of meth addiction that consumes many people in his Pennsylvania coal mining town from 9/11 and the nearby crash of United Flight 93 in Shanksville to the Quecreek Mine disaster in Somerset the following summer.
ISBN 978-0-375-85681-5 (trade) — ISBN 978-0-375-95681-2 (lib. bdg.) —
ISBN 978-0-375-98937-7 (ebook) — ISBN 978-0-375-84609-0 (pbk.)
[1. Methamphetamine—Fiction. 2. Drug abuse—Fiction. 3. Junior high schools—Fiction.
4. Schools—Fiction. 5. Supermarkets—Fiction. 6. United Airlines Flight 93 Hijacking Incident,
2001—Fiction. 7. Coal mines and mining—Pennsylvania—Fiction. 8. Coal mine accidents—
Pennsylvania—Fiction. 9. Pennsylvania—Fiction.] I. Title.
PZ7.B6236Pl 2011
[Fic]—dc22
2010050651

The text of this book is set in 11.25-point Goudy Old Style.

Printed in the United States of America
September 2011
10 9 8 7 6 5 4 3 2 1

First Edition

For Amanda

Frosty the Snowman knew the sun was hot that day.

So he said, "Let's run, and we'll have some fun

Before I melt away."

4

I wrote a journal last year, but it got destroyed. A lot of things got destroyed last year. So this is my best shot at bringing that journal back to life. It was supposed to cover one school year. Instead, it covers one of the most devastating things that can happen to a people, and to a place—a plague year.

—Tom Coleman, March 27, 2002

Newsweek—Anytown, USA, can be turned into a meth den almost overnight. Take Bradford County in northeast Pennsylvania, a place law-enforcement officials nationwide now refer to as "Meth Valley." Five years ago a meth cooker from Iowa named Les Molyneaux set up shop in Towanda, a town of 3,000 along the Susquehanna River. Hardly anyone in Towanda had heard of the drug, but by the time Molyneaux was arrested and pleaded guilty in 2001 to conspiracy to manufacture meth, he'd shared his recipe with at least two apprentices. From there, "it just spread like wildfire," says Assistant U.S. Attorney Christopher Casey. Today police have identified at least 500 people who are using or cooking the drug in Bradford County, and the actual tally is probably "significantly worse" than that, Casey says. The drug has seduced whole families and turned them into "zombies," says Randy Epler, a police officer in Towanda. "I see walking death."

September

Monday, September 10, 2001

I was staring through the window of Dad's van when I saw the shopping cart, stranded like a lost dog at the corner of Sunbury Street and Lower Falls Road. The green plastic trim and the white Food Giant logo identified it as one of ours. Maybe a customer had wheeled it, illegally, to a house around the corner, unloaded it, and then wheeled it back to that spot in an effort to say, *I didn't really steal this. I was just borrowing it. You can have it back now.*

Whatever. It wouldn't be there for long. Bobby Smalls would pass this way in ten minutes. He would spot the cart and then comment bitterly about the person who had left it there, since he'd have to retrieve it as his first job of the day.

Dad turned right and our van bumped across the dark expanse of blacktop in front of the supermarket. The Food Giant sign was still in its low-wattage setting, glowing like a rectangular night-light for the town of Blackwater. Dad is the general manager of this Food Giant, and he spends most of his waking life there. Although it was still an hour before opening and the lot was empty, he backed our Dodge Caravan into an outer space—a requirement for all employees. He asked, "Do you want me to leave it running, Tom?"

"No. I'll just open a window."

"Okay. I'll leave the keys in case you change your mind. I'll be about fifteen minutes, provided the system is up."

I yawned, "Okay," and lowered the electric window before he could turn the key.

Plan A was that Dad would drive me to school, which meant I would get there way early, before anybody, which meant that no one would see me being dropped off by a parent. This was infinitely better than plan B.

In plan B, Mom would drop me off later, in front of everybody, which meant that I might as well be wearing a yellow patrol boy vest and carrying a Pokémon lunch box.

But first we'd had to stop at the Food Giant because the Centralized Reporting System had been down the night before, so Dad hadn't been able to input all his sales figures, reorders, et cetera, and send them to the corporate office. In theory, he would input those figures now, and we would be gone before the opening shift arrived at 6:45.

I watched him walk across the large, rolling parking lot. The Food Giant was built, like much of Blackwater, on the uneven landscape of Pennsylvania coal country. If a shopping cart got away from you in this lot, it could roll for fifty yards, building up to a speed of twenty miles per hour before it crashed into a parked vehicle. That could do some serious damage, as any cart retriever would tell you.

Dad disabled the alarm, unlocked the automatic doors, and slipped inside. I opened my PSAT prep book, hoping to get in a few minutes of study time.

But that was not to be.

First, I looked up and saw Bobby's mother drop him off, fifteen minutes early, as usual. He was wearing his green Food Giant slicker in case of rain. (Bobby was always prepared. The Boy Scouts just said it; Bobby lived it.) After listening impatiently to some final words from his mother, he pushed away from the Explorer and started walking back toward Sunbury Street and that abandoned cart. Mrs. Smalls drove on to her job at the Good Samaritan Hospital.

Then, just as I had returned to my book, a louder engine sound disturbed me.

A black tow truck, driving too fast, bounced across the parking lot and took a hard left at the ATM. Its high-mounted headlights flashed right into my eyes. Then the driver killed the lights and backed up to the front of the store.

A man in a hooded sweatshirt and a black ski mask jumped out on the passenger side. He reached into the back of the truck and rolled out a metal hook so large that I could see it clearly from two hundred feet away. He wedged the hook into a slot in the ATM and gave the driver a hand signal. The truck lurched forward, creating a god-awful sound.

I was now sitting bolt upright and staring at them. They were trying to rip the ATM out of the wall and make off with it— steal the whole thing and crack it open later for the cash inside.

Suddenly, to my right, I saw a figure approaching. It was Bobby Smalls. He came running back clumsily in his green rain slicker, without the cart. He started waving his arms and shouting at the robbers.

I thought, *Oh no, Bobby. Not now! Keep away from them!* I slid over into the driver's seat and grabbed the steering wheel, trying to think what to do. I started pounding on the horn, making as big a racket as I could.

The driver, dressed in the same type of dark disguise, stepped out of the truck. He was holding a strange object. It took me a few seconds to realize what it was—a compound bow. He then produced a feathered arrow, nocked it, and aimed it right at Bobby's short, advancing body.

The beeping horn got Dad's attention. He appeared behind the glass in the entranceway, looking bewildered. He pulled the door open and stepped outside, holding out one hand toward Bobby like a traffic cop trying to get him to halt.

The bowman changed his aim from Bobby to Dad and then back again. Was he going to shoot one of them? Or shoot one, reload, and get the other? Or was he just trying to scare them?

I couldn't take the chance. I cranked the car key and hit the gas pedal. The old van roared like an angry lion. I yanked at the gearshift, still revving the engine, and dropped it into drive. The van took off with a squeal of spinning tires and rocketed across the parking lot.

The bow-and-arrow guy turned toward me and froze like a deer caught in the headlights. Then he aimed the bow right at me. I thought, *Can an arrow pierce the windshield?* He must have asked himself that same question and decided it could not. He lowered his weapon, tossed it into the cab, and climbed back into the driver's seat.

I continued to accelerate toward the truck, closing the gap quickly, like I was going to ram it. (Honestly, I had no idea what I was going to do.) By now, the other man had unhooked the cable and had scrambled inside the cab, too.

The truck lurched forward and drove right at me, like in a deadly game of chicken. I hit the brakes and steered to the right, throwing the van into a wild skid, stopping just feet away from the frozen-in-place figure of Bobby Smalls.

The tow truck continued across the parking lot and shot across Route 16, accelerating away into the darkness.

I turned off the van's engine, threw open the door, and hopped out.

Suddenly everything was quiet.

Dad came running from his spot by the door. He had a frantic look in his eyes. He started waving his hands back and forth to get Bobby's attention. "Bobby! Bobby, are you okay?"

Bobby didn't answer. He was fumbling around under the

green plastic slicker. He pulled out a cell phone and held it up. "I got to call my mom."

Dad nodded. His face was perspiring. "Yes. Yes." He turned to me. "And you, Tom? Are you okay?"

"Yeah. Sure."

"That was smart thinking—honking the horn like that."

"Thanks."

"But driving right at them? Where they could shoot you? Not so smart."

"I thought they were going to shoot Bobby. And you."

Dad looked at me curiously, like the second part of that had never occurred to him. "Me?" He shook all over, like he'd had a sudden chill. "Well, thanks, then."

Bobby was now angry at his phone. His stubby fingers had punched in the wrong number. He was about to dash it to the ground when Dad stepped forward and calmly took it away. "I'll call your mother, Bobby."

Dad quickly pressed some phone keys. Bobby seemed confused. "You know her number?"

"Sure. I call her all the time."

"You do?"

"Yeah."

"Why?"

"To tell her what a good job you're doing."

Bobby's eyes widened upon hearing the praise. He loved praise. He thrived on it.

Dad spoke into the phone. "Hello, Mrs. Smalls? It's Gene Coleman at the Food Giant. Yes. Yes, Bobby's okay. But we've had an . . . an incident here, an attempted robbery. Bobby helped to chase the robbers away."

Dad listened for a moment. It seemed like he was getting an

earful. "Sure. Sure, I understand. We'll probably be outside by the front door." He hung up and told Bobby, "Okay. Your mother's on her way."

"What for?"

"To check to see that you're all right."

"I'm all right."   .

"I know. She just wants to make sure. Can I use your phone to call the police?"

"Yeah. Go ahead."

Dad called 911 and spoke to an operator. I craned my head forward to make eye contact with Bobby. I asked him, "What were you thinking there, dude? You could have gotten killed."

Bobby answered loudly, impatiently, as if the answer was obvious. "They're thieves!"

"Yes, they're thieves. I'll bet they're murderers, too. I'll bet they'd have murdered you if you'd gone a step closer."

"I'm not afraid of stupid thieves!"

"He had a bow and arrow, Bobby. That's a deadly weapon. You should be afraid of that. All you had was your cell phone."

"If they're so brave, why are they wearing ski masks and covering up with hoods? They're just thieves, that's all. Stupid thieves!"

Five minutes later, the police and Mrs. Smalls arrived, at the same moment, from opposite directions.

Two police officers got out of the car and split up. One interviewed Dad, Bobby, and me. The other examined the ATM and walked around the lot, looking for evidence.

I told the police officer what I knew, trying to sound no-nonsense and coplike: "It was a black tow truck. It didn't say anything on the side. Two men were in it. They had ski masks on. They had a homemade bow. They had at least one arrow. They took off when I drove at them. They went out the same way they came in."

Bobby gave a much more spirited account of what had happened, and of how stupid the two thieves were.

Mrs. Smalls took Bobby's pulse, temperature, and blood pressure right there in the parking lot, much to his annoyance. She seemed satisfied with the results, but she did explain to my dad, "Bobby's system is delicate, Mr. Coleman. It's all part of Down's syndrome. He may appear to be fine, but that can be deceiving. He can't take too much stress. Down's patients are very susceptible to heart attacks and strokes."

My dad nodded solemnly. "Yes, ma'am. You do what you have to do with Bobby. Take him home for a rest if he needs it."

Bobby threw up his hands in frustration, so his mother quickly added, "No. That won't be necessary. But no more excitement today, Bobby. Okay? You take it slow today."

Bobby grumbled, "Yeah, I'll take it slow." He pointed to the store. "I'll be like Reg the Veg today. I'll take it slow. Real slow."

The sun was now rising behind the store. By seven, the back parking spaces started to fill in with employees from the early shift. Gert, the head baker, marched straight to the front door, with barely a sideways glance at us or the cops. So did Walter from customer service. Mitchell, the head of the meat department, veered over our way and slowed down to listen, but he never really stopped.

Uno did, though. He's the assistant manager, and in charge of opening up. He looked at my dad and held his hands out wide, as if to say, *What gives?*

Reg the Veg stopped, too. He's the produce manager. He pointed at the police car and whispered hoarsely, "WTF, man?"

I replied, "Robbery attempt. On the ATM."

11

Reg started hollering, at no one in particular, "WTF, man! WTF!"

Uno, whose name is really John Rollnick, was a little more focused. "Did anybody get hurt, Tom?"

"No." I added, "But Bobby could have. My dad, too. The robbers were ten yards away from them, and they had a compound bow."

Uno shook his head. "Wow. A compound bow? I know guys who hunt with those. Do you think they were guys from around here?"

"I have no idea."

I stood around talking to people for a while longer, telling them what I knew about the incident. Eventually, I heard the sound of a car creeping up behind me.

I turned and saw a green Taurus. My mom was at the wheel, and my sister, Lilly, was sitting next to her.

Plan B was obviously in effect. Dad must have called home.

I walked back to the Dodge van. It was straddling two spaces, like it had been left there in mid-skid. I pointed to the far side of the parking lot, calling to Mom, "Pick me up out by the road." I climbed in, started the van, and drove it carefully to its original space.

Uno, Reg, and Bobby went inside to do their opening checklist jobs. Dad went in to call the corporate office. Mom got out of her car and hurried into the store behind him, and she didn't come back out for a long time. (She was freaking out in there, I'm sure.)

I spent the time thinking about this: The day could have begun horribly, with two murders. Or even three if they had shot me through the windshield, or rammed me in that game of chicken. The Food Giant could have a huge gash in its front wall, where the ATM had been ripped out, and a lot of money stolen.

But none of that had happened.

I took a moment to give myself credit. I had driven the thieves away. It could have been a horrible day, or a much-worse-than-it-turned-out-to-be day. A day that destroyed lives.

Instead, from here on out, it would be a normal day.

Mom finally emerged, climbed into the Taurus, and drove up to get me. As I slid into the backseat, she caught my eye in the rearview mirror. "Your father said you did a brave thing, Tom."

I nodded. "Thanks."

"No, I'm not saying that. Your father is. I'm saying you did a dangerous thing. And an illegal thing. You don't have a driver's license."

Lilly interrupted her. "What is this? You told me that Tom saved Dad's life!"

"Yes, I did say that," Mom conceded. "But I didn't know the circumstances."

"Circumstances! Who cares? He saved Dad's life."

That silenced Mom for a while, which is no small task. We exited the parking lot and headed west. Soon we were on Sunbury Street and passing our own house—a white, two-story duplex set in a row of houses and businesses. The buildings on Sunbury Street tend to reflect our mining-town roots. We have lots of churches and bars and funeral homes.

At the end of the street, Mom remarked casually, "Don't forget that counseling-group meeting after school, Lilly."

Mom has always been active in our schools, volunteering for anything and everything. Mom rode with Lilly and me on all of our field trips—east to Philadelphia and the Liberty Bell in fourth grade, west to Pittsburgh and the Fort Pitt Museum in fifth grade, and so on. She keeps in touch with the front office at the high school just in case she can chaperone something, just in case she's needed. And that's how she found out about the counseling group.

Lilly snarled, "I'm not going to that thing!"

We reverted to silence, but it was a heavier silence. Mom had approached dark territory. She had nearly spoken about the great unspoken event of the summer, which was this:

About two months ago, on a hot July night, Lilly and a friend from Lewis Street had been sitting on that friend's porch. A policeman had approached them, claiming that a neighbor had complained about the smell of marijuana.

Lilly got scared and immediately confessed to the crime. The friend took a different approach. She denied any drug use, and claimed that Lilly was crazy and was always telling lies.

Then Lilly, offended by those comments, actually reached under her chair and pulled out the remains of a half-smoked joint. She held it up and protested, "I am not lying!" (She chose honor over self-preservation, I guess.)

The police called Mom to pick Lilly up, and the incident got submitted to the local district attorney's office. He decided it was a waste of time to prosecute Lilly and her friend for such a small amount of marijuana, and the whole thing, legally, went away.

But that did not get Lilly off the hook. Not even close. Mom took her to our family physician, Dr. Bielski, who prescribed an antidepressant which I don't think Lilly actually took. She probably could have used it, though, as Mom kept her a homebound prisoner for the rest of the summer, allowing her out only for work. (I was at home, too, but it was by choice. Dad had finally gotten me a Nintendo 64. I had spent the summer mastering Super Mario Brothers 3, Donkey Kong, and Mario Kart.) Then, just to be sure, Mom signed Lilly up for a substance-abuse counseling group after school.

Lilly tried, "I'm never going to smoke pot again. There's no reason for me to go and sit with a bunch of stoners. That might actually be worse, you know? I'll learn more about being a stoner. I'll make stoner friends. I'll learn how to lie about using drugs!"

Mom was not moved. "You'll learn no such thing."

Lilly tried, "You just don't trust me!"

"That's not it, Lilly," Mom assured her. "Your father and I have both told you that we trust you—"

"Right. Then why are you still punishing me?"

"This counseling group isn't about punishment. It's about information. You need to understand about addiction."

"Addiction? I took two puffs on a joint, and now I'm some crack whore standing on a street corner?"

"Don't overdramatize."

"I'm not an addict!"

"No. But your father was a drinker, until he quit. And your uncle Robby was a drug addict, and it killed him."

I said, "I thought Uncle Robby was an alcoholic."

"It's all the same. He was addicted to alcohol and drugs. That's what gets transmitted in your genes, and in your DNA; that's part of your family inheritance. You could have the same addictive personality."

Lilly suddenly turned to include me. "Okay. So it's in Tom's genes, too?"

I answered, too casually as it turned out, "Yeah. We both have some evil drug zombie inside us, waiting for the chance to bust out."

Lilly announced, "Then shouldn't Tom go to the meeting, too?"

Before I could even protest, Mom replied, "Yes. I think that's a good idea."

It was my turn to snarl. "I'm not going to that thing!"

Mom continued: "You should go to the first one, Tom. If you don't think it's worthwhile, then you can stop. Lilly, though, will keep going."

"That's not fair!"

"That's what your father and I decided. You know that."

"I have to keep going until when?"

"Until further notice."

"Because of stupid Uncle Robby?"

Mom warned her, "Don't speak ill of the dead." She added, "I bet your cousin Arthur will be there. If he isn't, he should be."

Our cousin Arthur, Arthur Stokes, was Uncle Robby's son. He's kind of a thug. Mom was right on that count—he should be there. He could probably use some counseling.

But I could not.

I accepted my fate silently, though. I would attend one meeting, and one meeting only. I quickly changed the subject. "Arthur is in my English class."

Mom made a face in the rearview mirror. "How can he be in your class? Isn't he with you, Lilly? Isn't he a senior?"

"He said the office screwed up his credits, and he has to take two English classes this year or he can't graduate. He says it's because he flunked Shakespeare."

Lilly stopped sulking long enough to remark, "So he has to sit there with you ninth graders?"

"Yeah. Can you imagine the shame?"

She smiled unpleasantly. "I can't."

Mom asked, "So is Arthur going to graduate or not?"

"I guess so. If he does everything that Mr. Proctor says."

"Well, that's a shocker. People in that family rarely make it through high school, never mind college."

Lilly challenged her. "*That* family? It's *your* family, you know. His father was *your* brother."

Mom backtracked. "I meant that side of the family."

Lilly pressed her on it. "Oh? I'm sorry. Did someone on *our* side of the family, someone like you or Dad, just graduate from college? Did I miss that? If so, congratulations."

Mom continued backtracking. "I meant that we both graduated from high school. Your father and me."

Lilly corrected her. "It's 'Your father and I.'"

I decided to defend Mom. "It can be either one. Like 'Your father and I want to talk to you, Lilly.' Or 'Don't talk back to your father and me, Lilly.'"

She told me, "Butt out, Tom. Go read your vocabulary book," and the morning's conversation ended for good.

By then we were climbing up into the foothills. As any old person around here would tell you, we were on the road that the coal miners walked on their way to work. Some days, they'd walk up here before the sun rose, work all day in their subterranean world, and walk home after the sun had set.

Such reminiscences were supposed to inspire the kids around here, I guess. But inspire us to what? To be coal miners? They lived in a world without sun, like mole people; like people on the dark side of the moon. Not all that inspiring.

Soon the piles of black slag and rusting machinery gave way to a nicer landscape of farms, creeks, and woods. This was my favorite part of Blackwater (the part that wasn't, technically, Blackwater).

Mom pulled into the Haven Junior/Senior High campus at 8:45, exactly thirty minutes late. She let us out next to the statue of the Battlin' Coal Miner—our school mascot—a tall, thin guy with a pickax over his shoulder.

Lilly hurried up the ramp and disappeared under the arch of the entranceway. I took my time, gazing at the distant mountains from the high elevation of our campus.

It was a beautiful view, on a beautiful day, and I was in no hurry.

I still had about a half hour remaining with Coach Malloy. Coach Malloy, at least in our family, was known for two things— being the worst teacher at Haven and being the father of Reg "the Veg" Malloy, from the Food Giant. My school day began with ten minutes of Coach Malloy for homeroom, followed by fifty-five more minutes of him for social studies.

After a final look around, I entered the front office and stood at the junior high counter. None of the student assistants paid the slightest attention to me, like I was some invisible boy.

Finally, Jenny Weaver came out of the principal's office. She was always nice to me (to everybody, really). She asked, "What do you need, Tom? A late pass?"

"Yes, please."

She tore one off a pad and handed it to me. "There you go. See you in Mr. Proctor's class."

"Okay. Thanks."

"Bye!"

I headed out into JH1, the junior high hallway, and was soon standing outside the door of my first-period class. I slipped in and found a seat in the back row. One glance up front confirmed what I had expected: Coach Malloy wasn't looking. He never saw me come in. (This early in the year, he probably didn't even know who I was.)

Coach Malloy was in the middle of a long, rambling complaint about "the geniuses who purchased whiteboards for Haven Junior/Senior High." According to him, he was part of a "select group of teachers who had been given one of these boards to test." But the test, at least for Coach, was not going well.

The whiteboard is a high-tech classroom aid. It's about four feet high by six feet wide. It can be rolled on wheels. You write on it with special erasable markers.

The cool feature is that you can press a button and a vertical bar starts to glide across the surface. As it glides, it copies every word that has been written. Then you press another button, and it prints out a piece of paper showing exactly what was on the board.

Mr. Proctor writes on his a lot. If you miss a class, he gives you a printout of what the whiteboard said that day. That way, you know what you missed.

Coach Malloy uses his whiteboard like it's a cork bulletin board. He attaches papers to it with Scotch tape, papers like the varsity football schedule. (Football's a big deal in Pennsylvania, but not so much in Blackwater. That's because we never win.)

Today's assignment, attached to the top of Coach's whiteboard, just said "Pick up homework sheet on way out."

The class was devoted to one of Coach Malloy's favorite lessons—supply and demand. He has been teaching this lesson for thirty years. (Lilly and my cousin Arthur had already told me about it.) He brings in fifty candy bars, which he sells to fifty students for ten cents each. He lets the students eat the candy in class. The next day, he brings in *ten* candy bars and, because many students now want them, he raises the price to a dollar, explaining, "It's supply and demand. If demand goes up and supply stays down, the item becomes worth more."

He'd started the lesson on Friday, so this was day two, the day when demand for candy bars exceeded supply. Some kids were surprised that the candy bars now cost a dollar.

And only those with extra money were able to afford them.

Okay. Got it. Lesson learned: no candy for the poor kids.

The class ended with Coach Malloy holding up a mason jar, opening it with a *pop*, and sticking in a spoon. He pulled out a faded-looking, shrunken strawberry and commented, with his mouth partly full, "My son Reg plants a garden every year. We have fresh fruit and vegetables in the summer, and we have canned fruit and vegetables in the winter."

He put the jar down, wiped his mouth with a paper towel, and announced, "Come Thanksgiving week, I'll be selling jars of fruit preserves just like this one. The cost will be five dollars per jar. The sale will begin on Monday, November nineteenth, and it will last through Wednesday, the twenty-first. So be ready with your money. Demand is always high, and supply is limited."

The bell rang right after that, and the students started for the door. I walked up front to drop off my late pass and take a homework handout. Just as I got to the door, a big senior, a football player named Rick Dorfman, came in the other way. (Football players stop in to see Coach Malloy a lot.) He plowed right through, making me back up into the classroom.

Normally, I would let something like that go—him being a senior football player and me being a freshman bagger at the Food Giant. But today I felt like a hero. I had foiled a robbery. I had saved lives. So I heard myself snap at him, "Watch out!"

I started to go, but I immediately felt a hand grab the back of my shirt collar and snap my head back. The senior kept his grip on my shirt and turned me around so I was facing him, with my twisted-up collar now acting like a tourniquet around my neck. He spoke in a very low, quiet voice. "What was that, you little pissant?"

I looked toward Coach Malloy. If he knew this was happening, he didn't let on. He spooned another strawberry into his mouth.

"I just asked you a question," Dorfman reminded me.

I could feel the blood pooling in my head, above the tourniquet. I squirmed to break free, but his grip got even tighter. He opened his mouth to speak again, but then he suddenly stopped.

His eyes darted to a spot behind me. His grip on my collar loosened, so that I could breathe again.

I staggered and then turned around.

Arthur was standing there. My cousin, Arthur Stokes.

He was a menacing sight, as always, dressed in camo and black boots. His head was shaved as close as his face, which always had razor burns where he had scraped over his acne. His eyes looked like gray steel, and his voice was steely, too, when he said, "Is there a problem here, Dork-man?"

Dorfman's mouth twitched upward into something between a smile and a sneer. He muttered, "Keep out of this, Stokes."

Arthur pointed at my shirt collar. "Hands off the merchandise. Understand, Dork-man? Or I shall visit the wrath of God on you."

Dorfman took a step back, out of Arthur's reach. He nodded his head up and down, one time. "Forget it. Forget you."

Arthur nodded his head the same way. "Forget me? That would be stupid. Real stupid. Of course, nobody ever said you weren't stupid."

Dorfman then turned his back on us and faced Coach Malloy.

The coach had put down his fruit jar by now. He had clearly been watching, and listening, but he hadn't done a thing to help.

Arthur jerked his head toward the hallway and told me, "Come on."

We started down JH1 alongside a slow stream of kids. Most of them were about a foot shorter than Arthur. (I was only about six inches shorter, but with about half his muscle mass.) I kept craning and rubbing my neck, trying to loosen it up, trying to tell if Dorfman had snapped a vertebra.

Arthur finally asked, "You okay, cuz?"

I tried to keep my voice calm. "Sure. Yeah."

He gave me a quick nod. "I heard what you did at the Food Giant today."

"You did? How?"

"Buddy of mine in first period. He stopped in on his way to school. He talked to Uno."

"Really?"

"Yeah. Uno said you were like an action hero out there."

"What?"

"Like Rambo."

"Like Rambo? No."

"Like James Bond in a spy-pimped minivan or something."

I was surprised that I could laugh. "Yeah. Maybe that."

"I didn't know you could drive."

"I can't. Not for eighteen months."

"But who's counting, right?"

"Right."

We arrived at Mr. Proctor's door, and I followed Arthur inside. If Arthur was embarrassed to be there among ninth graders, it didn't show.

Mr. Proctor is both a first-year teacher at Haven and a grad student at Blackwater University. He's working on his master's degree in English. He told us that he is from Philadelphia but he likes it better out here. (He didn't say why, and I couldn't imagine.)

Anyway, he teaches ninth-grade English. Ninth grade plus Arthur Stokes.

Last week, the first week of school, he got my attention by covering all of early American lit in just a day. He summed up the Puritans in two sentences: "They suffered, and they died. Let's move on to something good."

That was it. I loved it.

In Friday's class, he had had a brief discussion with Arthur about Shakespeare. He asked him, "Mr. Stokes, what did you like or dislike about Shakespeare?"

"Uh, I disliked that I couldn't understand it. It wasn't in English."

"Sure it was."

"Yeah, but like Old English."

"No. Shakespeare is neither Old nor Middle English. It is modern English." He smiled. "Didn't you at least like all the sex and violence?"

"Maybe if I'd understood it."

"Because I need to assign some Shakespeare to you this year," Mr. Proctor explained. "The rest of you will have to wait for it." Then he pointed to someone in the back. "Yes?"

A girl's voice answered, "I really like Shakespeare."

"Good. What plays have you read?"

"All of them."

Mr. Proctor sounded impressed. "You have? All thirty-seven?"

"Yes," the girl assured him. She sounded very confident.

As those two continued to talk, Mr. Proctor passed out copies of a paperback book. When I got mine, I read the title, *A Journal of the Plague Year.*

"This is a classic novel by Daniel Defoe, who also wrote *Robinson Crusoe*," Mr. Proctor explained. "In this novel, people are getting killed by something mysterious." He switched to a spooky, horror-movie voice. "Is it God? Is it the devil?"

Then he answered his own question: "No. It is a disease that spreads through London in the year 1665."

The confident girl from the back asked, "Did you say this is a novel?"

"Yes."

"But it's called a journal, and it reads like it's nonfiction."

"It does seem like nonfiction, yes. The author *was* in London that year, and he did keep a journal. What you are holding is a story based on all that, but written afterward. It *is* a work of fiction."

I finally turned around to match that girl's voice with a face. She was really cute. And smart. And, as I mentioned, confident.

Mr. Proctor held up a memo. "Before we begin, I want to tell you about a change in the language arts curriculum this year. You are expected to write a lot, about four thousand words per month."

Arthur let out a low whistle.

A new kid in a very tight Pittsburgh Penguins T-shirt raised his hand. He asked, "How many words is that a day?"

"I don't know. I'll let you do the math. One way you can achieve that total, though, is to write a journal for me for extra credit. So pay attention as you read this book. Think about how Daniel Defoe documented the history of a people and a place."

The Pittsburgh Penguins kid asked, "What if you don't have a journal?"

Mr. Proctor smiled. "A journal can be anything—a notebook, a pad, even loose papers that you clip together."

The kid seemed relieved.

Arthur muttered to me, "No way. That's too much work."

But I didn't think so. I had a new notebook from the Food Giant school supplies section, a small one that fit in my back pocket. I kind of liked the idea of a journal.

The Pittsburgh Penguins kid asked, "What if we write a whole lot and then we lose it?"

Mr. Proctor squinted at him, but then he explained patiently, "You can just tell me you did it. I'll believe you."

The kid sounded amazed. "Really?"

"Yeah." He looked around. "You guys wouldn't lie to me, would you?"

The kid laughed and answered goofily, as if for the whole class, "Oh no! No, we wouldn't do that!"

Mr. Proctor then picked up a black erasable marker and wrote one word on the whiteboard: *plague*. "Okay, tell me, what is a plague?" No one said anything, so he looked at his seating chart. He asked that new kid, "Ben Gibbons, what is a plague?"

"Uh, it's a really bad thing."

Mr. Proctor laughed. "It is. It's a *really* bad thing. So what are some really bad things that can come in plague form?" He turned to the whiteboard and assumed a writing stance. Still, no one said anything, so he wrote the word *disease*.

Then the cute girl in the back spoke up. She rattled off a list as Mr. Proctor wrote frantically to keep up: "Frogs. Locusts. Hail. Darkness. Death of firstborn males."

Mr. Proctor muttered, "Good. Good. Some of the ten plagues of Egypt, from the Bible." He pointed at the paperback. "Does anyone know what Daniel Defoe's plague was called?"

He looked at the girl, like she was the only one who had any chance of knowing. When she didn't venture a guess, he told us, "The bubonic plague. It decimated London, England, in 1665." He looked around the room. "But what about nowadays, in the year 2001? What kind of plagues do we have now?"

He answered his own question again, before any of us could. "AIDS? Swine flu?"

Mr. Proctor put down his marker. He pointed out the window. "Listen. I have been reading about a new plague. And they do use the word *plague* to describe it. It is a plague of drug use, right here in small-town Pennsylvania. The drug is called methamphetamine. Has anybody heard of it?"

Nobody answered. Nobody had, I guess. Not yet.

"Okay. Well then, let's go back a few hundred years and see what's going on in Daniel Defoe's England." Then Mr. Proctor began to read *A Journal of the Plague Year* aloud.

The drug-counseling group that Lilly would attend every Monday, and that I would attend one time only, was held in a large conference room inside the school's main office. In the middle of the room, there was a long table with about twelve chairs around it. There were another dozen or so chairs set back against the walls, nearly ringing the table.

By the time I arrived, the wall chairs were already filled, forcing me to be the first kid to sit at the table. I looked at the table's only other occupant, an attractive woman dressed in a dark blue suit. She wore an expensive necklace, earrings, and watch. Her hair was swept up in a style that I would call French (although I'm not sure why). I figured, correctly, that she was the leader of the group.

I watched Lilly enter the room. Her nostrils were pulled back as far as they could go, like she was entering the smelliest place on earth. She took the seat opposite me. Then, as Mom had predicted, Arthur walked in. His face betrayed no emotion at all as he took the seat right next to me. I turned, but I hadn't said a word when he told me, "Shut up. This gets me out of football practice."

I glanced quickly around the room, seeing how many of the wall-huggers I could recognize. Many were high schoolers. Some actually looked like stoners, with scraggly hair, tattoos, piercings, heavy-metal T-shirts. But some were a surprise to me as, I am sure, Lilly and I were a surprise to them.

Jenny Weaver was there, which *really* surprised me. She's basically the perfect kid—Student Council representative, honor roll member, office assistant. She's also in most of my classes.

Chris Collier was there, too. He was president of the Junior High Student Council last year, but I don't think he's running this year. At least I haven't seen his name on any posters in the halls.

Angela Lang walked into the room. She was carrying her own folding chair, which she set down by the door. Angela had been my "girlfriend" back in the sixth grade, although we never actually went on a date. Our whole relationship went something like this:

> *Angela:* Do you want to go out with me?
> *Me:* Okay.
> *Angela:* I think we should break up.
> *Me:* Okay.

And she has barely spoken to me since.

Finally, and best of all, that cute girl from my English class walked in and stood next to the leader. I had a much better view of her now. She did not look like the girls from around here. She had bright blond hair and a golden tan. She had blue eyes and very white teeth. She actually seemed to sparkle.

The leader woman reached over and touched the girl's golden arm. (I suddenly wished I could do the same.) She directed her, for some miraculous reason, to the chair next to Lilly.

The leader then cleared her throat softly and spoke. "Before we get started, I would like to announce that I do not have the plague. Any of you who would like a comfortable seat around the table, please join us now."

No one moved.

The woman went on: "Okay. My name is Catherine Lyle, and I am a mental health professional. I have a master's degree in counseling from USC." She stopped for a moment, wondering whether she had to explain that to us. She concluded that she did: "The University of Southern California." Then she added, like it was some big deal, "My husband is Dr. Richard Lyle."

We just stared at her. Arthur muttered to me, "Didn't he play linebacker for the Steelers, back with Mean Joe Green?"

Catherine Lyle explained, "He is a well-known lecturer in the field of psychology."

Arthur continued muttering, "What? He works in a field? Hey, I might know him, then."

Mrs. Lyle told us, "I just want you to know how much I appreciate this opportunity to put my degree to work. And I hope this group will be a benefit to all of you."

She pointed at the door. "First things first: As a counselor, I adhere to a code of ethics. We will have strict confidentiality in this room. Does everyone know what that means?"

Arthur said loudly, "What we say in here stays in here."

"Yes. That's very well put."

Arthur liked that. His scarred cheeks reddened.

Catherine continued: "If I see you in public, I will not acknowledge you. If I did, people would think, *That person must be*

28

in counseling, and that's nobody's business but ours. So if I do not say hello at Starbucks, I'm not being mean; I'm just following my counselor's code of ethics."

I'm sure I wasn't the only one thinking, *We don't have a Starbucks here, lady.*

She opened a large leather notebook with gold-trimmed pages. She slid a silver pen out of a slot in the middle, clicked it, and said, "Now let's go around the room. Please say your name and one quick thing about yourself so we can get to know each other." She turned and looked at Chris Collier. He shrugged and said, "I'm Chris Collier, and I work at the Strike Zone."

Catherine Lyle beamed a white smile. "Now, what is that? A batting cage?"

Chris looked confused. He answered, "No. It's a bowling alley."

"Ah. Of course."

The next kid, a high school stoner, mumbled his name as Terry something, but he didn't add anything else. He looked so stressed-out that Mrs. Lyle changed her mind on the spot. "Okay. Let's say that the one quick thing about yourself is voluntary. You're free to just say your name." She smiled kindly at Terry and moved on.

All around the wall, kids started mumbling their names and nothing else.

When the kids sitting in the wall chairs were finished, Catherine Lyle looked at me to start at the table. I said, "I'm Tom Coleman, and I work at the Food Giant."

"I'm Lilly Coleman. And I work there, too."

"I'm Arthur."

Finally it was the cute girl's turn. "I'm Wendy, and I am new here at Haven."

Catherine Lyle concluded by saying, "Thank you all. I know

that was difficult for some of you. It's difficult to talk about your-self, isn't it? You think no one really wants to hear about you and what you are feeling, but that's not true. Not in here.

"In this group, we will talk about low self-esteem, low expec-tations, and many of the other factors that can lead to teenage drug abuse. But I will not be doing all the talking. If we're going to have a successful group, you'll all need to talk, either in the large group or in smaller ones. I will be inviting some guest speak-ers to come in, too."

She consulted her notepad. "Finally, I want this group to be an information resource for you. Information is power when you are dealing with drugs and addiction. I'd like to ask for a volun-teer to do a report on a drug that has recently emerged in this area—methamphetamine."

Most kids looked away. I could have researched that word on our Gateway computer and written a report on it if I'd been plan-ning on coming to another meeting.

The cute girl finally raised her hand and said, "I'll do it."

Catherine Lyle said reluctantly, "All right, Wendy. Thank you." She stood up very gracefully and moved her hands in a cir-cling motion. "I know it is easier to talk to a few people than to many, so let's arrange ourselves right now into groups of four."

The cute girl took the initiative. She held out her arms so that they encompassed Arthur, Lilly, and me. "How about if the four of us form a group?"

I replied eagerly, "Sure. Okay."

Arthur just frowned at her.

Lilly didn't even do that. I could tell by her eyes that she had checked out completely.

Still, the girl smiled gamely and told us, "I'm Wendy Lyle. And . . . you guys must all be related, right?"

I smiled back. "How did you know that?"

She pointed to Lilly. "You two have the same last name, and the same face." She looked at Arthur. "And I've heard you call him 'cuz' in English class. Am I right?"

"You are," I assured her, then added, "That's very perceptive of you."

She beamed at me, so I tried, "And you have the same name as our group leader, but *not* the same face."

She gave me a short finger point. "That is very perceptive of you. Catherine is my stepmom. We just moved here for my dad's job. He's a professor at the university."

Arthur said sourly, "My dad's a drunk."

Wendy looked right at him. "I'm sorry. I hope that will change."

"I don't think so. He's dead."

She kept looking at him. "Sorry again."

I liked how Wendy kept her cool in the face of this open hostility from my cousin, and the open indifference from my sister. I didn't know why they were being so rude. Because she was an outsider? Because she was cute? Because she was kind of a teacher's pet? I turned to Arthur, determined to ask him what his problem was, but I stopped when he waved at someone outside.

Looking through the window, I saw Arthur's stepfather, Jimmy Giles.

Jimmy is a wiry, scraggly guy who always looks like he just woke up. He was standing in the school office, wearing a threadbare jeans jacket. Jimmy's brother Warren was out there with him, jangling a set of keys. (Jimmy had his driver's license revoked by a judge, so Warren has to drive him around.)

Warren is a handsome guy of about forty. He's the same age as my dad, but he looks a lot younger. Warren was wearing a jacket, too, but his was striking. It was green satin with gold lettering on the back. When he turned, I saw that the lettering said *Haven High Football*.

I asked Arthur, "What's your stepdad doing here? And Warren?"

Arthur nodded toward Catherine Lyle. "A judge sent Jimmy to this counselor lady."

"Yeah? Really? So is he in our group?"

"Nah. He's here to do community service."

Since Arthur wasn't exactly answering my question, Wendy Lyle added, "My stepmom asked him to talk here today."

"About what?"

"He's talking about drugs. About what they did to his life."

I looked at Arthur. "That doesn't sound like Jimmy."

"What doesn't?"

"Well, public speaking."

Arthur smiled. "You just might be surprised about that."

Catherine Lyle walked over to the door. She had a very classy walk, like a model. She opened it and spoke softly, "Mr. Giles? Are you ready?"

Jimmy nodded and entered the room. Warren stayed outside, watching through the glass.

Mrs. Lyle told us, "It takes courage to face an addiction and to overcome it. I'd like to introduce you to someone who is facing that challenge right now. Actually, I will let him introduce himself and tell you about his own experiences getting into, and then getting away from, drug addiction."

She smiled sweetly and reclaimed her seat. Jimmy Giles stood by the door, avoiding eye contact with us. He seemed to be talking to himself for a few seconds. Then he pulled a white note card from his pants pocket and started to read from it.

"I am here to tell you about my experience so that it does not become your experience." He cleared his throat and continued. "Any dumb animal can learn from a mistake. If a horse walks into an electric fence and gets a shock, it don't walk into that fence again. It learns from it. But humans can also learn from *others'* mistakes. I hope that's what will happen today."

Catherine Lyle encouraged him. "That's an excellent point."

Arthur suddenly spoke up, as if he were at an old-time-religion camp-revival meeting. "Amen, Jimmy! Well told."

Jimmy grinned at Arthur. Then he looked at the rest of us. His nerves seemed to melt away as his glance passed from face to face. When he spoke again, he was relaxed. "I should tell you my name is Jimmy Giles, and I'm from Blackwater. I have worked as a wildcat coal miner, on and off. I have worked as a mover"— he looked back through the door—"with my brother Warren. We move kids in and out of Blackwater University. We also sell Christmas trees."

He paused to clear his throat. From my side view, I could see his large Adam's apple bob up and down.

"I got involved with marijuana in junior high school." He looked around at the walls of the room. "At *this* junior high school, in fact. I started smoking it when I was twelve, and I was still smoking it three months ago when I got arrested for the second time. If I get arrested a third time, I go straight to jail."

Jimmy hung his head, as if looking back into his days at Haven Junior High. "Here's what I learned between then and now—what I learned the hard way." He suddenly pointed at Wendy. "Miss? Name something that you love to do."

"Me? I read. I read a lot."

"Okay." He pointed at me. "What about you, Tom?"

I answered, "Uh, play video games. Nintendo 64."

"Okay. Got it. Now let me break it down for you.

"You love to read, miss. And then you get high, and you love to read even more when you're high.

"And you love to play video games, Tom, and then you get high, and you love to play video games even more when you're high."

He looked from Wendy to me. "But then something bad happens." He pointed at Wendy. "You find that you *don't* love to read anymore when you're not high. It's not good enough." He switched to me. "And video games? You don't love to play when you're not high. No way. It's not good enough."

Jimmy stopped, then said, "Now, here's the really awful part.

"Miss, you soon realize that you don't love reading anymore even when you *are* high. And Tom, you don't love video games anymore, high or not. You don't love *anything* anymore. Not books, not games, not even getting high.

"But you keep getting high anyway because . . . well, that's what you do." He glanced at the kids against the wall. "Right, stoners? That's what you do, so you keep on doing it. Even though you hate it now. You have officially arrived at zombieland. You don't love anything. You don't like anything. You don't care about anything. It has all been taken away from you . . . by drugs."

A few of the stoners nodded at him.

Arthur suddenly said in his tent-revival voice, "Preach, Jimmy!"

Jimmy looked at Arthur. His voice started to rise. "I am thirty-eight years old, with a wife and kids, and I have a job that only pays minimum wage. And I have had some jobs that paid *less* than minimum wage. What can I thank for that?"

Arthur answered, "Drugs. You can thank drugs for that."

Jimmy went on. "I am a professional driver, licensed for any vehicle up to fourteen tons. Yet I have to get driven around in my pickup like I'm some two-year-old. What can I thank for that?"

Arthur's voice dropped this time. It was barely audible. "Drugs. You can thank drugs for that."

"My wife, and my son, and my stepson live on a piece of land that has been condemned by the United States government as unsafe for human habitation. What can I thank for that?"

This time, Jimmy looked around the room at all of us.

And we knew what to do. We replied, softly, raggedly, "Drugs. You can thank drugs for that."

This call-and-response continued for a few more minutes. Jimmy and Arthur did that old-time-religion thing, and, to my amazement, the whole group responded to it. Warren stood by the door watching us, smiling broadly.

When Jimmy finally finished, Catherine Lyle stood up. She delivered a very nice, very sincere thank-you to him, and we all applauded. Then she announced, "That's it for this week—just a short meeting, a getting-to-know-you meeting. I hope to see you all back here next week."

I walked outside with Arthur, Jimmy, and Warren. Warren was laughing. "I could hear you two through the door! You were doing that fire-and-brimstone stuff, right?"

Arthur conceded, "I reckon we were."

Warren winked at me. "You keep away from me with that. I don't want nothing to do with burning. I don't even want to hear about burning."

Arthur grinned. "Yeah, I know. Okay."

I glanced at Jimmy. He seemed nervous and withdrawn again. He muttered, "Thank you, Arthur. And you, too, Warren." He looked at me and explained, "They helped me write that stuff on the cards."

"But you delivered it, Jimmy Giles," Arthur told him. "The spirit was speaking through you."

And maybe it had been, but it wasn't now. Jimmy didn't say anything else. He climbed up into the passenger's seat of his Ranger pickup and just stared straight ahead.

As usual, Mom was waiting for Lilly and me after school in the car riders' circle. She drove us from Haven to our jobs at the Food Giant. Then she went home to cook dinner. (Mom calls that being "a traditional housewife.")

Lilly walked ahead of me into the store. She passed the customer-service desk and ducked into the employees' lounge, where she'd change into a green-and-white smock, pick up a cash drawer, and open up register three.

The Food Giant only has three registers (so it isn't all that giant). Two older ladies named Del and Marsha run registers one and two during the day. They get replaced by high school kids at around 4:00 p.m.

I walked into the anteroom outside the men's room, where all the brooms are stashed and the green slickers are hanging. As soon as I did, I heard voices on the other side of the door. I recognized Reg's wise-guy drawl. I recognized Bobby's voice, too. Hearing those two together was never good.

Reg went out of his way to bust Bobby's balls wherever and whenever he could. As a result, Bobby truly despised Reg.

I opened the door and stepped into the actual men's room, with the toilets and all. Bobby and Reg were both standing in front of the sinks, talking to each other's mirror images.

Reg immediately included me in whatever he was up to. "Here's Tom. If you don't believe me, ask Tom."

Bobby, still in his green slicker, shook his head adamantly. "I ain't asking nobody."

The door pushed open behind me, bumping me aside. Uno walked in and continued on to the urinal. He called over his shoulder, "Ask what?"

Uno always went along with Reg when it came to pranking Bobby. (I didn't. Well, except when it was something really funny.) Reg replied as if he were Coach Malloy handing out an answer sheet. "I am trying to explain to Bobby that the produce department is having a promotion—Chiquita Banana Week."

Uno confirmed that right away. "Oh yeah, Bobby. It's Chiquita Banana Week."

Reg continued: "As part of the promotion, we are asking each bag boy to carry a Chiquita banana in his pocket and to ask each customer if she would like a Chiquita banana."

Uno sputtered. He flushed the urinal to cover up the sound of his laughter. I started laughing, too, so I turned away from the mirror.

When I looked back, Bobby's round face was scrunched up.

Uno joined them at the sink. Bobby said warily, "Come on. Is that true?"

Uno assured him, "That is one hundred percent true, Bobby."

"So, is Tom going to do that tonight?"

Reg answered quickly. "The promotion doesn't start until tomorrow, Bobby. Tomorrow morning at seven. Tom will have a banana in his pocket tomorrow afternoon. And if I know Tom, it will be a sizable one."

Uno laughed so hard that he had to plunge his face into the sink and splash water on it.

I had to turn away again, too. But I also started to feel uneasy.

There were rules about bustin' them on Bobby. Rule one was that you couldn't do anything to hurt Bobby. Rule two was that you couldn't do anything to hurt the store. I was pretty sure this violated rule two.

I made a mental note to tell Dad about it. He would talk to Bobby in the morning. He'd talk to Uno, too. He probably wouldn't bother with Reg, though. They didn't call him "the Veg" for nothing.

I stepped back into the anteroom and grabbed a broom. My first job was usually to take one lap around the store with a wide push broom.

At broom level, the Food Giant is one large square divided into seven aisles. The floor is red-and-white linoleum. It is old, and cracked in places, and faded from thousands of moppings (many of those by me).

The ceiling is actually very high, probably twenty-five feet, but you can only see that if you are back in the storeroom. Out front, it is covered by a white drop ceiling, which, unfortunately, shows water stains from roof leaks.

Seven lines of fluorescent lights extend from the dairy and meat cases in the back to the registers in the front. The left wall is all frozen foods, so the floor there is the most messed up, again from leaks. The right wall contains the bakery and the produce department, which can also be messy.

Aside from the registers, the front part of the store has a customer-service desk, a line of soda, candy, and ice machines, and a corral area for the shopping carts.

When I finished my sweeping pass, I went outside to take Bobby's place in the parking lot. He was standing next to a white metal cage that holds propane tanks for grills. (His mother always picks him up there.) When Bobby saw me, he pointed out two carts left out near Route 16.

Reg emerged, fumbling with his truck keys. He called over, "Don't forget about that promotion tomorrow, Bobby. I'm countin' on you."

By the time I had walked all the way out to the road and back, both Bobby and Reg were gone. I wheeled the carts inside and crammed them into a lineup along the front wall. The Food Giant has fifty carts. But at any time, a dozen or so might be scattered across the parking lot (or stolen, or borrowed and abandoned, like this morning).

Dad was now running register two, so I went over to bag for him. Uno came up and stood next to me, apparently to bag for Lilly, although there was no one in her line. Uno got his nickname around sixth grade, or whenever puberty was, because only one of his testicles had descended. I'm not sure I would have bragged about that, but he apparently did. He still answers to the nickname, but lately I have heard him introduce himself as John. I guess if you live in Blackwater, anything that makes you stand out in any way is considered good.

Now, like most guys, I don't really think of my sister as a girl. I mention this because so far I have described her pretty much as an angry, snarling monster. And she can be that. But other guys, who are not her brother, seem to find her attractive. And she can act attractive around them.

Uno had asked Lilly to her junior prom last year (or, more likely, *Lilly* had asked *him*, but she won't admit it). He had just turned twenty-one and was legally an adult. Lilly, at seventeen, was legally a child.

Mom was horrified.

Dad said yes at first, but then Mom freaked out, and he had to change his vote to no. So Lilly didn't go to the prom.

╬

Mom returned to the store at 6:30 to pick us up. She does that every school day so we can go home, eat dinner, and do homework. Dad used to go home then, too, but lately he misses dinner more often than he makes it.

Today it would just be Lilly leaving, though. I had to stay and work. The produce truck had arrived late, due to a flat tire. Reg was gone for the day, and Dad couldn't reach him, so I had to stay and unload it.

They didn't call him "the Veg" for nothing.

I stacked produce crates until closing time, which is 9:00 p.m. Dad took two bakery rolls and filled them with lunch meat for our dinner. We ate them as we worked for another half hour, cleaning up, straightening up, locking up.

It was nearly ten when we finally got home. Fortunately, there was a big open space on Sunbury Street not far from our door. Dad parallel-parked the van into it.

The front doors on our street sit almost on the sidewalk, and the houses extend almost to the alleyway behind. This leaves very little room for backyards. Ours is taken up by a carport, a metal shed, and a cement slab that holds a gas grill (a Coleman, like us).

Since the houses are so close to the sidewalk, lots of people have turned their ground floors into some kind of business. On our block alone, we have a beauty parlor, a pet groomer, and a travel agency.

So far, our house is still just a house.

Dad opened the front door, and I followed him into the parlor. It's basically a living room, with a couch, a TV (which always

40

has my Nintendo 64 plugged into it), and our computer. Mom insists on calling it "the parlor," though.

After the parlor comes the dining room, dominated by a large wooden table and four chairs. That's where I have sat and done my homework since kindergarten (and Lilly has sat and avoided doing her homework since kindergarten). Beyond that are a big kitchen, the back stairs, and the back door.

Dad and I trudged directly up the front stairs. At the top, he veered off into his room with a low "Good night, Tom."

My parents' bedroom sits directly over the parlor, just feet away from the traffic on the street. After that comes our one, much-fought-over bathroom, and then two more bedrooms—my small one and Lilly's large one.

And that is it. Well, we have an unfinished basement with a washer and dryer, and an unfinished attic with boxes of Christmas stuff. But that is it.

I entered my bedroom wearily, not even bothering to turn on the light. With the skill of a blind man, I pulled off most of my clothes in the dark and dropped them in a hamper inside my closet.

I crawled into the same bed that I have been crawling into since I was five. My feet now extend several inches beyond the end, uprooting the covers every night.

If I had turned on the light, I would have seen my Florida college collage on the back wall. It's a collection I have put together myself: pictures of beautiful green campuses, pictures of smiling young people at FSU, UF, UCF. Beautiful warm places that I would like to live in someday.

Places that are far from here.

Tuesday, September 11, 2001

Today was a full plan B day, with Mom dropping us off in a crowd of kids at 8:10. Lilly and I exited the car quickly, with our heads down, like guilty criminals dodging the media.

I hurried inside, turned left down the junior high corridor, and went straight to homeroom. I flopped into a seat near the front and stared at the TV set mounted in the corner. Its screen displayed a test pattern of colors in vertical lines—ROY G BIV. Its speakers gave out a low hissing sound.

The desks around me soon filled up with bleary-eyed ninth graders. Haven Junior/Senior High is filled with working-class white kids. We only have a few Puerto Ricans, and no blacks. Most of us live in Haven County because someone, somewhere on the family tree, was a coal miner. Most of those miners were white Europeans, so most of us are, too.

At 8:25, the test pattern disappeared and was replaced by the unsmiling face of Mrs. Cantwell, the principal of the junior high side of the campus. Mrs. Cantwell was all business. "Good morning. Let us rise and recite the Pledge of Allegiance and remain standing for the playing of our national anthem."

We straggled to our feet, covered our hearts, and recited the pledge. Some kids kept their hands on their hearts for the national anthem, but most let them drop and started to fidget, stretch, and yawn.

Then, when the music stopped and we all sat back down, something wonderful occurred. Wonderful for me, at least.

Mrs. Cantwell's glowering face disappeared and was, after a moment of darkness, replaced by the face of a smiling, beautiful girl.

My heart nearly stopped beating.

It was her. It was she. Whatever. It was Wendy.

What was she doing on the TV, smiling that white, white smile? She said something about the upcoming school elections, and about this week's football game against Mahanoy, and about a fund-raiser. But I couldn't really take it in. I was too shocked. Too excited.

I thought about what I could say to her in second period. I even jotted some things down, like *Hey, you looked great on TV,* and other variations of that.

Then the TV blinked off, bells rang, and Coach Malloy's social studies class began. I pulled out the homework sheet that I had finished over breakfast. He went over it slowly, methodically, death-inducingly. He covered the topic "The Three Branches of Government" exactly the same way Mrs. Kerpinski had in fourth grade. The kid behind me, Mikeszabo, had not finished his, so I let him copy mine. Coach didn't notice.

Mikeszabo and I go way back. He had been in Mrs. Kerpinski's class, too. He was one of two Mikes in that class—Miklos Szabo and Michael Murphy. She always called them by their full names—Mikeszabo (the *s* is silent) and Mikemurphy—so I've called them by those names ever since.

Mikemurphy is a problem kid now. He gets suspended a lot. He gets caught with stuff on campus—cigarettes, a hunting knife, a can of beer. From stray comments I've heard from Mom and Dad, I get the idea that Mikemurphy's parents are heavy drinkers.

Coach finally finished his lecture. He looked at the wall clock. "Tell you what—you can have free time to work on other assignments from now until the bell rings. Then don't forget to pick up your worksheets on the way out."

A few kids took out pens and loose-leaf binders (I was one of them). But the majority, including Mikeszabo, did what Haven Junior High kids had done in Coach Malloy's class for a generation. They put their heads down and went to sleep.

After class, I managed to pick up my worksheet without getting into any confrontations with angry football players. I turned left in the hallway and spotted Arthur's shaved head in the crowd. Apparently, he was waiting for me, letting the river of freshmen eddy around him on either side.

When I got right next to him, he leaned forward and whispered in a no-nonsense voice, "Something's going down, cuz."

"What?"

"We're under attack."

"Who is? Am I? Is it Dorfman?"

"No. Shut up and listen. The United States of America is under attack. We just heard about it in first period. You didn't hear?"

"No."

"Two jet planes, big ones, full of fuel, hit the World Trade Center in New York City. One plane hit tower one. Then, fifteen minutes later, another hit tower two. Hijacked planes, man, exploding like bombs. Death and destruction everywhere."

"My God!"

"It could be happening in every city in America. Right now. It could be happening here."

I thought about that for a second. "No. Not here."

He agreed. "No, probably not. But every major city, every important target. The United States is under freakin' attack."

We turned into Mr. Proctor's classroom. He had his back to us, and he held a TV remote control in his hand. Keeping his eyes on the screen, he repeated several times, "Everybody take a seat."

Arthur and I sat in two desks up front, right under the TV. The screen showed a jet, moving impossibly fast for its altitude, slamming into one of the twin towers.

Wendy Lyle took the seat next to me, but I barely noticed. (And I completely forgot about her earlier TV appearance.)

As we watched and listened, things just kept getting worse. CNN announced that a plane had crashed into the Pentagon in Washington, D.C. I thought Arthur was going to jump out of his chair at that news. He clenched his fists like he wanted to punch somebody.

The TV announced that all planes flying in United States airspace had to land immediately or they would be shot down, to which Arthur shouted, "Hell, yeah! Payback!"

Then, right before our eyes, the first tower in New York City crumbled to the ground, just disintegrated into dust. Mr. Proctor whispered, "My God. That building is full of people."

It was amazing, and shocking, and News with a capital N. We all stayed glued to the television. Here is a summary of what happened:

8:46: Flight 11 crashed into the North Tower of the World Trade Center.

9:03: Flight 175 crashed into the South Tower of the World Trade Center.

9:37: Flight 77 crashed into the western side of the Pentagon.

9:59: The South Tower of the World Trade Center collapsed.

At 10:15, the scenes of destruction and carnage suddenly faded away and Mrs. Cantwell's face appeared. She told us, "Due to the national emergency, Haven County has decided to close all schools and to send students home for the day. We ask you to stay where you are, in your second-period classes, until the buses return. We will call for the bus riders first, after which we will call for the car riders. Students with no ride home should report to the auditorium."

Mrs. Cantwell's face faded and CNN returned. At first, I could not believe what I was hearing. The CNN anchors, who should have been talking about New York City and Washington, D.C., were talking about us instead. About Somerset County. About western Pennsylvania.

We were under attack?

I turned to Arthur. "Pennsylvania?"

He waved me off—"Shut up"—and continued to glare at the screen.

A plane had just crashed in Somerset County, Pennsylvania. Basically right next to us. It could have been in Haven County. It could have been right here—on our school, on my house, on the Food Giant.

Mr. Proctor looked at me and said, "Remember today, September eleventh. It's going to change everything."

He raised up the remote and clicked to different channels. The horrible news was everywhere, and it just kept coming. A car bomb had detonated outside the State Department Building in Washington, D.C. There were mass evacuations going on in New York City and Washington.

Then, just before 10:30, the second World Trade Center tower followed the first, disintegrating before our eyes, killing everyone still trapped inside, including all the firefighters and police who had run in to save people.

I turned around and looked behind me. Most kids just looked stunned, like this was way too much for them to handle.

That Ben kid kept saying stuff like "My dad's gonna be really pissed. Supermad. Like furious."

Jenny Weaver sobbed as she stared at the TV. "All those people, thousands of them, they all have families."

And me? What did I feel? I know this is strange, but I was secretly thrilled by the reports. We had *never* been part of the big story, the news headlines. Never. And now we were part of the biggest story to happen in my lifetime. It was happening right here. "Pennsylvania," the reporters kept saying. And I felt connected to the big world, to the real world, for the first time. This was happening to *us*, and it was being recorded in *my* journal.

At 10:45, an announcement came on for bus riders to go to the bus loop. At eleven o'clock, car riders were told to gather out front at their drop-off spot. I figured that Mom would be tuned in to all this and would be there, but she was not. Neither was Arthur's mom, my aunt Robin.

I hung out with Lilly, not speaking at all. Then I heard Arthur's voice behind me. "Payback time, cuz! This is it. Vengeance is ours, saith the Lord!"

Lilly asked him, "What are you talking about?"

"Vengeance. Payback. I'm talking about a military response. They'll be needing a lot of men, and I'll be one of them."

"A lot of men to do what?"

"To get whoever did this!"

I shook my head in total confusion. I asked, "Who *would* do this, Arthur? And why? It seems so crazy."

Arthur shrugged. "Who knows? Who cares? It's a matter of honor now. We're going after them. We're gonna kick ass and take names, cuz. The wrath of God will descend, and the infidel will be slain. Amen."

When I looked closer, I was surprised to see that Lilly had been crying. She asked me, "Does this mean they'll close the Food Giant today?"

I shook my head. "People will be panic-buying. Who knows when there'll be more food deliveries. All planes are grounded. Maybe all trucks—"

"Tom!"

"What?"

"Just yes or no. Will they close the damn store?"

"No."

"That's all you have to say."

✢

Mom pulled up at 11:15. She told us, "Your father called. He said the store is a complete madhouse."

We drove straight to the Food Giant parking lot. It was crowded and chaotic. Mom eased the car into a parking space. "They say we may not be getting groceries for days. I have to stock up."

As we wended our way through the lot, I saw Dad and Bobby corralling carts. I hurried over to join them.

As soon as he spotted me, Bobby pointed and cried out, "Tom was there! He told me to do it. Didn't you, Tom?"

I had no idea what he was talking about. The planes? The World Trade Center?

But then it hit me.

"Oh my God!" I stopped and stood with my mouth hanging open. I had forgotten all about the prank on Bobby. I had forgotten to tell Dad.

Bobby's stubby finger stayed aimed at me.

Dad maneuvered a train of carts my way. He looked really pissed off. When he got close enough, he said through clenched teeth, "Of all days to pull a stunt like this! With our country under attack!"

"It was yesterday, Dad. We didn't know—"

Bobby screamed, "You did know!"

"I mean about the attacks." I half whispered to Dad, "Oh my God. What did Bobby do?"

Dad snarled, "He did what he was told to do."

I cringed.

"Mrs. Mercer came up to me at eight, before all . . . this happened. She told me that Bobby had said something inappropriate. Did you put him up to it?"

"No!"

"Did you know anything about it?"

"Yes, I knew," I admitted. "And I meant to tell you. I just forgot. I'm sorry."

I told Bobby, very sincerely, "I am really sorry."

"You're a liar! You're like Reg the Veg!"

"No, I'm not. I'm not like Reg. And I'm not lying."

"Yesterday! You lied yesterday. You told me it was the banana promotion."

"No, I didn't. I just . . . didn't tell you that it was a lie. I just stood there. I let it happen. I'm sorry."

Dad looked at me with great disappointment. "Did you really think that was a funny joke, Tom?"

"No. No, sir."

His eyes swept the parking lot. "Well, we have more serious things to worry about now. Bobby, do you accept Tom's apology? Can we all get to work?"

Bobby was quick to forgive. (He always is, except when it comes to Reg.) He shrugged. "I accept it."

"Okay. Please, both of you, get these carts into the store."

Dad took off, nearly running, and squeezed through the entranceway between clumps of shoppers.

Bobby and I threw ourselves into a frenzy of cart collecting, and bagging, and wheeling groceries out. All fifty carts were in use, and all were full of groceries, and all three registers were running.

The frenzy did not let up until 6:00 p.m. By then the shelves were about three-quarters bare. Dad and Uno had restocked them steadily throughout the day, but the stockroom, too, was now reduced to just a few cartons and lots of empty wooden pallets.

Mom came back at 6:05 and took Lilly home, but Dad wanted me to stay. (He was still mad about the Bobby prank.) I wound up working until 10:30, over ninety minutes after the store had closed. Uno (who was also in Dad's doghouse) and I had to sweep the front, the storeroom, and the parking lot.

By the time we were driving home, though, munching on our deli sandwiches, Dad had let the Bobby thing go. He wanted to talk about something else. He said, "I had to fire Vincent this morning."

"What? Why?"

Dad shook his head in mild disbelief. "He was stealing."

"Stealing? Stealing what?"

"Cleaning supplies."

"Really?"

"Yes. And over-the-counter drugs. Boxes of cold medications." Dad pondered that. "Cleaning supplies and cold medications. Isn't that a weird combination?"

I told him, "Yeah." And I thought it was.

But I wouldn't think so for long.

October

Monday, October 22, 2001

Mr. Proctor said September 11 would change everything, and he was right.

Everyone everywhere was freaked out all the time, waiting for the next terrible thing to happen—for the White House to blow up, or the Empire State Building to topple over, or Walt Disney World to go up in a nuclear mushroom cloud.

None of that happened, but it felt like it *could* happen. All of it. And other things that we had not imagined, like we had not imagined the jetliner attacks in New York, and Washington, and Somerset, PA.

The drama that unfolded over western Pennsylvania had become an instant legend: The passengers on the flight, all strangers to each other, heard on their cell phones what the hijacked planes were doing in New York and Washington. And they decided not to let it happen again. They banded together and stormed the cockpit. They overpowered the hijackers and prevented another devastating attack, and they gave their lives in the process. In tribute to them, thousands of people were now heading out to the remote farmland where the plane went down.

In homeroom, Coach Malloy actually rose to the occasion. He described the shock he'd felt as a child when President John F. Kennedy was assassinated. He described the shock his parents had felt when Pearl Harbor was destroyed by Japanese bombers.

In English class, Mr. Proctor focused more on the present. He talked about "the zombie-like tone" of the September 11 aftermath:

—New Yorkers wandering around, coated from head to foot with white powder.

—Xeroxed pictures of missing people stuck up on every lamp-post.

—A monstrous pile of death—smoking and wheezing—in the heart of America's greatest city.

We finished reading *A Journal of the Plague Year*. I didn't like it very much because I couldn't understand the language. Nobody could. Fortunately, Mr. Proctor explained what was going on.

"People were dropping like flies in London," he said. "Death walked among them. Death stood on every corner. What was killing people so indiscriminately? They had no idea, no clue that it was fleabites and airborne germs. They would remain clueless about such things for another hundred years."

I thought, *Okay. They were stupid. But what about us? Are we any smarter? Are we any less clueless about what is killing us? Out of the sky? Out of nowhere? Not really.*

It had been six weeks, and we still had no idea who had attacked us, or why, or when they might attack us next.

The drug-counseling meetings got suspended after September 11. When they started again, though, I was back in my seat in the conference room, staring at Wendy, hoping to talk to her.

Catherine Lyle opened the first meeting in October by saying, "Hello, everybody. Welcome back. We've lost a lot of time, so I'd like to jump right to Wendy's research report. If you recall, I asked her to look into a powerful new drug that has appeared in Blackwater. The drug is called methamphetamine. Wendy?"

Wendy had a pocket notebook, too, just like mine. She opened it, but she never looked down as she launched into her speech. "Methamphetamine, as a street drug, is called 'meth,' and sometimes 'crank.'

"Depending on what sources you consult, methamphetamine was first made in Germany in 1887, or in Japan in 1893. Farmers used it to feed cattle to accelerate their growth. Methamphetamine was first used by *people* during World War Two.

"Japanese kamikaze pilots took methamphetamine to psych up for their suicide attacks. German pilots and tank drivers used it for the same reason, calling it 'flier's chocolate' and 'tanker's chocolate.' Methamphetamine helped soldiers accelerate their fighting skills. It also accelerated their deaths."

Wendy looked at her mother. "So what is methamphetamine doing here in Blackwater, Pennsylvania, in 2001? No one knows. The answer could be that it's a very cheap way to get high. With some training, you can make it yourself out of easy-to-find ingredients, but the process for making it is very dangerous. The ingredients are highly combustible."

Wendy paused, apparently finished, so Arthur interjected, "I hear people are stealing Sudafed and ammonia and other stuff to make it. They can get what they need right at the Food Giant, even the propane to cook it up with."

"Who told you that?" Lilly asked.

"Uno," Arthur answered.

She corrected him. "He wants to be called John now."

Arthur shrugged. "Okay. No problem."

Lilly shook her head and added, "Wow. Meth. That sounds like the worst drug *ever*."

Several kids around the room agreed with her comment, including Arthur, who said, "Amen to that."

In conclusion, Wendy Lyle produced some gruesome photos from her notebook. The photos showed meth users—people who had lost their teeth, and their hair, and were all covered with red sores. She held up one photo that I couldn't even look at. It was a man or a woman—I couldn't tell—who had tried to make meth at home and had gone up in flames. Horrible. Gruesome.

Mercifully, she stashed the photos away. No one spoke for a minute; then Mrs. Lyle changed the topic. "I have been speaking to Mrs. Cantwell about this group and about some things we could be doing. I am pleased to tell you that she has granted permission for us to take our first field trip."

Arthur muttered, "Must be to that field her husband works in."

Mrs. Lyle consulted her notebook. But before she could speak again, Ben Gibbons raised his hand. She looked at him and smiled. "Yes?"

Ben *really* changed the topic. He said, "I have pica disorder, Mrs. Lyle. Have you ever heard of that one?"

Catherine Lyle looked puzzled. "I'm not sure. Would you like to tell the group about it?"

Evidently, he would. "As a little kid, I ate a lot of crayons and pencils and chalk. I still do. I eat wood—nontreated wood. I eat coal—anthracite and bituminous. I eat plain old dirt."

Arthur told him, "That is messed up, dude."

"Yeah, I know. That's why it's a disorder."

Catherine Lyle nodded. "I *have* heard of it. But do you know why it's called pica?" she asked.

"*Pica* means 'magpie,' in Latin. I guess a magpie will eat anything."

She thought for a moment. "Well, Ben, that is very interesting. But it sounds like an eating disorder, and this group is about substance abuse."

Ben looked nervous, like he was afraid she was going to kick him out. "It is?"

"Yes."

"Well, this pica thing could lead to substance abuse! Who knows what else I might eat in the future? Maybe pills or something."

"That may be true," she assured him. "It could be what we call a 'gateway' to other problems."

Ben looked relieved. "Yeah."

"Gateways are openings that lead to drug abuse. Think about it. Nobody just wakes up one day and says, 'I'm going to become a drug addict.' Do they?"

"No."

Catherine Lyle continued: "The good news for drug abusers is that, with medication and with counseling, they can quit.

"The real problems occur *after* they quit. That's when they must face their triggers. Triggers are the temptations that lead drug addicts back to using. A trigger can be as large as the loss of a loved one, or as small as the loss of a football game.

"The big question is, Why do these triggers exert such power over addicts? Why do people go back to drugs when they *know* they are destroying their lives, as well as the lives of those around them? These triggers must be very powerful indeed."

She looked at the group. "Who can give us an example of a powerful trigger? Okay, Ben?"

"War!"

Everyone waited for more. Arthur asked him, "War what, dude? You mean like the Civil War? World War Two? Vietnam?"

"No. Like going to war."

Catherine intervened. "Certainly. People who go to war are under tremendous stress, as are their family members. What are some others? What are some triggers that happen in your lives?"

A senior girl, who I had never heard speak before, suddenly blurted out, "Abuse."

"Yes. Abuse at home causes tremendous stress."

Ben asked her, "Do you mean getting hit by your parents? Like a punishment?"

There was a pause. I didn't think she was going to respond, but then she did. "No. I mean sexual abuse."

Everybody froze, including Mrs. Lyle. Then she picked up the silver pen and wrote something in her notebook. After a few more seconds of silence, she said quietly, "That is a very powerful trigger, yes." She looked at the girl. "We should talk more about it."

Then she looked at the rest of us, "Okay. Can we name any other triggers?"

No one could, until Lilly raised one finger. "What about just . . . boredom?"

Mrs. Lyle seemed relieved to have a safer topic. "Yes! Boredom can be a trigger. And some people turn to drugs when they are bored. But that doesn't work, does it? So what are some things that *do* work against boredom? Let's hear some ideas."

Nobody said anything for a few seconds. Jenny finally came up with one. "Jesus?"

"Okay. Good."

Arthur suggested, "Football."

"Yes. Those are two." Catherine Lyle waited for a third, but it wasn't coming. She finally took it upon herself to add, "Okay. What about dance? Or horseback riding? Or martial arts training, like tai chi or tae kwon do? What about learning how to play a musical instrument? Or taking up painting, or sculpture, or pottery?"

Arthur laughed ruefully. He spoke for the group. "We don't have a lot of that stuff around here."

Catherine Lyle didn't understand. "What stuff?"

"Any of the things you said. We got, basically, football and bowling."

That got a small laugh. He added, "And Jesus," and got a bigger laugh.

But not from Catherine Lyle. She replied seriously, "Oh, I'm sure there are many things to do if you look. There certainly are things to do up by the university."

She stopped there. I could tell by her face that she finally got it. She wasn't "up by the university" now. She was twenty miles, and a whole world, away.

So she moved on. "Ben, as you suggested, one major trigger is a catastrophe, like a war. Or like what happened on September eleventh. Many people are still very stressed about the events of that day, especially the events that happened near here."

She placed a blank sheet of paper on the table. "As a result, I have organized a field trip to the flight ninety-three crash site in Somerset County. If you would like to see that site—perhaps to pay your respects, perhaps to face your fears—please sign up for the trip. It will be after school on Wednesday."

We then broke into our small groups. Wendy looked at me and smiled. "We're going in my dad's Suburban. That holds, like, twelve people. Do you want to come?"

"Sure."

"How about you, Lilly?"

Lilly shook her head. "No. I have to work."

Wendy moved on. "How about you Arthur? I know your stepfather will be going."

"Yeah? How do you know that?"

Wendy answered simply, "My stepmom told me."

Arthur challenged her. "But isn't she forbidden, by a strict code of confidentiality, from talking about what a client says?"

Wendy was ready for him. "Yes, she is forbidden. Unless the client releases her from that, which your stepfather has done."

Arthur looked doubtful. "He's released her? He didn't mention releasing anybody to me."

"Well, ask him about it. He also gave her permission to discuss his fears in group."

Arthur might have responded, but he got distracted.

We all did.

Rick Dorfman opened the door and looked inside. He spotted Catherine Lyle and walked up to her. He said in a low, miserable voice, "I guess I'm supposed to come here."

Catherine Lyle whispered, "Are you the one Officer O'Dell told me about?"

He shrugged. "I don't know."

"Well, is this a court-ordered case?"

Dorfman twitched uncomfortably. "I don't know."

She asked him patiently, "Did a judge, as a condition of probation, require you to join this substance-abuse group?"

Dorfman looked around at anyone within earshot, including me. He answered angrily, "Yes."

Arthur whispered, "Not surprising. Dork-man's a big 'roids user. Everybody knows that."

"What?"

"'Roids! To bulk up for football, you know."

Lilly asked, "What are 'roids?"

"Steroids—HGH, progesterone. They bulk you up. Without them, Dork-man's really, like, five foot two and ninety pounds."

I laughed, which I probably should not have done. Dorfman turned and glared at me.

Catherine Lyle told him, "Welcome to the group."

He growled, "Just tell me what I gotta do."

"You don't have to do anything."

Dorfman's mouth curled up into a menacing smile. I had seen that smile before, and I started to worry. He said, "Look, lady, why don't you stop busting my balls and tell me what to do?"

Arthur reacted immediately. He pushed his chair back, like he might have to move fast. Rick Dorfman saw that.

Catherine Lyle remained calm. "As I told you, you are welcome here. You may join any group you like. You are welcome to take part or not, as you see fit."

But Dorfman was already moving back toward the exit. He held out the middle finger on each hand to the group. And after suggesting that Catherine Lyle do something that was anatomically impossible, he stomped out of the room.

Arthur rose up out of his chair. He seemed on the verge of going after him, but he didn't. Instead, he asked, "Are you okay, Mrs. Lyle?"

She seemed surprised by the question. "Why, yes, Arthur. Thank you."

Then she turned the incident into some counseling. "Let's take a moment to analyze what just happened here. Obscene language and physical intimidation are two elements of abuse. How do we deal with that? By turning to drugs? Or alcohol? Does that really deal with it?"

She stopped so we could shake our heads or mutter no.

"No. Because that's not dealing with it. Is it?"

Lilly had been tapping her pencil nervously on the table. She stopped and asked, "So what about a nasty jerk like that? I get them at work sometimes. What should I do?"

"In a situation like that, you should always ask yourself, Who owns this problem? In this case, that young man clearly owns the problem, not me. He is going to have to figure out how to solve it. The problem was not mine when he walked in, and it is not mine now that he has walked out, no matter what crude thing he has said or done to try to make it mine. He still owns it."

Lilly said, "That's good advice. I'm gonna use that."

Mrs. Lyle gave her a big smile, and the meeting broke up on that positive note.

When I arrived at the Food Giant, Bobby was at register one, bagging groceries for Marsha.

As always, he was bagging them quickly and efficiently. He wasn't saying a word, either to her or to the customers. He never did, except when there was a new bag boy to train. Then he delivered a pitch that came word for word from the Food Giant training tapes. Stuff like "Tell a customer there is no tipping, and that loading bags is a courtesy. Do not mix a package of frozen food with a box of cereal. The customer will get home with a wet box, and they won't be happy with us. Push no more than five carts at a time. Otherwise, you might damage the carts, or a customer's vehicle, or yourself."

This could get annoying, especially on the third or fourth recitation. I think we lost a few bag boys because of it.

As I grabbed my green slicker, it occurred to me that there had been *no* new bag boys for quite a while. Or new cashiers. Or new assistants behind the customer-service desk, or the meat or bakery counters. None.

Why wasn't Dad hiring anybody? Why was he working double shifts, and adding hours for Lilly and me, without pay? (I should say that, technically, we do get paid. Dad and Mom put money into our college funds, but still . . .)

I had just stepped outside when I heard shouting by the back spaces. Bobby was pointing at the bottom of a man's cart, so I ran out to see what was going on.

The man was short, stocky, and balding. And he was quite indignant, claiming, "I didn't know anything was under there! I didn't see anything."

Bobby countered with, "What do you mean you didn't see anything? It's right there. You had to see it."

"Somebody else left these," the guy insisted. "I was just getting a cart to go in the store!"

He was clearly lying, and Bobby knew it. "No, you weren't. You weren't going *in* the store; you were coming *out* of the store."

The guy had heard enough. "I don't need to stand here arguing with an idiot."

Bobby fired back, "You're the idiot. Stealing stuff. Only an idiot steals!"

I stood close behind Bobby. The guy's car had lettering on the back window that said LEHIGH UNIVERSITY. He had a bumper sticker that said MY CHILD MADE THE DEAN'S LIST AT POTTSTOWN ELEMENTARY. I figured that he was from eastern Pennsylvania, a long drive from here.

I examined the supplies under his cart—jugs of ammonia and rubbing alcohol, boxes of Sudafed and Actifed.

The guy threw up his hands, releasing the cart. It started to roll downhill, so I ran and grabbed it. He jumped into the driver's seat, cranked the engine, and peeled out, driving way too fast.

Bobby watched him go, shaking his round head disapprovingly.

I wheeled the cart up to him. "That guy was upset, Bobby. You need to be more careful with people like that."

"He needs to not steal!"

"True. But I don't want you getting hurt out here. And I know my dad doesn't, either."

"I ain't hurt."

"I know. But you could have been. That guy could have pulled out a rifle." Bobby's eyes widened. I added, "Or a bow and arrow."

"Yeah? Yeah. Don't tell your dad. Okay?"

"Okay."

"Because he'll call my mom. And she'll come and take my blood pressure. And maybe make me go home."

"Okay."

I gathered two more carts, slammed them together, and pushed them toward the entrance. Suddenly I gripped the handles and pulled the train of carts to a screeching halt.

I couldn't believe my eyes! There, just inside the glass, looking way too stylish for the Food Giant, were Catherine and Wendy Lyle.

I was thrilled. But then, just seconds later, I was horrified. I thought of my dad at the front in his white shirt and tie, and my sister at the register in her Food Giant smock, and myself running around in a green slicker. Could I look any dorkier?

I left the carts for Bobby.

I peeled off my slicker, lowered my head, and ducked inside. I scooted along the left edge of the store, not stopping until I was back in the storeroom, peeking out through its small square window. Peeking out like a stalker. Like a total loser.

But soon my desire to talk to Wendy won out over my shame. When I saw the Lyles turn down the cereal aisle, I hurried out and set myself up near the end cap, rearranging boxes on the shelf.

I heard Wendy announce in that perky TV voice, "Hey, it's Tom!"

I turned and tried to look surprised. Catherine Lyle wheeled her cart the other way, but Wendy stayed behind. She sounded surprised. "You work here?"

"Yeah."

"But . . . don't they have, like, child labor laws here? Don't you have to be a certain age to work?"

"Oh, yeah. I don't work here officially. My dad's the manager, so I work, you know, under the table. He puts money into my college fund."

She didn't seem to like that. She muttered noncommittally, "Oh."

That was followed by a long, agonizing silence, during which my mind froze up. Wendy finally spoke. "Seems like we're in a different context here, Tom."

"What?"

"You and me. When we're sitting in Mr. Proctor's class, or in group, we can talk about books and drugs and all. But here"—her blue eyes darted up to the cereal boxes—"we're just standing in front of the All-Bran with nothing to say."

I picked up on that as best I could. I pointed to the shelf and asked her, "Did you know that Mueslix, All-Bran, and Fruit 'n Fibre are all made by the same company?"

She seemed mildly interested. "No. I didn't."

"So are bran flakes, Special K, and Product 19."

"Really?"

"Yep. It's all Kellogg's. And"—I pointed to the next aisle—"did you know that Mountain Dew, Sierra Mist, and Slice are all made by Pepsi?" Then I pointed even farther afield. "And that

Reese's peanut butter cups, Cadbury eggs, and Heath bars are all made by Hershey's?"

Her pretty face oscillated back and forth slightly, indicating no.

"It's true. It's like . . . we think we're making choices in the supermarket, but in reality, there's not much choice at all."

Wendy's blue eyes bore into mine. She told me, "That's kinda deep."

I smiled. "Thanks."

Her mouth twisted into a frown. "But do you really believe that?"

I stopped smiling. "Believe what?"

"That there's not much choice?"

I didn't understand. "For what?"

She looked toward those distant aisles. "Not much choice for your life. You know—for where you live, for what you do."

"I sure hope there's a choice. I don't want to stay here."

She looked interested again. "No? You want to move somewhere else?"

"Yeah! I've been sending away for college brochures, to places I think I can get into. You know, if I work hard. And they're all in Florida."

"Florida?"

"That's about as far from here as you can get."

"Yeah." She hesitated for just a moment. "We've lived there."

"Really? Where?"

"Melbourne."

"Was that a nice place?"

"Yeah. It was nice. But I liked California even better. San Diego. That's where my mom lives now."

"Oh?"

Then she came right out and told me: "My dad left my mom for Catherine, back when Catherine was a grad student. My mom's remarried now, to a naval officer, and she travels all over the world." She assured me, "So it's all cool."

Catherine Lyle reappeared at the front of the aisle. She turned her cart toward us. Again she avoided eye contact with me, but not with Wendy. She waved for Wendy to join her at the register.

Wendy said, "I guess we're through shopping. I'll see you in second period tomorrow."

"Yeah. In our old context."

"Right. Good word. Use it three times and you'll own it."

"I know." I thought, *She must read the same PSAT workbook I do!*

I watched her walk away. She had that model walk, too.

A minute later, Dad stopped at the end cap and stared at me curiously. He said, "You're due for a break, aren't you, Tom?"

I checked my watch. "Yeah, I am. Can I get the keys to the van?"

Dad fished in his pockets. "Sure."

I took the keys and walked out, way out, to Dad's parking space. I was hoping to study some vocabulary and I thought the van would be the safest place, but I was wrong. I had just opened the book when Reg appeared at the window, lit cigarette in hand. He asked me, "Uncle Tom, did you rat me out with your dad?"

"What are you talking about?"

"About that Chiquita banana thing?"

"No."

"No? Then it must've been Uno. He's the type. He's lacking in the testicular department. You know?"

"Yeah. I guess."

Reg flicked an ash away. "What are you doing out here?"

I showed him the book cover. "Learning new words."

"For school?"

"For a test."

"For one of my dad's tests? I got the answers to those if you ever need 'em. They're the same tests every year."

"No. For the PSAT. I'll take it next spring."

He took a deep drag. "Uh-huh. What's that?"

"It's a test that colleges use to give out scholarships."

"So this is about money?"

"I guess so. Yeah."

"I hear that. It's all about money. Or the lack thereof." He pointed his free hand at the book. "What are the words? Let's see if I know any."

I resigned myself to a vocabulary lesson with Reg. "Okay. *Obviate*."

"What's that mean?"

" 'To anticipate and prevent.' "

"Give me an example."

I looked at the store in the distance. "Like if you think someone is going to shoplift, and you have an employee follow them around, you *obviate* the need for a cop."

"Because you anticipated what might happen. You thought it through."

"Right."

"I hear that. Give me another one."

"*Obdurate*. It means 'hardened in feelings.' "

"Like you're a hard-ass."

"I guess so."

"Got it. Give me one more."

"*Obsequious*."

"Never heard that one."

"Me, either." I read the definition. "It means 'fawningly attentive.'"

"What-ingly attentive?"

"I guess, like you're falling all over somebody, praising them."

"Like you're kissing their ass."

"Yeah. That's it."

Reg flicked his cigarette away. "Okay. Good. I'm gonna use those words."

"Use them three times and you'll own them."

"Is that right?"

"That's what they say."

We both watched Lilly and Uno walk out of the store arm in arm, heading toward us. They stopped at Uno's Jeep, six spaces away.

Reg called out, "Hey, Uno! Use that three times and you'll own it, bro!"

Uno scrunched his face and called back, "What?"

Reg just laughed evilly.

Lilly snarled at him.

I wondered what Lilly was doing walking that way with Uno. Last year, I might have blackmailed her about this, threatening to tell Mom. But not anymore. What Lilly does now is her business. Especially after work. Especially with Uno.

Mr. Proctor said it: Everything is changing.

Wednesday, October 24, 2001

As I approached my homeroom today, I spotted the hulking figure of Rick Dorfman standing by the door. I slowed down, assuming he was going in or out, but he just stood there, so I continued on.

That was a mistake.

He was waiting for me. As soon as he spotted me, he started clenching his fists. When I got within arm's length, he reached out, grabbed the back of my neck, and force-walked me inside.

Coach Malloy wasn't in there. The few kids who were quickly backed away.

Dorfman twisted me around until my face was directly in front of his. His eyes were ablaze with anger. With hatred. I was instantly terrified.

He spat out some words, spraying saliva in my face. "I been thinking about you, Coleman. You little nerd, you joke, you nobody! You think you can laugh at me?"

I remember feeling surprised that he knew my name. Otherwise, though, I lapsed into craven-coward mode. I shook, and I stammered, "N-n-no. I wouldn't. You don't understand."

He switched his grip to the front of my neck, grabbing me with both hands and squeezing, like he really might kill me.

Suddenly someone screamed at him. A girl's voice. That caused him to loosen his grip.

It was Jenny Weaver.

She looked every bit as angry as Dorfman. "Get your hands off him! And get out of here. You don't belong in here!"

Dorfman released his grip, but he didn't leave. He just took a step back.

Unafraid, Jenny screamed at him again. "Get back to the high school side, or I'll call Officer O'Dell!"

Dorfman's face muscles twitched, like he had a spasm.

Suddenly the mad-dog glare went out of his eyes, like a light switching off. He lowered his head and bulled his way out the door, knocking Ben Gibbons three feet back into the hallway.

Jenny took my elbow and walked me to my seat like she was helping an old man at a nursing home. She asked, "Are you okay, Tom?"

I reached up to my throat and tried to swallow. I couldn't answer.

She asked, "Do you want a glass of water?"

I shook my head no. I couldn't even look at her. I sat there in total humiliation, as red as a tomato, and on the verge of crying. I felt like everyone was staring at me.

I looked up at the TV. I imagined Wendy Lyle was staring at me through the screen as she delivered the morning announcements: "Tom Coleman today proved that he is a sniveling coward and a total wuss. Please join me in laughing at Tom about his ultimate humiliation. Now let's all rise to say the Pledge of Allegiance."

I didn't regain my normal breathing until halfway through first period.

And Coach Malloy didn't notice a thing.

I guess Wendy didn't notice anything, either, when she entered Mr. Proctor's room, although I still had a big red welt on my neck. She started right in, as if nothing was wrong. "I was talking to Mrs. Cantwell about the academics here. I've been trying to convince my dad that Haven's not so bad. He calls it 'a school for coal miners.'"

I choked out, "Oh?"

"She started telling me about her top students. Guess who's the number one student, academically, of all the incoming freshmen."

I shrugged.

"Tom Coleman." When I didn't reply, she added, "That's you, right? The kid who works at the supermarket?"

Trying to be funny, I flipped open my notebook. "Let me check."

She laughed. "Does everybody know this but me? Does everybody know you're number one?"

I shrugged again. "*I* didn't even know."

"Well, congratulations! You stay number one, Tom Coleman!"

I said, "I'll try." And suddenly I felt a lot better.

Mr. Proctor started class by pulling out a poster, unrolling it, and taping it to the whiteboard (Coach Malloy–style). It was a movie poster with screaming teenagers on it. It was black and white except for the slime-green title: *Night of the Living Dead*.

Mr. Proctor pointed to the board and explained, "This is the original poster for *Night of the Living Dead*, a cult horror movie that was filmed right here in western Pennsylvania.

"George Romero, a college student from Pittsburgh, was shooting commercials and bits for a kids' show called *Mister Rogers' Neighborhood*. But he had something else in mind. Something very dark, and noncommercial, and non-kid-friendly—*Night of the Living Dead*.

"This movie is not set in Transylvania, with some foreign-sounding Count Dracula as the monster. No. It's set in a town like yours, with regular people as the monsters. Regular people who had been your neighbors and your friends and your family just a week ago, but who are all bloodthirsty zombies now.

"We will watch this movie over the next two class periods. Then I want you to write an essay comparing and contrasting *A Journal of the Plague Year* to *Night of the Living Dead*."

He popped a video into the slot beneath the TV screen. Blaring, evil zombie music filled the room. It was cool stuff, but I thought, *No way is this part of the county curriculum. Mr. Proctor's going to get in trouble.*

Near the end of class, Mr. Proctor stopped the video to point out, "Karen, the cute little girl in the movie, is already infected with the zombie plague, but no one knows it. She'll wind up devouring her own mother and father. That seems pretty bizarre, right? And unbelievable. But let me tell you, I think *I've* seen zombies walking around at the college." Then he added darkly, "Meth zombies."

Arthur raised his hand immediately. "Yeah. I've seen meth zombies around, too, Mr. Proctor. Around my house. We definitely have them in Caldera."

Hands shot up all around the room. Other kids started to say similar things—that they had seen meth zombies around Blackwater. As I listened to their stories, I realized that I had seen one, too. I raised my hand, and Mr. Proctor pointed to me. I contributed this:

"One night last summer, just after closing time, I was doing a roundup in the parking lot. A guy was sitting next to a cart, just staring at me. His eyes were black, his mouth was hanging open, and he had all these rotten teeth.

"It was like I was looking into the eyes of a corpse. I went in and told my dad about the guy, but by the time we walked back out, he was gone. My dad said, 'He was probably drunk. Just sleeping it off.' But I've seen drunks before, and this was something else."

Mr. Proctor nodded. He continued to listen to our stories intently. People were still telling them when the bell rang, and he had to say, "Okay. That's enough for now. I'll see you all tomorrow for part two of the movie."

Arthur walked out behind me.

He started talking, like to himself. "So, let me make sure I've got this right. Dork-man went after Mrs. Lyle in the counseling group, and then he went after young Tom before school today. My God! He's attacking the women and children!"

That was mildly offensive. I asked, "Who told you that he attacked me?"

"Jenny Weaver. Why? Isn't it true?"

"Yeah. It's true."

"So who saved your sorry ass this time?"

"I guess it was Jenny."

"No way! She didn't mention that part." Arthur doubled over with laughter. He finally managed to say with real respect, "Those Weavers, man. They are awesome. When I was little, they came up to Caldera every Thanksgiving with food, and they came up every Christmas with presents. For the poor people, you know?

"Some people would get pissed off about that, like it was an insult. Like *Who asked you to give me stuff?* But my mom never did. She took what they offered and was glad to get it. The Christmas presents were always crap—like Dollar Store stuff. But still, it was something to open."

He stopped at the senior high stairs. "But back to Dork-man. What was it about?"

"I don't even know. I think he's just basically insane."

"Yeah. Could be. Could be genetic. Jimmy Giles had a hassle with Dork-man's old man a couple of years ago. The old man was insane."

"A hassle about what?"

"Jimmy got behind on payments on his big Ford, the F250. The bank sent Dork-man's father out to get it."

"Why him?"

"Dork-man's father is repo."

"What's that?"

"What's that? Man, you rich kids don't know crap! The repo man works for the damn bank. He sneaks out to your house in the middle of the night, hooks up your truck, and hauls it away. Like Santa Claus in reverse. There's no lower creature on earth than the repo man."

I pointed out, "So that makes Dorfman the son of the lowest creature on earth."

"Yeah. That's about it. He's like a repo man without a truck." Arthur shook his bald head. "Did you hear he's off the football team?"

"No. For what, drugs?"

"Nah. Coach wouldn't know about that. Dork-man stopped showing up at practice. Then he came to the game on Friday and sat on the bench, pouting like a girl because Coach wouldn't put him in. Then he quit." Arthur started up the stairs. "I'm gonna miss him, though. He was the only senior who was worse than me."

I was surprised at this sudden flash of humility. My face must have shown it, because Arthur immediately added, "We're talking about the skill stuff here—throwing, catching, kicking. For raw power, for pure destructiveness, like the wrath of God, I'm still the best."

"Good!" I called after him. "Glad to hear it."

✢

Lilly actually offered to work a longer shift so I could go on the field trip. Or was it to spend more time with John/Uno? Whatever, it was decent of her.

Everyone gathered in the high school parking lot at 3:00 p.m. Wendy, Jenny, Mikeszabo, Ben the Penguin, and I were there from the junior high side. Arthur and at least two of the stoners were there from the high school side.

Jimmy Giles was there, too. I overheard him telling Catherine Lyle quietly but firmly, "I always have to be near an exit wherever I am. Just in case I get panicked."

She assured him, "Certainly, Mr. Giles. I understand."

"Can I sit up front next to the door handle?"

"Yes. That would be fine."

The Suburban was like a cross between a van and a luxury car. It had two bucket seats up front and a big console between them. Behind those seats were three rows of bench seats, each wide enough for three people.

Jimmy opened the front passenger door and claimed his place. Mrs. Lyle opened the side door, indicating that the rest of us should pile in.

Arthur went first. He stepped up and maneuvered his way to the back row, sliding over to the left window. A high school stoner followed him and took the seat by the right window. Then Jenny, Mikeszabo, and Ben climbed in and filled the next row.

I think Wendy was planning on sitting next to her stepmother. She frowned when she saw Jimmy up there. Catherine Lyle pointed her to the seat behind the driver.

I was still standing outside, not sure what to do. I climbed in, thinking I would take the empty seat next to Arthur, but Wendy surprised me. She leaned over, grabbed my sleeve, and pulled me into her row.

And that was just fine with me.

I started to strap myself into the outside seat, leaving a space between us. Wendy shook her head no and patted the seat right next to her, within actual hip and arm contact, so I slid over.

I heard the sound of Catherine Lyle closing the door behind me. Then she got in, knelt on the driver's seat, and looked back at us. "Before we go, I just want to say that I hope you all will benefit from this field trip. I have spoken to people at the university who have driven out to the flight ninety-three crash site. They said we will be met by volunteers there. The volunteers are people who actually saw what happened. They have set up their own schedule so that there will always be someone around to tell the story to visitors.

"We need to keep in mind that the site is still a crime scene. Federal investigators have sectioned off the areas where we are and are not allowed to be."

Catherine Lyle swiveled back, sat down, and started the Suburban. She pulled out of the parking lot and headed west for the turnpike.

Wendy looked out the window, but she spoke to me. "Okay. So here's your chance to explain something to me."

I was happy to do anything for her. "What?"

Wendy held up a letter. It was from a private school in Schuylkill County. She pointed to the return address and demanded to know, "How do you say this word?"

I pronounced it for her. "*Skoo-kill.*"

Her nose crinkled. "How do you get that? I'm thinking *Sky'll-kill*. Like the sky'll kill you. Like it's raining down death or something."

"No. It's *Skoo-kill.*"

"What language is it? It's not English."

"I don't know. Pennsylvania Dutch?"

She pronounced that to be "weird." She put the letter away and pulled a paperback out of her large bag.

I asked, "What are you reading?"

She held up the book for me to see. "*The Picture of Dorian Gray*, by Oscar Wilde. Have you read it?"

"No."

"You should. It's about a handsome young man who does horrible things. But those things don't show up on his face like they do for most people. Instead, they show up on a portrait he has hanging in his house."

"Cool."

"Well, more like creepy," she pointed out. "That's like heroin addicts. You know? They're the best-looking drug users by far. Heroin actually preserves the outside of their bodies. But of course they're rotting inside. Like Dorian Gray."

"You seem to know a lot about drugs."

"Well, it is the family business. Now, at the other extreme, you have the meth addicts."

"Are they the worst-looking?"

"For sure. Their teeth fall out. Their hair falls out. Their skin erupts. It's horrible, and it all happens very quickly."

"So if you had to date an addict, it'd be a heroin user?"

She looked at me curiously. "I sure wouldn't date a meth user. Their sex drive is down to zero." She smiled mysteriously. "Your sex drive isn't down to zero, is it, Tom?"

I froze. My hands started to tremble, but I clenched my fists to cover that. "No. No, I'm above zero."

"You are?"

"Yeah."

"Then why haven't you asked me out yet?"

"Uh . . ."

"This would be the perfect opportunity. I mean, if you're interested."

"Uh, yeah, I'm interested. I just don't know how that would work," I explained. "I mean, I don't drive."

"Oh. Well . . . what about meeting somewhere? Like a mall? We could meet at the food court. You could buy me a smoothie."

"Uh, we don't really have a mall around here."

"You're kidding."

"No."

"Okay, then." She thought for a moment. "I'll have to invite you to my house. We're having a Halloween party on Friday night. My dad is really into Halloween. We always have a big, wild party."

"I'd still have a problem getting there."

Wendy was starting to lose patience. "Come on. You must know someone who drives." She turned herself all the way around, like her stepmother had done, and pointed to Arthur. "How about him? Your cousin. Does he drive?"

"Yeah."

"Does he live near you?"

"Sort of. He lives in Caldera."

Wendy blinked. I could tell she didn't know what that meant. I asked, "Have you heard about Caldera?"

"No."

I looked back at Arthur and then up at Jimmy. "It's famous around here."

"Yeah? Why?"

I lowered my voice. "Well, because it's on fire. Seriously."

She looked interested.

"Caldera used to be a strip mine," I explained. "Then it became a landfill dump. But instead of compressing the trash, they burned it. Big mistake. The trash was sitting on top of a vein of anthracite coal, which caught fire and started to burn. For years.

"People started noticing that their basements were feeling hotter, and smelling like sulfur. Just about everybody cleared out of there. The U.S. government condemned the houses and sent in the Army Corps of Engineers. They put most of the fire out, we think. It still flares up sometimes."

Wendy pointed surreptitiously to Jimmy. "But those guys still live there?"

"Yup."

Wendy shook her head at the weirdness of that fact. She muttered, "People make such strange choices." Then she didn't say anything else. After a minute, she opened her book and started to read. I passed the time thinking up interesting things to say when we started talking again. But she just kept on reading.

We finally exited the turnpike and began to drive down old country roads. We passed a scrapyard with more wrecked cars than I'd ever seen in my life. There must have been a thousand of them.

We turned left and bumped along a narrow gravel road. As soon as we crested the hill, I saw a brown car ahead—an older sedan, sitting on a muddy lot. A woman got out of the car, opened an umbrella, and walked over to us. She introduced herself. "Good afternoon. I am a local volunteer for the crash site."

A light rain started to fall as she launched into a prepared speech.

"United flight ninety-three came in from the north. The workers over there in the scrapyard were the last ones to see it. It flew in just forty feet over their heads, upside down, with its jet engines screaming. The plane held seven crew members and thirty-seven passengers, including four hijackers. Most of you know by now what happened.

"The four hijackers had seized control of United ninety-three approximately thirty minutes after takeoff. The passengers and crew were able to make secret calls from the plane. They learned from their loved ones that other planes were being used as bombs in a coordinated assault against our country. So they decided to take the plane back. They charged the cockpit and overwhelmed the hijackers. They lost their lives when the plane crashed, right over there. But their brave actions prevented another devastating attack, probably against the United States Capitol. Both houses of Congress were in session in the Capitol that morning. Our entire representative democracy was gathered there.

"And think about this: Do you know how those passengers decided what to do? They took a vote! Like in a democracy. And the vote was to take the plane back and stop whatever evil plan was unfolding."

The woman seemed genuinely moved by the story, even though she must have told it a hundred times.

"So people started coming out here to say thank you any way they could—by laying a wreath, or saying a prayer, or just bearing witness."

The woman pointed to the exact spot where the plane had crashed. It was raining pretty hard now. We could barely make out a field in the distance.

Suddenly Jimmy growled, "I can't see it. I can't see anything!"

He yanked his door open and tumbled out. He bent into the rain and started walking toward the crash site. Our hostess's umbrella was now flapping in the wind, and she was getting soaked. She told Catherine Lyle, "He's not allowed to go out there! No one is."

Catherine turned on the wipers. We all watched Jimmy push on to the edge of the field. Catherine asked, "Should I go after him?"

Before the woman could answer, though, Jimmy stopped.

He fell to the ground, on his knees, in the driving rain. He leaned forward slowly, until his outstretched palms and then his face were pressed against the ground. I believe he was praying.

The woman said, "As long as he doesn't go any farther, I guess it's all right. If he does, though, I'll have to call the police." She turned her umbrella so that it covered her head, and she worked her way back to the car.

Jimmy did not go any farther. After about five minutes, he got up, clapped some of the mud off his hands and knees, and returned to the van. He opened the door, letting a cold squall of rain blow in. He flopped back onto his seat, soaking wet. His face and the front of his jacket were streaked with mud.

Catherine asked us, "Does anybody have a towel?"

I thought, *Why would anybody have a towel?*

She called, "Is there one in the back, Arthur?"

Arthur twisted himself so he could see. "No. There's no towel back here. There's a toolbox, and some kind of lantern-flashlight thing."

She asked, "Mr. Giles, do you want me to stop somewhere and get you a towel?"

Jimmy shook his head no very slowly, like he was in a trance.

Catherine Lyle said, "I'll turn the heat on high." She turned it on full blast. Then she executed a sloppy K-turn and we started back along the gravel road, leaving the volunteer behind us in her car.

After a few miles of country roads, we were back on the highway. Catherine asked, "How are you feeling, Mr. Giles?"

He didn't answer. I saw Catherine exchange a fearful look with Wendy in the rearview mirror as we drove on in silence.

Jimmy finally did speak, his voice low and haunted. "Those people on the plane were doomed from the start. All of them."

I thought about those passengers trapped in that plane with, literally, no way out.

He added, "We're just like them. We're doomed, too. We're trapped, too. All of us."

Arthur called up to him, "Amen, Jimmy. You take her easy now."

Other kids muttered encouraging words, too.

The Lyles, stepmother and stepdaughter, looked at each other again. Did they think Jimmy was crazy? Maybe.

But I can tell you, the rest of us did not.

Friday, October 26, 2001

Dad left early today to help Reg unload a shipment of pumpkins. Mom made breakfast, like she always does. It was Quaker instant oatmeal for Lilly, and Life cereal for me (both products of the Pepsi food conglomerate).

I had my PSAT prep book next to me, opened to the vocabulary section. I read the words softly to myself: "*Laconic*, 'terse in speech'; *languid*, 'sluggish from fatigue or weakness.'"

Mom sat down at the table with us. Her eyes were shining; she was eager to talk. "So, Lilly, you're graduating this year. What are your plans?"

Lilly just shrugged, which is never a good move with Mom. "I asked you a question, and I would like an answer, please."

Lilly spoke through a mouthful of oatmeal. "I don't know."

"You must have thought about it." Lilly chewed silently. Mom tried, "Well, what would you *like* to be doing one year from today?"

Lilly's mouth was empty when she replied wearily, "I don't know. Why don't you tell me what I should be doing one year from today? That'll save us all some time."

Mom turned to me with a martyred look. Then she turned back to Lilly and said, "Well, I hope you will be continuing your education. That's what your college fund is for."

"No way! I am through with school, forever. I have done my time."

Mom said, "Okay. You have worked hard to graduate from high school. But what do you want next in life? A job?"

Lilly answered (laconically), "Sure."

"So you'll need a skill."

"I have a skill. I'm a Food Giant cashier. Why not just pay me to do that?"

"We do pay you," Mom protested. "We pay into your fund."

"Or maybe Kroger would pay me. And not into a fund."

"They wouldn't pay you much, believe me. You have to have a real skill to make real money." Mom got to the point. "Mrs. Nalbone's daughter Kellie took a course to be a dental hygienist. Now she's got a good job, in Dr. Wojahowitz's office."

This did not have the desired effect on Lilly. She screwed up her face in a look of horror. "A dental hygienist! You mean she puts her hands in other people's mouths? Oh my God. That is so disgusting."

Mom quickly added, "There are other courses, too. You could be a nurse's aide."

"That's even worse!"

I said, "Yeah. What do you stick your hands into in that job?"

Mom was losing her composure. "Lilly! Please. You need a way to support yourself."

Lilly smiled. "I'll just do what you did. I'll be a housewife, a traditional housewife."

Mom shook her head emphatically. "No. You're too young for that. Too young to get married. Too young to be serious about a boy. You're barely eighteen. You shouldn't even be thinking about marriage. You should be dating lots of different boys."

Lilly laughed. "Oh, right. And where would I be finding these boys? At school? Uh, no. At work?" She held up her index finger. "Let me see: There's Mitchell, in the meat department, but I think Del has her eye on him."

I closed my book and smiled.

Mom said, "Mitchell is too old for you."

I added, "Anyway, Reg says Mitchell is only interested in his own meat."

Lilly rolled her eyes. "Yeah, Reg the Veg. Now, there's a real catch."

Mom frowned deeply.

"And then there's Bobby."

"Lilly! We don't make fun of Bobby."

"I'm not making fun of him. I just don't want to leave him out."

Mom got to the point. "I don't think there's anyone at the Food Giant for you."

"How about John?"

"Who?"

"John, the assistant manager?"

"He's too old for you."

"He's twenty-two."

"And you're barely eighteen."

"I am legally an adult. It would be legal for me to date him."

"What? He asked you on a date?"

"He did, in fact. Yesterday."

"When he was supposed to be working?"

"He was working. He was setting up the Halloween display, and I said that I always loved Halloween, and he said he did, too. Then he asked me to go to a Halloween party."

"A party? Where? At a bar somewhere? You're not old enough to go to a bar."

"At the Hungarian church."

"At a church?"

"In the basement. He volunteers with the youth group there. He's chaperoning the party, and he asked me to come."

"He's Hungarian?"

"No!"

Mom looked trapped. "Your father is always hiring new people. Young people. You can find a boy closer to your own age."

"Like who?"

"Well . . . what about that Vincent boy? He seemed nice."

"Dad fired Vincent," I informed her.

"Fired him?"

"Yeah. A month ago."

"For what?"

"Stealing."

"He stole money?"

"No. Cleaning supplies and cold capsules." Mom looked confused, so I went on. "People are stealing those things to make meth."

That didn't help. She looked even more perplexed. "What is that, Tom? A drug?"

"Yes. A very addictive drug that you can make yourself, at home, using those supplies. We learned about it in our counseling group."

"You're not supposed to be learning how to make drugs in that group! You're supposed to be learning how to say no when people offer you drugs."

Lilly formed her mouth into a small O. "I said no when you offered me drugs."

"Me? What are you talking about?"

"The Adderall?"

"Lilly! That was from Dr. Bielski, not me. He said you needed it because you were sluggish!"

Lilly turned to me. "What does that word mean?"

"*Sluggish* means you act like a slug. Like a slow, soft worm. It's like *languid*. That's one of my words today."

"Great. I'm like a worm."

Mom corrected me. "It means 'depressed,' Lilly. The doctor prescribed that medicine because you were acting depressed."

She agreed. "Yes! I *am* depressed. I am depressed because I hate school. I have always hated school. But soon I will be through with school, and I will no longer be depressed."

Mom looked up at the wall clock. Her eyes were no longer shining. She exhaled loudly. "Okay. Put your bowls in the sink." She looked at Lilly. "It's time to go to the place that makes you so depressed." She looked at me. "And the place that teaches you to make drugs."

Mom's breakfast talk had not gone as she'd planned.

Wendy sat next to me today in Mr. Proctor's class. She picked up right where she had left off, talking trash about Pennsylvania, and Blackwater, and Haven. She said, "Even the people with homes around here look like they're homeless. Does everybody dress right out of the tool department at Sears?"

I looked down, embarrassed, at my own generic, nondescript clothes. "Well, we don't have much choice."

"People always have a choice. The women choose to wear men's clothes here—baggy jeans and work shirts." She raised her eyebrows to make a point. "Here's what I think: It all stems from the weather. If the weather is depressing somewhere, then the people who live there get depressed, especially in the fall and winter. It's called seasonal affective disorder.

"Depressed people don't care what they look like, or what their houses look like, or what their cars look like. It all filters down. This place needs serious medication."

"It needs drugs?"

"Yep. On a massive scale—lithium, Valium, Prozac. Like a

crop duster needs to zoom over Blackwater and spray it with antidepressants."

I laughed. "Sounds like it's worth a try."

"Definitely. This is not normal. You should see how people live in Florida."

"Yeah? I'd like to."

"It's always warm there, so you have to wear shorts, and T-shirts, and swimsuits. You have to show your body. There's no hiding it. You can't get by being all flabby and pasty and unhealthy-looking. California is like that, too. You can't be hiding under Sears all-weather farm clothes."

I asked her, "How many places have you lived?"

"Three: California, Florida, and—*ta-da!*—Blackwater, Pennsylvania."

"I guess I don't have to ask which is the worst."

"Let's see. Blackwater would come in at number one in that category, yes. And, curiously, at numbers two and three, as well. It's that bad."

All this time, I had figured that Mr. Proctor was deep in thought. He was standing by the whiteboard, but, as it turned out, he was listening to us. He took a step forward and said directly to me, "Blackwater, Pennsylvania, is the center of the world. It is the most important place in the world."

Wendy's face screwed up into a you've-got-to-be-kidding-me expression. She said, "Come on, Mr. P. Even the name is awful. It sounds like black death. Black Death, Pennsylvania."

"But that doesn't make it black death. *You* make it what it is."

I think Wendy wanted to rebut that point, but Mr. Proctor didn't let her. He told the whole class, "Okay! Let's start. I need everybody's attention up here."

He wrote today's vocabulary word and sentence on the white-

89

board: *au pair—an exchange student with household duties. The au pair pared a pear for the pair of pères.*

Wendy conceded, "That's awesome, Mr. P."

We all wrote it down and worked in our vocabulary books for ten minutes.

Then Mr. Proctor passed out another book. It wasn't a novel, though. It was a play titled *The Roses of Eyam*, by Don Taylor. He held the book high and told us, "This is a play about the bubonic plague. The roses in the title refer to the rose-shaped blotches that appeared on a plague victim's skin. These blotches, and a sudden sneezing fit, signaled the beginning of the end. You may have heard of this before without realizing it."

He flipped up both index fingers, as if he were conducting music, and recited, "'Ring a ring of roses, a pocket full of posies. A-tishoo, a-tishoo, all fall down.'

"And they did all fall down. In some towns, every man, woman, and child fell down. Dead. Every one."

He continued: "*Eyam* rhymes with *dream*. Or *scream*. It is the name of a village in England."

He looked at Wendy as he went on. "You may not like our village of Blackwater too much. You may think it is the worst place in the world, and you can't wait to get out of here. But before you go, consider the villagers of Eyam. They really *were* in the worst place in the world because, in the year 1666, death arrived in their village.

"The bubonic plague. The Black Death. When they realized what was happening, the villagers' first instinct was to run for their lives and take their chances out on the road. But their second instinct, their higher instinct, was to stay where they were; to keep the plague confined to their village for the greater good of mankind.

"More than half the villagers died because of that decision, died horribly. It is likely that many of them would have lived had they run for it. But it is also likely that some of them already had the plague. And they would have spread it, unchecked, throughout the countryside. They would have set off a chain of events that killed thousands.

"So this is a play about choice, and responsibility, and being connected to mankind as a whole." He looked at me. "And maybe it's about blooming where you are planted; about playing the hand you are dealt; about getting lemons and making lemonade. All those things."

He pointed out the window. "Are there better places than Blackwater? Maybe. Are there worse places? Yes, most definitely."

—✠—

At the end of class, Wendy ripped a page out of her planner. She wrote down her address and phone number and handed it to me. "Here. Don't lose this. I'll talk to your driver right now."

She sidestepped in front of Arthur before he could exit. She said, "Arthur? May I call you that?"

"That's my name."

"Sorry for the late notice, Arthur. I am inviting you to a Halloween party at my house. Tonight."

Arthur shrugged, but he answered, "Okay."

"Can you make it?"

"I guess."

"Good. Can you drive Tom?"

Arthur looked at me. "Sure."

"Good." Wendy turned to include me. "You will both need to wear costumes."

Arthur replied, "I don't have a costume."

I said, "I don't have one, either."

Wendy thought for a moment. "You two could go as a team, you know? The brain guy and the muscle guy. The brain guy rides on the muscle guy's shoulders—like Master Blaster in *The Road Warrior*."

Arthur's lip curled up. "What's that?"

"It's a cult movie," she said. "Or like *Freak the Mighty*."

I explained, in case Arthur didn't know, "That's a book. A little kid rides on a big kid's shoulders." Then I added, "Or like Banjo Kazooie."

It was Wendy's turn to look puzzled. "What's that?"

"Video game. It's the same idea. Smart bird rides on dumb bear's shoulders."

"Yeah."

Arthur looked offended. "I ain't doin' that. I'm smart *and* strong. I don't need Thomas here for my brain. And I sure ain't lettin' him ride on my shoulders."

Wendy smiled. "Fine. Those were just suggestions. A lot of the college guys are coming as zombies. All you have to do is wear something that makes you look like you just crawled out of the grave. Most guys around here dress like that anyway."

I told Mom a version of the truth: that some of the kids from the counseling group had been invited to Mrs. Lyle's for a Halloween party. I didn't mention that it was at Blackwater University. Lilly, after some serious pleading, backed me up. Or at least she didn't rat me out.

So, at 7:00 p.m., I was standing outside on Sunbury Street in the dark, wearing my grossest climb-out-of-the-grave zombie clothes.

I expected Arthur to pick me up in Jimmy's truck, but he

pulled up in a three-door midnight-blue hatchback. I opened the passenger-side door. "What's this?"

"This," he explained with pride, "is a 1997 Geo Metro."

"You just got it?"

"Just picked it up. I ain't even been home yet."

"Cool."

"It's a genuine Chevrolet, cuz, even if it is made by Suzuki."

Maybe I shouldn't have asked, but I did. "How did you ever pay for this?"

He answered as if it should be obvious, "With my money."

"Your money? But you don't have a job."

"I have something better than a job. I have an income."

A dark thought crossed my mind: *Does he mean an illegal income, like selling drugs?* But I was totally off base there.

"From the Social Security Administration," he explained. "I get a check every month. It started on the day my father died, and it will end on the day I turn eighteen."

I was relieved. I asked him, "When do you turn eighteen?"

"February second. That's two/two. And check it out: Next year, it will be two/two/two. Deuces wild, man! That's what I'm gonna have tattooed on my arm."

We rode in silence for a few moments through the chilly October night. As we rose up into the foothills, I asked him, "Would you mind turning the heat on?"

"Heat? Why do you need the heat on?"

"Let's see. . . . To survive?"

"But you're indoors."

"I'm inside a tin can. A freezing tin can."

"Well, this just ain't your night, cuz. The heat don't work. So I guess you're not gonna survive."

I resigned myself to a long, cold ride.

Our first stop was Arthur's house. This was my first trip to the condemned trailer where he lives with his mother and stepfather and stepbrother, Cody.

We turned off the highway and continued up a dirt road for about fifty yards. Arthur made a right turn, and we inched up a gravel hill. I saw a pair of trailers in the headlights. I stared at them closely, taking in all I could.

Aunt Robin's trailer was in front. It was made of white metal held together with some rusty screws. I'd say it was forty feet across and twenty feet deep—not a bad size. It had a painted brown door in the center, flanked by two windows covered with thick plastic sheeting.

The steps beneath the front door were improvised. They were made from two wooden pallets—like the kind Food Giant orders come in, but sawed off to fit.

A bright porch light illuminated a strange collection of items spread across the ground, Cody's baby toys and some other things. As we pulled closer, I could see orange plastic ducks and matching plastic rings, probably from a bath set. There were body parts from two or three Transformers, as well as Nerf balls, Wiffle balls, and a plastic bat.

I was shocked, though, by a few of the nontoy items.

These items had obviously been made from a stolen shopping cart—probably from the Food Giant. There was a low, square movers' dolly made out of four metal wheels and the slats from a wooden pallet. There was a half-full firewood basket, which had once been the main section of a shopping cart. It was missing its hinged, movable side. That's because that piece of metal was now the grill for a hibachi, sitting there on top of a ring of concrete blocks.

Bobby Smalls would have been horrified. But I had to admit it was all pretty clever.

I couldn't see Warren's trailer very well. It sat another thirty yards behind Aunt Robin's and on a higher elevation. It looked narrower by perhaps ten feet across. As far as I could tell, it had no debris around it.

We parked near the right corner of the first trailer and got out. Just as Arthur reached the front door, someone pulled it open from the inside. Arthur backed up to let Warren step out, followed by Jimmy.

They both smiled at me and said, "Hey, Tom," almost in unison.

Warren was holding an item I recognized from the Food Giant—a fifty-count box of Ziploc freezer bags. He pointed to the driveway and smiled hugely. "Whoa! Check out the new ride!"

Arthur grinned. "Yeah."

Warren asked Jimmy, "Is that the one you told me about, bubba? From Primrose?"

Jimmy nodded.

"Sweet." Warren winked at me, but he spoke to Arthur. "Now I don't have to drive you to football games? And sit there and watch you lose?"

"Nope. I guess not."

Warren then looked from Arthur to me. "So what are you two gentlemen up to tonight? You goin' joyriding?"

Arthur replied, "We're heading up to the college."

"The college? What for?"

Arthur smiled. "Tom's got a girlfriend there."

Warren poked my ribs with the box. "Is that right, Tom? You're dating a college girl?"

I protested, "She's not my girlfriend. And she doesn't go to the college. She just lives there with her family."

Arthur corrected himself. "I should say we are going to a party at the college, a Halloween party, invited by a friend of Tom's, who just happens to be a girl."

I nodded my approval. "There you go."

Warren asked Jimmy, "Remember the time we went up there, bubba? With Ralph? And the Cowley brothers?"

"I do indeed."

"That was some night."

"Amen to that."

I asked them, "Did you go there for a party?"

Warren replied, "Not hardly, young Tom. We went there for a fight."

Arthur, who rarely looked surprised at anything, looked shocked. "A fight? Why don't I know about this?"

Warren pointed at Jimmy. "Because bubba here never told you? So I'll tell you now. Here's what happened: Jim's buddy Ralph got beat up by two college boys. Beat up for no reason except that he was a townie.

"He was working at the Strike Zone, and these two frat boys showed up drunk. They were acting stupid, acting like they were better than everybody. Laughing at everybody. You know the drill."

Arthur nodded. "I do."

"So Ralph told them to leave. A few minutes later, he went out to make sure they were gone, and they jumped him. Beat him up real bad. So the next night, him, Jimmy, me, and some other guys went up there to take care of business."

"To the college?"

"Yeah."

Arthur asked, "How did you find them? There's gotta be a thousand people up there."

"It wasn't that hard," Warren explained. "They got those college bars on the main road, heading up to that big gold dome. We figured two drunken frat boys would be there drinking, and so they were! Ralph spotted their car after about five minutes. Then we all waited until they came out."

Warren smiled, remembering. "I believe it was a Ford Mustang. A bright red one. Jimmy took a tire iron to the front and back windows. We gave them college boys as good as Ralph got and then some. Then the bar owner came out, yelling that he had just called the cops.

"So we left them on the sidewalk, bleeding and crying for their mommies. We jumped into the back of Jimmy's truck and peeled out of there."

Jimmy added somberly, "Somebody coulda got my tag number. I kept waitin' for the cops all the next day. Waitin' to get arrested."

Warren told him, "Don't matter if you got arrested or not. We did what we had to do."

Jimmy agreed, "Yeah."

"They hit us, so we hit them back."

"Amen."

Arthur nodded angrily. "Yeah, I hear that."

Warren raised up his Ziploc box in a friendly wave. "Well, enough townie history. You guys have a good time up there. Don't drink and drive. Don't play with matches. All that stuff." He started up the incline to his trailer, calling, "Anybody needs me, I'll be at the Drunken Monkey."

I followed Arthur and Jimmy through the door. Arthur veered

left toward his bedroom. He pointed to the right and said, "Go sit in there. I need to find me some zombie rags."

I said, "Okay," and walked into the living room. It was surprisingly large—with a long cloth-covered couch along the right wall, a big TV straight ahead, and a pair of recliner chairs to the left.

Aunt Robin was sitting on the floor in front of the chairs. She is a small, feisty lady with long black hair and multiple ear piercings. She was playing with Cody—a cute, squirmy boy about two years old.

She looked up at me, "Why, Tom Coleman! As I live and breathe!"

I waved awkwardly. "Hi, Aunt Robin. Hi, Cody."

"Did I just hear you're going to a party?"

"Yes, ma'am."

"No drinking or drugs!"

"No, ma'am."

I had seen Aunt Robin often over the years—at the Food Giant and at other public places—but I had never been in her living room before. Nobody ever said it out loud, but we all knew that Mom and Aunt Robin did not get along. Going way back. We had never spent a holiday together, or any other day, for that matter.

Jimmy walked in from the kitchen holding a jar of Gerber's baby food and a spoon. He grinned at me, but he spoke to Aunt Robin. "Here I am, out bustin' my butt at work all day, and I got to come home and work here, too?"

Aunt Robin got instantly riled, like this was an ongoing argument. "Don't you start that, Jimmy Giles! Especially in front of company!"

She shot an offended look at me. "Don't think I haven't been working, Tom. I just finished a job driving a school bus." She pointed a red nail at me. "The trouble is, you need a second job if you drive a school bus, because the pay is so low. But you can't get a second job because you always have to be on call for the school bus job."

Jimmy interjected, "But having one job was better than having none, wasn't it?"

She answered angrily, "No. Not that job. It was terrible. You never knew what they were gonna throw at you. Especially if you were new, like me. You might have to drive the gangbangers, or the teenage girls with the babies, or the just plain old troublemakers up to the county school. With no security on board. Just you.

"Or you might have to drive the retarded bus." She assured me, "I got nothing against those kids, Tom. They're just fine. But some of them need helpers with them, and they don't have helpers."

She stopped talking.

I felt like I should say something, so I commented, "Bobby Smalls has Down's syndrome. He's the bag boy at the Food Giant."

"Yeah. I know who you mean. But he's a smart one, right?"

"Yeah. He's real smart."

"Well, I'm not talking about him, Tom. I'm talking about these poor kids who still wear diapers. And they're big kids! I just couldn't handle driving them every day. Maybe that makes me a bad person, but it was just too sad for me."

Arthur came out of his bedroom. He was dressed pretty much the same as before, in his camo pants and boots, but he had ripped up an old white shirt and pulled it on over his hoodie. And he had smeared black stuff under his eyes, like football players do for glare.

He said, "Let's roll, cuz," and exited quickly, without a word to Aunt Robin, Jimmy, or Cody.

I muttered, "I'll see everybody later," and followed him out. But we could not roll.

A car had pulled in and parked behind Arthur's Geo Metro. A white Saab convertible.

Arthur was really annoyed, but he didn't say anything. We just stared at the car uncomfortably until we heard voices from above. Two tall college-age guys emerged from Warren's trailer. Despite the dim light, I could see that one of them had a Baggie in his hand. Of marijuana? Probably. They were all laughing about something. Then they exchanged some goodbye stuff, like "Later, bro," "Be cool," and so on.

Warren stepped back inside and closed the door. I don't think he even saw us.

But the college boys did.

They kept walking toward us, but the one with the Baggie stuffed it into the pocket of his Blackwater U jacket. They got into the Saab, backed out, and roared away down the road.

I opened my mouth to speak, but Arthur cut me off. "You didn't see that. You didn't hear that. You know nothing."

I agreed, "Okay."

Arthur opened the driver's-side door. "Do you understand what I'm saying?"

We both got inside. I assured him, "I don't even know what you're saying, because I didn't see or hear anything."

He mumbled, "Good. What Warren does is his business. Always has been."

"Okay." Arthur dropped the Geo Metro in gear, and we began a tense drive up to the party.

I guess you could say that Blackwater University is the most famous thing around here, but I had never heard a good word spoken about it in my life. The university people look down on us, and we hate them for it. That's the way it is, and always has been.

We drove for about twenty minutes, mostly through farms and woodlands, until the highway narrowed. Then we turned onto a two-lane road leading to the main gate. College-kid businesses lined both sides of the road—used-book stores, coffeehouses, trade-or-sell music stores, and several bars. (I wondered where, exactly, Warren and Jimmy had found those guys and beaten them up.)

We entered the campus and veered right, following a perimeter road around academic buildings, dormitories, and a wide quadrangle dotted with statues. I recognized that Venus-without-any-arms statue. She had been the victim of a frat boy prank, though, and was now wearing a pink bra. (I wondered if frat boys did that in Florida, too.)

The perimeter road took us behind the student center, where we veered right again and, technically, left the campus. We were now in a tree-lined area that held the fraternity and sorority houses and the homes of the university professors.

Arthur had not spoken all the way up, and he did not sound happy when he finally did. "What's the address of this place?"

I told him, and we slowed down to look at numbers. But that turned out to be unnecessary. It was obvious where the big Halloween party was taking place.

The Lyles' house was a large redbrick structure with a white porch running around the front and sides. College kids in costumes were hanging out on the porch and on the lawn, and they were moving in and out of the open front door.

We found a parking spot a block and a half away and started walking back through a crowd of partyers. Some were in real costumes—I saw a Spanish matador and a couple of Disney princesses—but most people had improvised like we had, and the prevailing costume was indeed zombie.

The first person I recognized was Catherine Lyle. She was standing, costumeless, on the front porch (which was, of course, *her* front porch). She was speaking to a young man about the plastic beer cup in his hand. The young man reluctantly poured the beer over the porch railing and onto the dirt below.

When Arthur and I mounted the stairs, Catherine Lyle looked up and met my eyes. But then her counselor ethics kicked in, I guess, and she looked away. Her frown deepened, though, as she realized that two more underage kids, very underage kids, were entering her house.

Some kind of rock music was playing as we walked into the wide foyer. To the left was a living room filled with people on couches and chairs. They were all smoking and drinking.

To the right was a dining room. There were snacks and sodas on one table, and a CD player, some CDs, and two kegs of beer on another.

I heard a familiar voice call out from the back of the foyer. "Hey! You made it!" Wendy Lyle was standing there (leaning, really) against a wall. She was wrapped in purple cloth. Like a genie, I guess.

A short guy with curly hair had his arms pressed against the wall over her head, like he had her trapped. He was wearing an eye patch and a purple sash with a plastic dagger stuck in it.

Wendy slipped out from under his arms and walked toward us just as Catherine Lyle walked back inside. Catherine stopped her long enough to say, "There is to be no underage drinking, Wendy. That goes for you and any of your friends." She then continued down a hallway to what I figured was the kitchen.

Wendy was not like herself. Not like herself in class anyway, or in the counseling group. She was smiling at everything. She told me, over the rock music, "One thing I will say about the town of Blackwater [she pronounced it BACKwahr], one *good* thing, is that they are really into Halloween. We were driving around, and we saw all of these . . . haunted houses. You know? Like people had gone all out to turn their houses into these . . . haunted houses."

I nodded. "Yeah. There are always a lot of those around."

"I guess because it already is a dark, old, scary place, people just go with it, you know? They make it even darker and scarier. You know?"

"Yeah. I guess."

She stopped talking. I tried to come up with something to say. The best I could do was to point to the walls. "This is a nice house. It's all brick?"

Wendy wrinkled her nose. "I guess. Aren't most houses brick?"

"No."

"No? What's your house made of?"

"Wood."

I had forgotten momentarily about Arthur. He was right behind me, and he suddenly spoke up. "I live in a trailer."

Wendy started to laugh hysterically. "My God! Do you hear that? Do you get it? We're the three little pigs! I'm brick, you're wood, and you're . . . I don't know. What are trailers made of?"

Arthur didn't answer. He walked into the dining room and stared at the snacks table.

Wendy laughed for a little while longer. She muttered, "Straw. That's it. They're made of straw."

I asked her, "What's with the purple? Are you a genie?"

"It's not purple! It's indigo. It's because *I* am an indigo."

I must have looked confused. Wendy added, "That's the color of my aura."

That didn't help me. She asked, "Have you ever had your aura read?"

"No. I don't know what that is."

"Every living thing gives off energy in an aura," she explained. "Like the aurora borealis. And every aura has a color." She tugged at my sleeve. "You could be an indigo and not know it. Tell me: Do you seem to have more empathy than those around you?"

I remembered my PSAT vocabulary. "Like can I put myself in someone else's shoes?"

"Exactly."

"Yeah."

"And are you more creative than those around you?"

"I don't know. Maybe. That's not too hard around here."

"Yeah. Right."

The conversation deflated after that. Wendy started looking around, maybe to find someone better to talk to. "So, where did you get your aura read?" I asked.

"Cassadaga. In Florida. My dad took me."

"Uh-huh."

"It's all spiritualists. It's a very spiritual place. You should check it out when you're down there."

"Yeah. Maybe I will."

"I know you will."

"How do you know that?"

Arthur rejoined us. He had a handful of Chex mix.

"Because I'm an indigo," Wendy said.

Arthur asked, "What's that?"

"It's the color of my aura."

Arthur tried to pronounce it, like it was a foreign word. "*In-DEE-grow?*"

"Indigo—like indigo on the light spectrum," I explained. "ROY G BIV."

Arthur asked, somewhat dumbly, "Roy Biv? Who's that?"

"Nobody. It's a mnemonic device."

Arthur rubbed at his eye, smearing one black line of makeup. "Huh?"

"A memory trick. ROY G BIV. Each letter stands for a color on the spectrum."

"Relax, cuz. I know what it is. I'm just bustin' them on you. I know all that stuff."

"Oh."

"I was good in science." He asked Wendy, "Indigo? So that means you're . . . what? Like a grape?"

Wendy didn't respond to that. She checked around furtively. Then she whispered to both of us, "Who wants a drink? We have beer. We have rum punch!"

Arthur made a dismissive gesture with his hand. He answered curtly, "Not me," and walked outside.

I shook my head. "No. I'd better not, either."

Wendy shrugged. She stepped into the dining room and grabbed two pieces of candy corn. "I love these. Love them, love them, love them."

She took me by the arm and led me back to that spot against the wall, the spot where the pirate had been. He wasn't there now.

She told me, "Open your mouth."

"Huh?"

"Just do it."

I complied.

She placed a piece of candy corn on the tip of her tongue. Then, out of nowhere, she leaned into me, like for a kiss. She slid her tongue and the candy inside my mouth. I took it off with my lips, letting them run down the length of her tongue.

It was incredibly exciting.

Wendy reloaded her tongue with another piece, and we did it again.

Then she looked at me expectantly. All I could manage to whisper was, "What was that?"

She whispered back, "It was . . . what it was. Did you like it?"

"Yeah."

She backed away, smacking her lips together loudly. "Let's get some more. For eating, though."

"Okay."

"No more taking advantage of me because I am drunk."

I laughed. "Okay."

She led me back into the dining room. Two guys were standing by the CD player. One was dressed in zombie attire. The other had on a long black robe and a white skull mask, a death's-head mask. The death's-head was saying, "Play something Midwest, man. I'm sick of this L.A. pop crap."

The other guy pointed to a stack of CDs. "Tell me what you want to hear, bro."

Wendy dragged me right up to him. She called out, a little too loudly, "Hey, Mr. P.!"

The death's-head mask turned around. It had big holes, so you could see the eyes and mouth inside. It was Mr. Proctor all right. Definitely. And he did not look pleased to see us. He managed to say, "Hey. What are you guys doing here?"

Wendy replied, "I live here! This is my house!"

"Oh, yes. Of course." We stared at each other for a few

seconds. Then he turned left and started toward the front door. "Sorry. I really don't think I should be partying with you guys."

I watched him go.

Just as he disappeared, I felt a hard tug at my arm. I turned and saw the pirate guy with the eye patch. He looked me up and down, but he spoke to Wendy. "Now, what's he dressed up like? A townie? Is he your little townie friend? A little townie who has to go home now?"

Wendy said, "Shut up!" But she didn't sound angry.

"Bye now, little townie friend." The guy turned his back on me. He told her, "You come over here and shut me up." Then he took Wendy by the wrist and walked her back to that same place against the wall. Then he leaned over her, just like before.

I started to panic. I wondered: *Should I go rescue her?*

Then I stopped wondering.

Wendy opened her mouth to him, revealing another piece of candy corn. She stuck out her tongue and held it there, dangling it in the air, just as she had done with me. The pirate guy knew what to do next. He covered her tongue with his whole mouth.

And there they were, the two of them, making out against the wall. Right in front of me, like I wasn't even there.

I felt the blood rising in my neck, and face, and ears, like when Rick Dorfman was choking me.

I stared for a few more seconds; then I tore myself away. I pushed through a crowd at the front door, looking for Arthur, hoping to get out of there as fast as I could. But I didn't see him.

So I found an open spot against the railing and stood there with my head hanging down. I was furious and ashamed and humiliated all at the same time. I gripped the railing and stared at the ground, hoping nobody would see me or, worse, say anything to me. I was a total loser, just a total coward loser.

After a few minutes, I sensed somebody grab hold of the railing next to me. Grab it clumsily, bumping me to the side.

I saw a girl's arm to my left, and the purple folds of a costume. It was Wendy. She may or may not have known that it was me standing next to her. She leaned over the railing and hurled very loudly, projecting a solid three-foot-long stream of vomit onto the dirt below.

My stomach turned at the smell, and the sight, of the pieces of candy corn. There they were, risen from the grave of her stomach. Undigested. Making me sick.

From behind me, I heard someone say, "Nice shot."

It was Arthur. "You ready to get out of here?" he asked. "Or did you want to, maybe, kiss her again?"

Before I could answer, I heard the sound of a large, boisterous group coming out of the house. Wendy suddenly snapped to attention. She hurried down the steps and took off into the night.

A man in a pirate costume called out, "Wait! Is that my daughter? Does my costume embarrass her that much? Come on, Wendy—I did leave off the codpiece!"

The group of mini-pirates around him started to laugh, and I realized this was Dr. Lyle. He had on a long blue velvet coat, a puffy white shirt, and a golden vest. He had on a feathered blue hat, too.

Dr. Lyle's bloodshot eyes suddenly turned toward Arthur. He squinted and then demanded to know, in a loud voice, "Now, what are *you* supposed to be? Let me guess: a homeless man with a sleeping disorder?"

The pirate boys laughed.

Arthur did not reply, so Dr. Lyle tried again. "No? Perhaps a coal miner who has tried, unsuccessfully, to wash his face?"

The boys laughed again.

Arthur cleared his throat. He answered, "Yeah, that's it. I'm a coal miner. You got a problem with that?"

Dr. Lyle leaned back, popping his red eyes open. "Certainly not. That is a great career for the new millennium. Coal miner. Yes, there will be a great demand for nonrenewable fossil fuel and those who can dig it up, I am sure." He looked at his boys. "Did you know that *clean coal* is an oxymoron? A self-contradiction?"

The boys replied with variations of *no*, so he continued.

"Like *wise fool*. Like *military intelligence*."

The boys laughed appreciatively. One of them snorted, and told him (obsequiously), "That is hilarious, Doctor."

I looked at Arthur. He was enraged. What would he do? I took a step down the stairs, hoping he would follow me, but he did not. Instead, he spoke up in his dumb voice. "Well, coal minin' isn't as fancy as doctorin', I guess." He held up a finger, like he had a thought. "Oh! I hurt my finger today, Doctor. Do you think you could look at it?"

Everybody froze. Dr. Lyle's nostrils flared out, as if he had detected an odor. He finally replied coldly, "No. I'm not that kind of doctor."

"Oh? What kind are you?"

Dr. Lyle answered abruptly, "Perhaps you should go home now."

Arthur joined me on the step. "Yeah. Yeah, perhaps. Perhaps to all that." He took off quickly toward our parking space, and I followed.

Dr. Lyle said one more thing to his boys, but I could not hear it. They all started laughing, so I concluded it was about Arthur.

Or about townies.

Or about coal miners.

November

Monday, November 5, 2001

Last week was pretty miserable for me.

Wendy did not come to school the first two days after the party. Maybe she had a really bad hangover. I was relieved because I had no idea what to do—about her, about the college guy, about the whole humiliating scene.

That guy had broken up the most beautiful moment of my life. He had pulled Wendy away from me. He had called me her "little townie friend."

So what was I supposed to do about all of that?

Wendy finally reappeared midweek, on the TV, giving the morning announcements. She was smiling and beautiful, as always. She talked up this week's football game against North Schuylkill. (And she pronounced it right.)

I took my front-row seat in Mr. Proctor's class and waited for her. She breezed in just seconds before the bell. She smiled at me and whispered a breathless "Hi," like nothing was wrong.

I smiled back. I don't know why; I just did. I couldn't help myself. But I did not speak to her. I didn't speak to her on Thursday, either. But by Friday, I had relented. I had basically forgiven her. She had kissed me, sort of. Twice. And then she had moved on.

It was what it was.

Make no mistake, though, I had not forgiven that scumbag college guy. I couldn't. Maybe that's how they do things in California, and in Florida—they forgive and forget and move on.

But it's not how we do things in Blackwater.

Mr. Proctor began with vocabulary. He picked up his marker and wrote this on the whiteboard: *docent—a museum guide. A decent docent doesn't descend to dissent.*

Wendy sounded as perky as ever. "Another good one, Mr. P.!"

We all started working silently on vocabulary. I finished mine quickly. I guess Arthur did, too, because he started whispering to me from my right side. "Did you hear, cuz? We're going on another field trip."

I stared straight ahead, but I whispered, "No, I didn't hear."

"Jimmy told his counselor lady that he's scared of going down into coal mines."

"Is he?"

"Yeah. Jimmy did some wildcat mining a few years back. The down shaft collapsed on him, and it took the other guys about an hour to dig him out. He was okay, but he quit mining. Anyway, he told Mrs. Lyle about it, so guess where we're going next?"

"A coal mine?"

"Got it. Over in Ashland."

Mr. Proctor interrupted us. He raised his voice and announced, "Okay! It sounds like you're all finished."

He returned to the whiteboard and wrote *annus mirabilis—the year of wonders*. He asked, "Who here remembers his or her Roman numerals?" About half of us raised our hands. "Okay. Call some out to me."

We did, and he started to write them on the board, apparently in random order: *C, L, X, V, I.*

He turned back to us. "Come on, what are the bigger ones? M is a thousand, right? What about five hundred? What is that?"

Nobody answered, until Wendy told him, "*D*."

"There you go!" He added *M* and *D* to the list. "That's it. And that's all of them. The Romans had no use for millions, or billions, or trillions. And frankly, neither do we." He pointed at the capital letters, and we learned that they were not in random order after all.

"The Romans only needed *these* numerals. And only once in human history would each numeral appear only one time, in descending order, to designate a year. The year was MDCLXVI. Who can tell me what that is in our numbers? How about you, Tom?"

He caught me off guard, but I managed to work it out aloud: "Sixteen hundred and . . . sixty-six."

"Correct! Good man! Sixteen sixty-six. It was expected to be the annus mirabilis, the year of wonders, and great things were expected to happen during it. However, because of what *did* happen during it, it has come down through history bearing another name. That name is . . ." He paused for effect before intoning in his horror-movie voice, "The plague year, 1666. One of the most deadly, destructive, devastating years in all of human history."

He paused to write *the plague year* on the whiteboard.

Wendy raised her hand. "Mr. P.? What would that be in Latin?"

"I am not sure," Mr. Proctor admitted. "I did look it up online"—he started to write again—"and I came up with three possibilities." He read them out: "*annus vomicam, annus pestis, and annus pestilentiae.*"

Arthur pointed out, in what I guess was his Wendy Lyle voice, "Mr. P.? They've all got *anus* in them."

A few kids sniggered.

Wendy turned and glared at him.

Ben said, "I like Annus Vomicam. It has, like, the plague and vomit in it."

Arthur turned to Ben and added, "And *anus*. And *cam*, like in *camera*. Like you have a camera in your anus to record when you're vomiting."

Ben replied, "Awesome."

Just about everybody laughed or groaned. Except Wendy. She threw up her hands angrily.

Mr. Proctor stopped the discussion, saying, "Okay. Okay. That one is particularly disgusting, yes. But so was the plague. Let's remember what we already learned about it from Daniel Defoe." He raised up his copy of *A Journal of the Plague Year.*

"The plague had devastated London the previous year. The English people *knew* they were in for it. They were aware of plagues that had ravaged Europe three hundred years before, when half the people in the Western world had died.

"Half the people in the world! Dead! For no apparent reason!

"Imagine what the plague would do to your town. Imagine half the kids in this school not showing up tomorrow, not because they were sick, but because they were *dead*. Half the members of your family not showing up for Thanksgiving dinner! Half the world . . . just . . . gone!

"It was devastating beyond belief. It appeared to be the end of the human race. Whole towns disappeared. Whole economies collapsed. There was no one left to bring in the crops, or herd the sheep, or milk the cows. Western society broke down completely, and it would stay broken down for generations to follow."

Mr. Proctor held up his copy of *The Roses of Eyam.* "That brings us to my play. My play needs actors." He looked right at me. "My play needs you.

"Now, do not worry if you have never acted before. I promise you, this will be a no-pressure production. All the actors will carry Bibles. Inside those Bibles will be your lines, typed out in big letters. You may simply read what you cannot memorize."

Wendy didn't like that, and she told him so. "That is so lame. Actors should memorize their lines."

Mr. Proctor shook his head. "It will be fine. The message of the play is what matters." He pointed his book at Wendy. "You know, I could see you and Tom Coleman in the lead roles."

Wendy smiled delightedly.

I did not. I replied right away, "I'm sorry, Mr. Proctor. I can't do it. I have to work."

He raised up one eyebrow. "It may not be the big time commitment you think."

"I have to work just about every day now."

Mr. Proctor seemed genuinely disappointed. "Oh. Okay. I'm sorry to hear that."

I thought, *Yeah. Me, too.*

He pointed to my right. "How about you, Arthur? I have a role in mind for you."

"What is it?"

"The Bedlam."

"Who's that?"

"He's a very important character."

Arthur cocked his head. He asked, like he was horse trading, "If I played him, would I get an A for your class?"

"Yes, you would."

"For both semesters? Because that's what I really need."

Mr. Proctor thought for a moment, but then he agreed. "Sure. Why not."

Arthur slapped his desk. "Then sign me up."

Mr. Proctor pointed his book at other students. "Ben, Jenny, you could have parts, too. Let's talk about it. I'd like this class to take as many parts as possible. The remaining parts will be filled by members of the Drama Club."

So, for the next fifteen minutes, everybody who was interested in a part got one.

Everybody but me.

Because I had to work. For no money. At a family business that my family doesn't even own.

†

After school, while we were waiting to go into the conference room, Arthur said, "Check this out: Jimmy Giles had on a white shirt and tie this morning."

"No way."

"Yeah. He's got a new gig with WorkForce." He explained, "They do day labor."

"I know. We use those guys at the Food Giant."

"Jimmy doesn't like it. He says it's like government work."

"What's that mean?"

"It means you don't really have to work. Close enough is good enough. That kind of thing."

"Got it."

Jenny came out of Mrs. Cantwell's office. She joined Arthur and me and whispered, "Did you hear? Mike Szabo's dad got arrested."

I was shocked. "No!"

"Yes. Out on the turnpike. At a rest stop."

"What did he do?"

Her voice dropped even more. "He tried to sell meth to an undercover cop."

"Meth? Are you sure?"

"Yeah. Mike told me himself. His mom was in the car when it happened, so they both got busted. Taken to the police station, the whole bit. Anyway, they're gone."

I was really stunned. "They're gone? What do you mean? He has no parents, just like that?"

"Yeah. They had no money for bail, so they're in the county jail, awaiting trial."

Arthur, always skeptical, demanded to know, "How did you hear this?"

"Like I said, I talked to Mike. And his parents talked to my parents from the jail. They asked if Mike and the twins could stay with us."

"The twins?"

"He has twin sisters. Two-year-olds."

I couldn't believe what I was hearing. "So they're all moving in with you?"

Jenny acted like it was no big deal. "They already have. The two little girls—Maggie and Dollie—and Mike." She looked around furtively. "Anyway, don't say anything to Mike. We're doing a presentation today. He's already nervous enough."

Mikeszabo walked in shortly after. He had three white posters rolled up under his arm. If he was broken up about losing his parents, it did not show on his face. He joined Jenny at the front of the room, where they huddled with Catherine Lyle.

The rest of us took our seats. (They were the seats we had taken the very first day, back on September 10. No one in the group ever deviated.)

Catherine Lyle began, "We have been talking about drugs and how they can destroy a community. Jenny Weaver suggested to me that we could do more than just talk. We could take action in some way; perhaps sell T-shirts that warn people about getting involved with drugs. I thought that was a great idea. So today Jenny, with Mike's help, is going to open our meeting. Jenny?"

Jenny and Mikeszabo stood up and unrolled one poster. It had a black-and-white drawing on it. The drawing looked like a robot bug, with round pods sticking out. Jenny said, "This is the molecule for dopamine. That's the hormone that sends feelings of pleasure to the brain."

Jenny held on to the poster while Mikeszabo unfurled the second one. The drawing looked like the first one, but with a slight variation. "This is the molecule for methamphetamine," Jenny explained. "As you can see, it is very similar to the dopamine molecule, similar enough to fool the brain into thinking it *is* the pleasure molecule.

"But it is not. And the brain won't stay fooled for long. The brain realizes it has been tricked by the meth molecule, and it shuts down. It refuses to send *any* feelings of pleasure to the brain."

Mikeszabo put down the second poster and unfurled the third. In its center was a drawing of some drug paraphernalia—pipes, cigarette papers, needles. On top of the pile were three giant blue letters: *NEO*. Underneath the pile were the words, also in blue, *Not Even Once*.

Jenny put down her poster and explained. "Your own brain, your own body, will turn against you if you mess with drugs. It will shut down your ability to feel pleasure. It will make your life so much less than it could have been. That's why we need to send out this message to everyone we can, in every way we can: NEO—Not Even Once." She bowed slightly. "Thank you."

The group applauded. Catherine Lyle positively beamed. Spontaneously, she said, "No, thank *you*! I would like to see this drawing, and this slogan, on a T-shirt. If it's all right with you, I will advance the money to get those shirts made."

Everyone approved of that.

Catherine Lyle then elaborated on the theme. "All it takes is one time for certain things—drugs, suicide, choking, sexually transmitted diseases. You don't get a second chance with these things. These are things you cannot do *even once*."

After thanking Jenny and Mikeszabo again, Mrs. Lyle switched gears. "Okay. Last month was Halloween, and we all got scared of vampires and zombies and other pretend monsters. Those were irrational fears." Then, attempting a joke, she added, "Unless you happen to know any real monsters." No one laughed. She went on. "This month we will face a real fear called claustrophobia. Who can tell me what that is?"

Wendy gave the answer right away: "Fear of confined spaces."

Catherine frowned at her, I guess for not letting one of us answer. She continued: "Fear can be a major trigger for drug use, or for a drug relapse. So our next field trip will be to a local coal mine in order to face the fear of confined spaces. Anyone who would benefit from that should sign up and come along."

I resisted the urge to look at Wendy. Was she looking at me? Was she thinking I would go, and sit with her, and be totally fascinated by everything she said and did?

Yeah. She probably was. But that wasn't going to happen. At least I didn't think so.

During my break at work, I grabbed my PSAT book and headed out back, hoping to do some vocabulary. But, to my surprise, Reg was there on the loading dock. He was standing with his back to me, posing like he was on a stage. His left arm extended outward, like it was the fret board of a guitar. His right arm was striking that guitar with sweeping blows. His voice, somewhat higher than normal, belted out the chorus of Ted Nugent's "Wango Tango."

He knew someone had joined him on the dock, because he stopped singing. But his arm crashed down on a few more chords before he turned to see who was there.

"Tom! Hey, I was just doing some Nugent for the fans."

"The fans?"

"Right. The produce. They love it, especially the potatoes."

Reg pulled out a Marlboro and lit it. He pointed to my book. "Okay, enough culture. What are the words today?"

I opened the book and read one aloud. "*Puerile.*"

Reg took a deep drag. "Sounds like *pubes*. Puberty."

"Close. It means 'childish, juvenile.'"

"That's me. What's next?"

"*Pusillanimous.*" Before he could put an obscene twist on that, I added the definition. "'Lacking courage, cowardly.'"

"Being a pussy, in other words."

"Right. In other words."

"That's a good one. What else you got?"

"*Pernicious.* It means 'highly destructive.'"

"Ah, no. No way. That's not me." Reg took a final, long drag, burning up about an inch of tobacco. "There's not a pernicious bone in my body." He pitched what was left of the glowing cigarette into the truck bay, then saluted comically and walked back into the storeroom with all that smoke still inside his lungs.

I did manage to memorize a page of words before it was time to go in. Then I stashed my book on a shelf, pushed open the door, and saw two people standing by the bakery—Reg and Bobby. Never a good combination.

Reg was holding up a plastic bottle of Gold Bond talcum powder. He was pointing to it and talking, like a TV pitchman. "Bobby, you need to try this. You owe it to your customers." He turned to include me. "Right, Tom?"

"What is this about?" I asked.

"I am trying to get Bobby to sprinkle some of this down his pants to relieve his chafing. I do it all the time, Bobby. I go through three or four bottles of this stuff every week. You owe it to your customers not to be irritable due to chafing in the crotch area. Did you ever hear the word *crotchety*?"

Bobby squirmed. "Yeah. I've heard that word. So what?"

"Well, that's exactly what it means. Tom knows lots of big words." He asked me, "Do you know the word *crotchety*?"

"Leave me out of this."

"It means some guy has neglected to take proper care of his crotch, and he has become crotchety, irritable, unpleasant to customers. Do you think that's good for business?"

I continued past them and got to work.

Reg, apparently, did not. Ten minutes later, he was at register two, bothering Lilly. I heard him say, "I can help you get a used car. Then we can go out together, now that you're legal."

Lilly, barely acknowledging him, muttered, "How do you know that?"

"What? That you're legal? Uno told me."

She didn't like that. "John said I was *legal*?"

"In so many words. He said you turned eighteen."

"That's not the same. Anyway, I wouldn't go out with you."

"Well, we wouldn't have to go very far. We could just go to the parking lot, to your car, where you could express your gratitude."

Lilly shook her head. She replied matter-of-factly, "You are such a pig."

"I am not a pig. I am merely puerile." He turned to include me. (I wished he would stop doing that.) "Right, Mr. Tom?"

"Leave me out of this."

"Come on, Lilly," Reg continued. "Why are you so mean? You don't talk like this to Uno."

"He's going by John now, not Uno."

"Why?"

"That's a boy's nickname. He's a man now."

"Yeah? You made him a man?"

Lilly was starting to lose her cool. "Shut up."

"Or did the other one finally drop?"

"Shut up!"

I looked over toward the customer-service desk and saw a stocky guy standing there. Something about him bothered me; it took me a second to realize why. It was Rick Dorfman. He was pointing at Walter and talking to him in an animated way.

Walter is a mild-mannered older guy. He's retired, after working thirty-five years at the post office. He smiles at everybody, but he wasn't smiling now. He looked scared. I thought about calling Dad to intervene, but Dorfman suddenly stopped pointing and talking, and stomped out of the store.

I got well out of his way, thinking, *Good riddance*.

A few minutes later, when Bobby came through the register line, I was sorry to see that he was carrying a bottle of Gold Bond talcum powder. I probably should have stopped him then and there, but I didn't. I was afraid that would only make things worse.

Reg called after him, "Now don't be stingy with that stuff, Bobby. Apply it liberally."

Bobby replied, "Yeah. Okay."

Reg waited until Bobby exited the store. Then he picked up the register phone and punched in the public-address number. He intoned, "Cleanup in Bobby's room!" and hung up. With a final chuckle, he stuck a cigarette in his mouth and walked outside.

Lilly turned to me. "He is a pig. Piglike. Not that other word."

"*Puerile?*"

"Yeah."

Lilly pulled out her cash drawer and waved to Dad. He came over and asked, "Are you ready to close?"

"I am way beyond ready."

Five minutes later, Lilly and I were standing outside, waiting for Mom. As we watched Reg drive away in his pickup, Lilly asked, "Did he show you that website?"

"Who, Reg?"

"Yeah."

"No. What website?"

"It was some gross thing, of course, just like Reg. John and him were looking at it on the office computer. John showed it to me, so I figured they showed you."

"No. Not yet, anyway."

"Some guy at Blackwater University made it. He put pictures of girls on there, and he rated them on what they'd do to guys on dates."

"What do you mean?"

"Like sex stuff."

"Really?"

"Yeah. It's gross. So, I was looking at some of the girls, and . . . that Wendy girl is on it."

I tried to remain calm. I just repeated, "Really?"

"Yeah. I saw her picture. She was wearing, like, a purple Halloween costume. I told John, 'Hey! That girl's in our counseling group. She's Mrs. Lyle's daughter.'"

"Uh-huh."

"She's like fourteen or fifteen years old. Right?"

"Yeah."

Lilly shook her head. "That's not right. I bet that's not even legal. It's like abusing a minor."

I chose my words carefully. "What does it say about her?"

"It says the same stuff about every girl on there. It has columns with check marks. She'll do this—like French kissing—but she won't do this—like, you know. It's gross, stupid guy stuff."

Suddenly I felt like somebody had cut open the back of my head and sucked out my brain. I was totally numb.

Then I got angry.

I got angry at Wendy. For flirting with me. For making me think I had a chance with her. For asking if I had a zero sex drive. (Yeah, maybe I did, after watching her puke up those candy corns. That'll do it.)

But I got more angry—enraged, violent angry—at that college guy. That scumbag. For calling me a townie. For making out with my girl—even if she was only my girl for ten minutes—and then posting lies about her on a website. A dirty sex site. What kind of scumbag would do that?

And, more important, what was I going to do about it?

Tuesday, November 6, 2001

I got to class early. I sat in the front row and stared up at the bars of the TV test pattern: ROY G BIV.

Wendy came in at the last second and sat next to me. I couldn't even look at her.

Mr. Proctor wrote out today's vocabulary word and sentence without comment: *eschew—avoid. The shrewd shrew eschewed the chute.*

Wendy, apparently, was not impressed. She didn't say anything about it. We worked in our vocab books for ten minutes. Then I couldn't take it anymore. I leaned my head toward Wendy and kept it there until I knew she was listening. Then I whispered in a quick, flat monotone exactly what Lilly had told me. Every word.

Wendy's blond head stayed frozen in place until the end of my monologue. Then she whispered back, "First of all, if I am on that site, that guy is lying about me."

"So you know about the site, and the guy? Is he your boyfriend or something?"

"That would fall under the category of none of your business."

I pulled away, angrier than ever. I leaned back and demanded to know, "It was that guy at the Halloween party, wasn't it?"

After a moment, she conceded, "Yes."

"You were making out with him."

She finally answered, "I was drunk. I was making out with you, too."

"Yeah. I remember. So, did he ask you out after that?"

"Yes, he did. He wanted me to go back to his room that

night, and I said no, and I guess that's why he's telling lies about me."

"So he did this as revenge?"

"I guess, yeah." After a long pause, she looked straight at me. She softened her voice. "Look, Tom, I'm really sorry about what happened at the party. I was drinking, and I should not drink. It's a problem for me." She added, "That's why I'm in the counseling group."

After a long pause, I finally managed to mumble, "Okay."

Mr. Proctor walked over and stood right in front of me. He rarely got annoyed at talkers, but he was today. He asked coldly, "Are you two finished?"

I answered for both of us. "Yes."

"Then let me get your attention up here." He raised his voice. "Let me get everybody's attention up here, please." Mr. Proctor pulled out his marker and stepped to the whiteboard. He drew a rectangle with a curvy right side. He called over his shoulder, "What does this look like?"

Ben answered, "A rectangle?"

"No. What state in the United States does it look like? I'll give you a hint: We're living in it now."

Several people chorused: "Pennsylvania."

"That's right. Your state. My state. Now listen to this, because it is important: Pennsylvania was once considered to be a Garden of Eden by Europeans. Many religious communities, utopian communities, settled here. They lived off the bounty of the land, in a Garden of Eden, just like the villagers of Eyam. Then, just as in Eyam, just as in Eden, something evil arrived, something so horrible that it was able to destroy everyone and everything.

"For the town of Eyam, that something was the bubonic

plague. For Pennsylvania, that something was methamphetamine. For both places, it signaled the start of a plague year."

He looked out at the class. "Those of you who are writing journals, I want you to keep this in mind." He picked up a leather-bound classic. "In *Paradise Lost*, John Milton describes man's fall from the Garden of Eden. So . . . who will tell the story of man's fall from the beautiful land that was Pennsylvania? Will it be one of you?"

He looked right at me. On another day, I might have been excited. I might have been honored. But right then I couldn't even register what he was saying.

I was in my own world, and it was a world full of pain.

All I could think about was that college guy. And what he had done to Wendy. And what he had done to me. And what he had said to me. And what I should do about it.

By the end of class, though, I had my answer. I turned and asked Arthur urgently, "Will you drive me to the college on Saturday?"

"Why?"

"I think I need to beat a guy up."

"Righteous! Who is it?"

"A guy who started a website."

"Really? Why?"

"He put lies on it about Wendy."

Arthur looked disappointed. "The Grape? Come on, cuz. Can't we come up with a better reason than that?"

"And he insulted me at the party."

"There you go. What did he say?"

"He called me her 'little townie friend.' And he told me to go home."

Arthur practically snapped to attention. "Oh, did he now?"

"Yeah. Can you help me? I've never done anything like this before."

"Definitely. You leave everything to me."

"No. No, I want to do this myself. I just want you to drive me there. And maybe help me find him."

"Yellow Corvette."

"What?"

"Are we talking about the dude who was making out with the Grape?"

"Yeah."

"Little curly-haired guy?"

"Uh-huh."

"I saw him get into a yellow Corvette."

"So we just need to find that?"

"Yeah. Then what?"

I heard myself say, "I'll take care of the rest."

I couldn't even look at Arthur. He might have been laughing at me. But he sounded serious enough when he replied, "I'll do whatever you need me to do, cuz."

The field trip to the Ashland coal mine began just like the one to the flight 93 crash site. There were three fewer passengers, though, since the high school stoners had not signed up.

Jimmy Giles was sitting up front again with his hand on the door. Catherine Lyle was driving. Wendy Lyle was sitting alone behind her, reading a novel. (Maybe it was another novel about someone who was beautiful on the outside but ugly on the inside.)

I was in the back row, next to Arthur. Jenny was right in front of me, between Ben and Mikeszabo. Her hair was hanging over the back of the seat, just inches in front of me. It looked and smelled really nice. Long and brown, with highlights. Very shiny.

In fact, all of Jenny looked nice. I haven't mentioned that before, but I should have.

Arthur was asleep with his head against the glass the entire way up there. I pulled out my PSAT book and tried to do some math problems, but I was way too distracted to work. I was still angry, scared, and pumped up about our plan to go after that college guy.

It wasn't long before we were cruising down the main street of a small town. Catherine Lyle found the mine quickly and pulled into its parking lot. It was a pretty small operation, with a gift shop, the mine itself, and a train ride. I guess it gets crowded some days, but on this day the lot was empty.

Mrs. Lyle parked the Suburban in a space right across from the gift shop and we trooped in. All the gifts in the shop—and there were hundreds of them—were based on anthracite coal. They even had coal candy.

A short, skinny woman with a pointed nose stood behind the cash register. We lined up in front of her and purchased tickets for the next tour. A guy in coveralls and a miner's helmet sauntered in and watched us, smiling. As soon as we all had tickets, he announced, "Are you ready to get to work? Okay, come on, then!"

He led us outside toward the mine entrance. A small engine was sitting there on railroad tracks. It had three yellow coal cars attached to it. The guy climbed into the engine cab and called out, "Hop on board, you coal miners!"

Wendy Lyle and her stepmother got into the first coal car. Arthur and his stepfather chose the second, and I joined Jenny and the guys in the last one.

The guide told us, "This is a real coal mine, folks, although no one is currently working it. It has been in operation in various forms for nearly one hundred years.

"We'll be following the tracks of the coal cars down into the mine, where the temperature is always fifty-two degrees Fahrenheit. We will get out, walk around, and see the sights common to coal miners approximately seventy-five years ago."

The little train took off with a lurch. We pushed through a pair of wooden doors, leaving the daylight behind. We rolled past walls of rocks and wooden beams, moving steadily downward, our way lit by a series of red lanterns hanging on the walls.

The guide pointed out, "Those lanterns are electric, folks, but back in the day they would have been kerosene." Then he added, "Those wooden beams you see won't really help you in a cave-in, though. Nothing will. They are there mostly to make noise before they crack. The miners had a saying: 'When the timbers start talking, you'd better start walking.'"

The train came to a halt in an open area crammed with prop items—tools, wheelbarrows, dummies of men and mules. The guide got out and walked over to a wall of pure anthracite. We followed and formed a semicircle in front of him.

"Seventy-five years ago," he began, "coal miners and their helpers would chip away at veins of anthracite just like this one. They would fill carts with it, and mules would drag those carts to the surface."

He pointed to Ben, Mikeszabo, and me. "The mules wouldn't stop there, though. They'd keep pulling the coal up the hill to the breaker house. That's where boys like you would be waiting. For ninety cents a day, you would sit in the breaker house and sort out the good coal from the rocks and dirt."

Mikeszabo looked at me and whispered, "That's not such a bad deal."

I whispered back, "No. That's more than I make."

Jenny asked the man, "What about girls? Could they do that?"

The guide was adamant. "No, ma'am! There were no breaker girls. Just boys. The girls were back home learning how to cook and wash and sew."

Arthur muttered, "Righteous."

Jenny sneered at him playfully. But then she complained, "That's not fair."

The guide repeated, "No, ma'am. But that's how it was, and everybody went along with it. Men and women. Boys and girls."

It was at this point that I first noticed Jimmy Giles.

He did not look well. His face was pale and he appeared to be sweating, despite the fifty-two-degree temperature. His eyes were darting around.

But everybody else was focused on the guide, who continued talking. "And while we're discussing what's fair and what isn't, here's a question: Who can tell me how many pounds are in a ton?"

Wendy answered before anyone else could. "Two thousand."

The guide nodded. "Well, you kids know that, and I know that, but the mine owners did not. They insisted that there were two thousand two hundred pounds in a ton. They called it a 'long ton,' and they made the miners add another two hundred pounds to every ton if they wanted to get paid."

As we all contemplated that injustice, Jimmy took a big step away from the group.

Catherine Lyle asked him, "Are you okay, Mr. Giles?"

He whispered hoarsely, "Doomed. I'm doomed to die down here."

"What's that?"

"I gotta get out!"

Catherine Lyle turned to the guide. "Where is the nearest exit?"

He looked puzzled. "Well, there's the way we came in, and there's the way we'll go out."

"This man needs to go out. It's an emergency."

I guess it took the guide a moment too long to respond. Maybe he was hoping to finish his speech—I don't know—but Jimmy could not wait. He squeezed behind the last coal car, got onto the tracks, and started back the way we'd come—walking first and then running.

The guide yelled, "Sir! You can't do that." He told us, "Everybody hop back in. I'll get us out right now."

We all clambered back into our cars, except for Arthur. He took off after Jimmy, scrambling as best he could over the wooden rail ties.

The train lurched forward and quickly picked up speed. We barreled around several curves before we hit another pair of doors and broke into the daylight.

The guide screeched to a halt, jumped out, and ran to the entrance. We all followed.

The guide pushed open the left wooden door and peered inside. He called over to us, "I see them! They're okay!"

A minute later, Jimmy and Arthur emerged, blinking in the sunlight. Arthur had his hand cupped under Jimmy's arm. Jimmy was covered with sweat and he was breathing hard, but he did manage to say, "I'm all right. I'm sorry, everybody. I'm sorry."

Catherine asked, "Is there anything I can get you, Mr. Giles? Some water?"

Jimmy nodded, so Catherine and Wendy took off for the gift shop.

Jimmy repeated, "I am really sorry. I guess I wasn't ready to go back down there. I messed up everybody's trip."

We all gathered around and assured him he hadn't.

"It's okay."

"We saw enough."

"Don't worry about it."

We moved toward the gift shop in a bunch. Catherine Lyle met us at the door. She was holding Jimmy's bottle of water. No one else had money, so we just stood around and watched him drink it.

I should say no one else had money except Wendy. She went back in and shopped for jewelry. She wound up purchasing an anthracite heart on a silver chain.

A black heart.

Yeah.

When we were all back in the Suburban, Jimmy apologized some more, and everybody reassured him some more.

Arthur, who hadn't said a word on the ride up, talked the whole way back. In a lowered voice, he told me, "Jimmy Giles was a wildcat miner when I first met him, but I don't think he did it for too long."

"Well, it'd be tough to be a miner if you were afraid of tunnels."

"Yeah. It's like if you were a roofer and afraid of heights."

"Or a sailor afraid of water."

"Right. So then Jimmy and Warren bought the flatbed truck. They hauled pine trees for the government, to make turpentine. They were supposed to haul a hundred trees at a time. They hauled maybe sixty, but they still got paid for a hundred. Jimmy used to say it was close enough for government work.

"Then they started moving college kids in and out of frats and dorms. They moved them in in September and moved them out in June. But you can't work for just two months a year, so they came up with the idea of the Christmas-tree run."

Arthur's eyes lit up. "And they let me in on that deal! On the day before Thanksgiving, we load up with Frasier firs and Douglas firs for seventeen dollars each," he explained. "Then we drive to a lot in Orlando and sell them for eighty to a hundred dollars each."

"Florida—that's cool. That's a cool profit, too."

"It can be, yeah. Unless there are problems. Last year, a Boy Scout troop staked out a lot next to us and really hurt our business. These Boy Scouts had an air horn that they blew whenever somebody bought a tree. That must be some kind of Florida thing. I never heard of blasting a damn boat horn over a Christmas tree. That horn was getting on my last nerve.

"One night, right before closing, Jimmy fell asleep in a chair tipped back against the truck. Two Boy Scouts crept over and blasted that air horn in his ear, making him crash to the ground, hurting his neck and ear something serious. Then they ran away, laughing.

"Jimmy and Warren and me all walked over and complained to the Scout master, some fat dude. A buncha Scout mothers started yelling that it wasn't true, like their precious little darlings would never do that, so the Scout master started saying it wasn't true, too. Then a bigmouth woman asked us, 'Why don't you go sell your trees someplace else? Let the Scouts make their money. They need it for camping and equipment and stuff.'

"Warren said, 'We rent this lot every year from Mr. Peterson. We pay good money for it, so we have a right to be here.' Then Warren called this Peterson dude and told him what was going on and told him to get out there and talk to the damn Scout mothers.

"Well, when Peterson arrived, he got all scared of the Scout mothers because they all had big mouths and they were all yelling and calling us liars and out-of-staters and crap. He backed down right away. He told us, in front of them, 'Y'all will just have to make the best of the situation. Let these boys sell their trees. It looks like they're about to run out. Then you can sell yours.'"

Arthur shook his head. "Well then, don't another shipment of Boy Scout trees arrive the next day?

"Warren called Peterson back. Peterson told him he was sorry again. He said it would never happen again, because a Jiffy Lube was going up on the Boy Scout lot. So we decided to let it slide, but it did hurt our business. Near the end, we were selling those trees for forty bucks each."

"That's tough."

Arthur assured me, "God will visit his wrath upon the infidel, upon those damn Boy Scouts, wherever they are."

I looked at him curiously. "Arthur, do you really believe all those things you say about God and heaven and hell and all?"

He seemed confused. "Of course I do. I live in Caldera, cuz. I know there's a hell. I grew up with it under my bed."

It was dark when we arrived back at the school. Mrs. Weaver was parked there, waiting. So was a guy who turned out to be Ben's father. (At least Ben got in the car and left with him.)

Arthur was giving me a ride home, which was a major concession from Mom. I was heading for his car when I heard a voice behind me.

Wendy's voice.

She hadn't even looked at me the whole trip, but now she was standing next to the idling Suburban, demanding to know, "Hey! What's going on with you?"

I mumbled, "Not much."

"Are you not talking to me or something? I thought we were good."

I answered as evenly as I could, "I thought *you* weren't talking to *me*."

She shook her head no. Then she shrugged in a *Whatever* gesture. She pointed over my shoulder toward the Geo Metro and said, "How about poor Mr. Giles, huh?"

I turned and looked. Wendy said, "Catherine has been working with him, trying to desensitize him, but I guess he wasn't ready. It was too much too soon."

I watched Jimmy talking to Arthur at the car. I finally answered, "Yeah. That was rough."

Wendy sounded empathetic. "It's so sad. He takes two field trips, and he has two breakdowns. If I were him, I wouldn't take a third."

I actually considered correcting her grammar, "If I were *he*," but I didn't. Instead, I said, "Well, they say you have to take it one step at a time."

She frowned at my cliché of an answer, but I didn't care. Then Catherine Lyle beeped the horn, causing Wendy to turn and glare at her. She wasn't even looking at me when she said, "Okay. I guess I'll see you tomorrow."

I didn't answer. I watched her climb into the passenger seat and ride away.

By the time I got over to the Geo Metro, Arthur and Jimmy were sitting inside with the engine running. Arthur opened his door. He leaned forward and unlatched the seat so I could squeeze into the back. He pulled me into their conversation right away. "So, cuz, I just talked to Jimmy, and we got a proposition for you."

"Really?"

"The Christmas-tree run this year is gonna start on November twenty-first."

"The day before Thanksgiving?"

"Correct. We will drive down to sunny Florida in the big truck. Jimmy and Warren will stay for twelve days"—he turned toward me—"but *I* won't. We are going to tow the Geo Metro, so that I can leave after *five* days. I'll be back on November twenty-fifth, the following Sunday, in time for school on Monday." Arthur paused for dramatic effect. "And Jimmy here says you can join us if you want."

I was astounded. "Me?"

"Yep. Jimmy says they will even pay you for your labor."

Jimmy confirmed this. "Three hundred dollars for five days' labor."

"Wow! Really?"

Arthur said, "Yeah. And it ain't hard labor, cuz. People point at a tree; you pick it up and tie it to their roof." He smiled and asked, "What do you say?"

I was thrilled. Three hundred dollars! Florida! But I must admit, I was a little scared, too. I didn't really know Jimmy and Warren, except as people my parents kept me away from. I asked, "Are you sure we would be back in time for school?"

"Yep. Most trees get sold the first few days after Thanksgiving. That's when they need our help. Jimmy and Warren will keep selling trees for another week after that. What they haven't sold at eighty bucks by then, they'll sell at forty and skedaddle."

Jimmy repeated, "Skedaddle."

Then I heard myself say, "Okay. Yeah. Count me in. Absolutely."

It all sounded really really great to me.

Of course, it would not sound great at all to Mom and Dad.

Mom tries to do a traditional Thanksgiving at our house. But here is how it usually goes: Dad, Lilly, and I work late at the Food Giant on Wednesday night. Dad goes in for a few hours on Thursday morning, too, to catch up on Centralized Reporting System stuff.

I get up early and play video games on the TV in the parlor (like Banjo Kazooie on my old Nintendo, or Super Mario Brothers on my N64). Mom has her portable TV in the kitchen, blaring the Macy's parade as she cooks. I'm not sure what Lilly does, but it probably involves hair and makeup.

Dad times things so he arrives at home just as Santa arrives at Macy's. We gather in the kitchen. We fill our plates with food and carry them into the dining room. We hold hands (which is always a bit awkward), and Dad prays.

Then we have dinner—just the four of us—because our only other relatives are Aunt Robin and her crew from Caldera, and Mom doesn't want them in the house.

It's a tradition, I guess, but it's a tradition that nobody seems to like, so why do we keep doing it?

I sure don't want to do it this year. I have a better idea.

I want to go to Florida.

I was hoping to plant the idea of the Florida trip at dinner—to plant it with Mom, at least, since Dad couldn't get away from the store. But before I even had a chance to speak, dinner took an awkward turn.

Mom suddenly asked Lilly, "So, are you and this Uno boy a serious couple?"

Lilly did not explode, as she normally would have. Instead, she answered calmly, even maturely, "He's going by his real name now—John."

"Good. *Uno* makes him sound like a Puerto Rican."

Then Lilly exploded. "Mom!"

"What?"

"What is the matter with you?"

140

Mom held out her hands. "What?"

"That's a racist thing to say."

"No it isn't. *Ooh-no* is Spanish. That's a fact. There's nothing racist about a fact."

Lilly stopped talking.

After a few minutes, Mom tried another line of conversation, as if the first one had never happened. "You know, your uncle Robby and your aunt Robin met when they were very young."

Lilly clenched her jaw.

"Robin snagged him when he was seventeen, and she was only sixteen. Some girls think they have to snag their men fast, because the bloom is quickly off the rose. Personally, I don't agree with that. I think a girl should take her time."

Lilly just stared at her food glumly.

Thankfully, the phone rang in the kitchen. I was relieved to get up and answer it. I leaned against the refrigerator and said, "Hello."

I heard a familiar perky voice. "Tom?"

"Yes."

"It's Wendy." She started in chattily, like nothing was wrong. "Did you hear Ben Gibbons on the ride home today?"

"No."

"He described eating a chair—a whole wooden chair—when he was two years old. It took him, like, six months, but he did it."

"No. I didn't hear him. I was listening to Arthur."

"Catherine says Ben is a classic example of a designated patient."

"What's that?"

"It's a disorder. Not as weird as pica, though. It's when a whole family—parents, siblings, everybody—has serious issues but won't admit it. Instead, they pick one family member to be the designated patient. They pretend that only that one family member has a problem, so the rest of them can pretend to be okay."

All I could think of to say was a generic "That sucks."

After a few seconds of dead air, Wendy finally got down to business. "Hey, I talked to Joel about that website. He was really embarrassed and, like, really sorry. He said he must have been wasted when he put me on there, because he didn't even remember doing it, and he didn't mean any of it."

I interrupted. "Joel? That's his name?"

"Yeah. He's one of Dad's top students. Really brilliant but, like, really immature."

"And he lives across the street?"

"Yeah, in one of the frats. Anyway, Joel promised he'd take the whole website down. Like, permanently."

I didn't respond, so she went on. "But, you know, none of that stuff about me was true. I don't even know what some of that stuff means. Okay? I am not like that. Okay?"

"Okay."

"So will you stop being mad at me all the time? And start talking to me again? Because now you know that none of this is true?"

I thought to myself, *I have no idea if this is true or not.* But I finally repeated that everything was okay.

After a pause, she answered, "Okay. We're good, then?"

"Yeah. We're good."

"Good. Well, see you at school."

"Yeah. Bye." I leaned against the refrigerator for one more minute. I let myself fantasize one more time about a kiss from Wendy Lyle. A beautiful piece of candy corn rising up toward me. The feel of her tongue in my mouth. Then I thought about that same piece of corn lying on the ground, in front of the railing. It's just not the same after it's been thrown up.

The Wendy thing was over.

But the Joel thing was not.

He had called me a "little townie." Then he'd made out with Wendy right in front of me, like I didn't exist. He would have to answer for those things. And for the website.

You don't do that kind of stuff around here and get away with it. Maybe in California, and Florida, but not here.

Saturday, November 10, 2001

I went in to work with Dad at 7:00 a.m. and stocked shelves for five hours.

Arthur picked me up in the parking lot a little after noon. The first thing he said was, "You ready to go up there and kick some ass, Tom?"

"Uh, yeah."

"*Uh, yeah?* What kind of answer is that? You ready or not?"

"I'm ready."

"Do you know what you're going to do?"

"Not exactly. I'll figure that out when I get there."

Arthur sounded doubtful. "Okay. So, we are gonna go to the campus and look for a yellow Corvette."

"Right. Wendy told me the guy lives in a frat house across the street from her, so it shouldn't be too hard."

"We just have to find the right frat boy and let the mayhem begin. Let the wrath of God befall him."

I gulped. "Yeah." Then I asked him, "Do you think we'll get in trouble?"

"I don't know. I don't care. This is a matter of honor, right?"

"Right."

"Then you got to do it. End of story."

"Yeah. I know."

We retraced the route we'd taken on Halloween—up the main road leading to Blackwater University, around the big quadrangle, then onto Wendy's street. This time, in the light of day, I could see that many of the brick houses were frats. They had banners with big Greek letters hanging over their front doors.

We passed the Lyles' house, with its three-sided porch, its

white railing, and the dirt below it. I wondered if they'd cleaned up that candy corn.

Up on the left, just as Wendy had implied, was a frat house with a yellow Corvette in the driveway. Arthur pulled the Geo Metro in behind it and turned off the engine. He looked at me expectantly.

I said, "What do we do now?"

He laughed out loud. "Well, I'd say we go inside."

"We can do that?"

"No, but we're gonna do that. Right?"

"Right."

Arthur leaned in front of me. "You sure you're up to this?"

"Yeah."

His gray eyes bored into mine. "First, tell me something: What's this really about?"

"It's about . . . personal honor."

"Okay. Righteous. Now, do you remember what he did to dishonor you?"

"Oh yeah."

"Okay. You think about that, right now, in detail. And you keep that thought in your head when we go inside."

"What if somebody stops us?"

"You let me worry about that. Tell me: Do we know the dishonorer's name?"

"Yeah. It's Joel."

"Okay. So we walk in there like we own the place. We are here to see Joel. Got it?"

"Yeah."

Arthur exited the car and set off on a determined march, his shaved head held erect, his black boots pounding on the sidewalk. I scrambled out and followed him.

We climbed the stairs, passed under a Greek banner, and stopped before a tall wooden door. Arthur grasped the glass door handle, turned it, and pushed.

The door opened.

Arthur and I stepped into a wood-paneled foyer. We didn't see anybody. We didn't hear anybody. He pointed silently to a staircase on the right. As we climbed the steps, I did start to hear sounds—a TV set, a stereo.

At the top, Arthur pointed again and smiled. There were several doors around the landing, and each had a nameplate telling who lived behind it. The first two had pairs of names. But the third had only one, and that name was JOEL.

The door was slightly ajar. I stepped in front of Arthur and leaned forward to hear. A faint rhythmic sound was coming from inside, a clicking sound, like typing.

I put my hand on the knob and paused, remembering the Halloween party, and Wendy, and my humiliation. I relived that moment, and then I opened the door all the way.

A curly-haired guy was sitting at a desk. It was Joel, all right, working at a laptop. A messy bed was behind him, and a row of gadgets—a TV, a stereo, an exercise bike—stretched from the right side of the room to the left. I stepped inside and said, "Hi, Joel. Do you remember me?" He cocked his head. I added, "The little townie?"

Arthur stepped in behind me and closed the door with a *click*.

Joel shook his head. He answered, "No. No, I don't. What are you doing here?"

I spoke slowly, haltingly. "I came here . . . to talk to you about . . . that night." I groped for something else to say. I was losing it. I came up with "And about a website that you put up. A website that . . . slandered the good name of a friend of mine."

I think Joel did remember me, and that night, because he replied, "Do you mean Wendy Lyle?"

"Yes."

"We talked about that. The website is gone. We're good."

"Yeah? Well, you and I are not good."

Joel closed the laptop and pushed back his seat. He looked warily at Arthur as he stood up. "You need to get out of here, both of you. Right now."

Arthur sniffed the air. "Have you been smoking in here, Joe?"

"Do you know how old Wendy Lyle is?" I asked.

Joel's eyes darted to Arthur and then back to me. "Yeah. She's sixteen."

"No. She's not. She's fifteen."

"Hey, what's the big deal here? I'm just messing around with my laptop."

"By talking about underage girls in dirty and disgusting ways?"

Joel pointed at the laptop and shrugged. "It's the Wild West out there. People can do whatever they want."

I informed him, "No. No, they can't." But then I had no clue what to do or say next. I turned to Arthur and pleaded with him silently to step in.

And he did.

He crossed over to the desk, scrutinizing the laptop like he had never seen one before. He muttered, "What is this here contraption for?"

Joel snapped at him, "Don't touch that!"

"Why?"

"Because you don't know the first thing about it."

Arthur pointed back at me. "Tom came all the way up here to talk to you, Joe."

"It's Joel. And you need to leave that alone and get out of here."

"We'll be leaving shortly, right after you apologize to Tom for calling him a townie. We don't like that word."

Joel's jaw dropped open. Then he spat out the words "Screw you!" But he didn't sound like he meant them.

Arthur picked up the laptop with his left hand and ripped it away from its power cord. With his right hand, he gave Joel a shove, driving him back toward the wall. He held the laptop up to me. "How do you open this thing?"

I located the button and popped it open. Arthur tossed the laptop down onto the floor and kicked it toward the corner. He said, "Block the door." Then he turned away from us.

I placed my left shoulder against the door and leveled a mad-dog stare at Joel. He tried to stare back, but he could not.

He caved.

He smiled goofily and said, "Okay. Okay, I apologize. I shouldn't have said that. Let's forget this."

Then we both heard an unmistakable sound. Joel looked over toward Arthur in the corner. So did I.

Arthur had his back to us. The laptop was on the floor in front of him, and he was urinating on it.

Joel sputtered, "Are you . . . are you insane? You can't do that!"

Arthur, still urinating, asked innocently, "What?"

Joel looked like he might cry. Or faint. He pointed to his laptop and squeaked, "That!"

Arthur zipped up and replied. "Well, why not? It's the Wild West. I can do whatever I want."

"You ruined my computer!"

Arthur pretended to slap himself on the head. "Computer?

Is that what it is? I thought it was a portable urinal. You know? For busy college guys who can't take the time to walk down to the bathroom?" He reached out and dried his hands on Joel's shirt, admitting, "I guess you were right. I didn't know the first thing about it."

Joel stammered, "You . . . you're going to pay for this!"

"No. I don't think so." Arthur walked to the door, opened it, and left.

Joel was just staring at the puddle on his floor.

I hurried out after Arthur. I whispered to him, "Come on! We gotta get out of here before he calls the cops."

Arthur shook his head calmly. "Nah. That guy won't call the cops."

"Why?"

"Didn't you smell the weed in there? It reeked of it. He's got too much to hide."

Arthur walked coolly across the landing, with me directly behind. As he descended the stairs, though, he picked up speed, and so did I. We were both practically running when we hit the front door—bursting outside and vaulting off the porch onto the ground. We ran to the car and dove in. Arthur gunned the engine, threw it into reverse, and peeled out.

As we raced past the Lyles' house, I couldn't contain myself any longer. I let out a loud *whoop!* Arthur laughed and held up his hand for me to slap. I did, and I started laughing hysterically.

Arthur took a hard left at the end of the street. He had circled the quadrangle and was back on the main road before I could finally speak. Babble is more like it: "Hey, well, you know, Arthur . . . you might have overreacted in there. Just a little bit!"

Arthur snorted. "Overreacted?"

"Yes, maybe. Maybe just a tad."

"You mean by pissing on his computer?"

"Yes. Yes, that is exactly what I mean."

"No. No, cuz. Overreacting would be, like, if I had pissed on his head."

"Oh, well. Okay. Yeah. Since you put it that way."

I sat back and let the incredible feeling flow over me.

I had done it. Or Arthur had done it, but I had been there, too.

We had now joined Warren and Jimmy, and Ralph, and the Cowley brothers, and every other townie who had ever been disrespected by frat boys and had come up here and had taken care of business.

And I absolutely loved that feeling.

Monday, November 12, 2001

Wendy did not act like she had heard about a townie raid on the frat house across the street, resulting in a score being settled, and her honor being defended, and some personal property being destroyed. I was a little disappointed in that, but only a little. The Wendy thing was over.

There was a change in Wendy's routine, however. She did not show up for the counseling group after school. Her seat remained empty across the table. Our small group now consisted of Arthur, Lilly, and me—all family, all Blackwater, all townie.

Catherine Lyle ran the group as usual, though. Today's topic was role models. She began by telling us, "If you have good role models, you'll do well in life." Her manicured hand pointed out the window. "So let's talk about people here in the community, people you know, who serve as good role models."

We just stared at her, so she said, "Okay. What jobs in the community automatically get your respect?"

We started to get the idea. Kids called out suggestions.

"Police officers."

"Firefighters."

"Doctors and nurses."

"Teachers."

Chris Collier added, "Student Council presidents." (I think he was kidding, but maybe not.)

Catherine Lyle nodded. "Good. Good. These are the jobs, and the people, we respect. These are our good role models."

A high school stoner asked, apparently out of nowhere, "Are all teachers role models?"

Catherine looked at us for an answer. When no one spoke up,

she replied, "Well, they *should* be. They sign up to be role models. That's part of the job description."

The stoner nodded. He asked, "If a teacher smokes weed, then, what should happen to him?"

Catherine Lyle opened her notebook and picked up her pen. She replied, "I would say he should be fired. If a teacher says one thing and does another—"

Arthur muttered, "Talks the talk but don't walk the walk."

"That teacher should certainly not be around children. It's one thing if you are teaching adults, but not children."

Ben said, "Anybody who takes one of those jobs, one of those role-model jobs, should have to live up to it. If they don't, they should get kicked out."

"Kicked out ain't enough," Arthur snarled. "They should get punished. They're putting themselves up as better than other people, but they're not."

Other kids agreed. They started talking about people in their lives, people they looked up to, who had let them down. The conversation went on like that, very seriously, for ten more minutes.

Then, as usual, Catherine Lyle changed topics.

She delivered some news in a perky voice, like Wendy on the morning announcements. "Next Monday, Dr. Richard Lyle will come speak to our group about new trends in substance-abuse treatment. Dr. Lyle—forgive me for bragging—is kind of a big deal. He gets paid thousands of dollars, plus travel expenses, to speak to groups all over the country. He is coming here for free, so let's really make the most of it."

Catherine then smiled her perfect smile, clicked her silver pen, and closed her leather notebook. She turned, out of habit, toward Wendy's seat, and she seemed disappointed to see that it was empty.

Monday, November 19, 2001

I had both Dad and Mom with me at breakfast, so I tried to work in the Christmas-tree idea. I started off conversationally, like I was talking about something else. I told them, "Arthur's last football game was Friday afternoon."

Mom replied, "Oh? That's nice."

"Yeah, I saw Aunt Robin at the school. She came to watch the game." I added, "She seems like a nice lady."

Mom didn't say anything, but Dad replied, "Sure. She is."

I heard Lilly coming down the back stairs. I waited until she had entered, selected an apple from a bowl, and started washing it before I continued. "I don't really remember Uncle Robby. What was he like?"

Dad said, "He was a nice guy."

Mom added, "He was. But he should never have gotten married so young. And never to Robin."

Dad turned away, concentrating on his shredded wheat, but he did murmur, "Well, he didn't have much choice."

Lilly picked up on that before I did. "What? Aunt Robin was pregnant? With Arthur?"

Mom nodded tightly. "Yes, that's right. And that was the beginning of the end for Robby. There he was, married to this child bride, who had the same bad habits that he had."

Mom started to get angry. "Robin didn't finish high school. She never got her GED. So after Robby died, what did she have? She had no job, no money, and a child to raise."

Lilly asked, "So how did she do? Was she a good mother?"

Mom backed off. "She tried, I guess. She would take Arthur to football; she would take him to church to hear those Holy Roller preachers."

"Really? What church was that?"

Mom looked at Dad, so he explained. "Some church in Cal-dera, in a double-wide. It got condemned along with everything else, so they had to move it. They put the whole thing on a flat-bed truck and hauled it away."

Mom grumbled, "Who would go to church in a place like that? It was unhealthy."

Lilly winked at me. "Maybe Hungarians," she suggested. "Or Puerto Ricans. I'll have to ask John." She looked at me for a laugh, or at least a smile, but I was way too stressed to react.

Dad said, "It was an evangelical church. It attracted all kinds of people. I think that's where Robin met Jimmy."

I responded as evenly as I could, "Jimmy Giles?"

"Right."

"Do you know him?"

"A little. He's not a bad guy. He had a drug problem, I guess. And some legal problems."

"Do you know his brother?"

"Warren? Yeah. Real smart guy. He was a pharmacy tech at Kroger."

"No!"

"Yeah. During college."

"He went to college?"

"He did, up at Bloomsburg, but I don't think he finished. He had some problem at Kroger—stealing pills, or underreporting pills, or misreporting. I'm not sure what."

Dad finally gave me my opening when he asked, "What are those guys doing now?"

"Oh, different stuff. They move college kids in and out of the Blackwater dorms."

"Yeah?"

"And they do some government work, hauling pine trees."

"For turpentine?"

"I guess so, yeah. And they sell Christmas trees down in Florida."

"Really?"

"Uh-huh. They've been doing it for a few years now. They make good money. And, uh, they asked me to work for them this year."

Dad froze in mid-spoonful.

Lilly bulged her eyes out at me and whistled softly.

I added quickly, "Just for five days, and they'll pay me three hundred dollars. That's sixty dollars a day. And really, two days are travel days, so that's a hundred dollars per working day."

Mom spoke up immediately. "No. You can't miss school."

"But that's the beauty of it. I won't! It's just Thanksgiving and the weekend. I'll be back in time for school."

I smiled and looked pathetically from Mom to Dad.

But Dad just shook his head. "I can't spare you at work, Tom. Not at Thanksgiving. It's one of the busiest times of the year; you know that."

Mom piled it on. "And you'd be on the road with those"— she struggled to find the right term—"drug guys."

I thought about Warren and that box of Ziploc bags. Were they to store food, or weed? Both, probably. Still, I tried to sound offended, like that was an outrageous lie. "Drug guys?"

"Yes! You heard what your father just said. They've both had drug problems."

"That was years ago! Didn't Dad have a problem back then, too?"

"That's not the point. You have school, you have work, and you have parents who won't let you get in a car with just anybody and take off for just anyplace. The answer is no."

I can't say I was surprised. The answer is always no.

I said as evenly as I could, "Okay. Forget it. It was just an idea." Then I took the stairs two at a time up to my room and, very calmly, got ready for school. But I was fuming inside.

———✠———

Mr. Proctor began class by describing his reactions to our journal entries. "These are great! Heartfelt and well-observed. I especially liked the ones about your town, and about coal mining, and about a place called Caldera.

"They got me to thinking. We have talked about Pennsylvania as a Garden of Eden, as a paradise. It has some of the world's most abundant farmland above, and it has some of the world's most abundant coal veins below.

"So picture this: It is glorious, sunny, and heaven-like up top, and it's sulfurous, burning, and hell-like down below. It's all here in one place. It's yin and yang. It's *Paradise Lost*.

"And, while we are speaking of great literature . . ." He picked up his script for *The Roses of Eyam*. "All the roles in my play have now been assigned. I want to thank everybody who auditioned."

He looked at Wendy. "Some of you showed great talent."

Arthur muttered behind me, "Grape talent."

Mr. Proctor heard him, and he called him on it. "What's that, Arthur?"

"Uh, I was wondering, sir, if I got that village idiot job. Did I?"

"Yes. I told you that before."

"And—I just want to double-check—if I play this part, I get an A in English?"

Mr. Proctor summarized, somewhat impatiently, "Yes. You have been assigned the part of the Bedlam, the village idiot. And if you learn that role and you play it on December thirtieth in the school auditorium, you get an A. Why? Are you having second thoughts?"

"No! No way. Oh, but I have to tell you: I'll be gone from November twenty-first to the twenty-fifth. Out of town on business. I won't be able to rehearse then."

"Okay. That won't be a problem."

"Cool. Then you got yourself an idiot."

Mr. Proctor held the script high. "The original production had over fifty actors. I have managed to pare it down to a dozen speaking parts, and I've cut the three acts down to one. But I have preserved the essence of the play, which, in my view, is this:

"One day, in the peaceful English village of Eyam, the plague arrives in a shipment of cloth. People start to die. At first no one knows what is happening. The plague starts to spread very rapidly, geometrically—two, four, eight, sixteen bodies a day. The people realize, to their horror, what is happening to them. But they also realize that if they let the plague move beyond their village, it will continue to increase, geometrically, until half of England is dead. To prevent that ultimate catastrophe, the villagers embark on something truly heroic: They stay in their own town. They do not run away. They stay and fight."

He stopped and looked at me, but I looked away. I had heard enough. Mr. Proctor could stay in Blackwater if he wanted, in his plague village, but I would not.

I had made up my mind. I was getting the hell out, with my parents' permission or not.

I was going to Florida.

✠

The counseling group started right on time, at least for us. But I could tell by Catherine Lyle's nervous glances at the door, and at her watch, that something was wrong. Our guest speaker, her husband, was not there.

Wendy, however, was. She was sitting in her old spot, smiling, waiting to hear her famous father speak.

Catherine Lyle improvised by saying, "I often start the meeting by introducing a topic. I know that some of you have things you want to talk about that I have *not* covered. So let's start today with a free topic, anything you'd like to share that you have not been able to."

Ben's hand shot up, of course. But some other hands did, too.

Catherine Lyle pointed to Jenny, who said, quite unexpectedly, "I would like to share that I have a problem at home. My father is a recovering alcoholic. I tried to hide that fact all my life. I get all A's on my report cards, and I'm on the Student Council, and I try really hard to act perfect, but that doesn't change the truth. I have a problem at home, a big problem. I always have."

Jenny stopped there.

Other kids nodded and said they understood her predicament.

I was shocked. The Weavers did seem to be the perfect family, but I guess that was Jenny's point.

Angela spoke up next. Her topic was very different. "My cousin drank bleach to pass a urine test with her probation officer. But she drank too much, or it was too strong, and it burned out the lining of her esophagus. So now she has to eat through a tube."

Another girl advised her, "She shoulda drank vinegar instead. Vinegar's supposed to work."

Lilly objected to that very strongly. "No! You shouldn't learn how to lie better. Or cheat better. You should stop using drugs. That's the only thing that works."

One of the high school guys was eager to share next. He didn't even wait to be called on. "My brother mugged an old man outside a bank, but they caught him because of his army coat."

Arthur sounded puzzled. "What do you mean, dude?"

"They caught him because the old man remembered the name on the army coat."

Arthur held up his hand. "Wait a minute. You're telling us that your brother mugged somebody while wearing a coat that had his *own* name stitched on it?"

"Yeah."

"Is he a moron?"

The guy looked offended. "No. He's an addict."

"That's the dumbest thing I've ever heard."

Ben agreed. "That guy's, like, too stupid to live."

But Angela came to his defense. "Come on! Addicts don't think."

The high school guy explained, "My brother was never good at anything. He even got kicked out of the army. So naturally, he's not a good mugger, either."

For the next ten minutes, people shared other anecdotes about the stupid, and deadly, and just plain sad things that had happened to users they knew.

All that talk stopped, though, when our guests walked in.

Catherine Lyle looked up at her husband, so we did, too. He was not alone. (Was he ever? How weird was that?) He had two students trailing him, two frat boys who were smiling very wide. They looked familiar, but I couldn't place them. Our three visitors walked to the head of the table and stared at us like we were some kind of lab specimens.

I hadn't seen Dr. Lyle since the Halloween party. He wasn't

wearing blue velvet now, just jeans and an old sweater. He had long gray hair tied up in a ponytail. You don't see a lot of that around here.

Dr. Lyle tried an opening joke. "We just saw your mascot outside, the Battlin' Coal Miner. We were thinking they might replace him with a statue that better reflects the local economy. We came up with the Battlin' Walmart Greeter."

He paused to let us all laugh, but we did not. We just glared at him. His boys did manage a low snigger, though.

Catherine Lyle reacted to this awkward moment by launching quickly into an introduction. "Now we come to the main part of our meeting. We are all grateful to have Dr. Richard Lyle with us today, along with, I see, some of his graduate students."

The frat boys exchanged a smirk. I hated those guys. We all did; I could sense it.

"Dr. Lyle has been a leader in his field for twenty years, holding professorships at the University of Southern California, the Florida Institute of Technology, and now Blackwater University. I have asked him to talk today about some exciting new treatments that are available to substance abusers. Please welcome Dr. Richard Lyle."

Dr. Lyle nodded at his wife and smiled at Wendy. "Thank you, Catherine, for inviting me here." He looked around at us. "Obviously, there is never a *good* time to be a substance abuser, but if you had to choose a time in history, this would be it. Psychologists and physicians and counselors have been working together throughout the last decade to develop some of the most effective and revolutionary treatments in medical history, treatments that have proven to be highly effective in their success-versus-relapse ratios.

"Substance-abuse centers in California and in Florida

now offer total-immersion programs to patients over a twenty-eight-day period. These programs include individual, group, and family therapy; relapse-prevention education; and trust building via team sports, horseback riding, rope courses, and other activities."

He then launched into a long list of places like the Betty Ford clinic where, basically, drug users could go and listen to people like him all day, and do activities, and get cured of their addictions. After about fifteen minutes, he wrapped it up by saying, "These programs are expensive, though. So my best advice to you is this: Get a job with good health benefits, benefits that cover drug treatment should you ever need it."

As soon as he stopped, Lilly raised her hand. She asked him, "Wouldn't the best advice be 'Don't do drugs at all'?"

Dr. Lyle looked confused. Then he smiled. "Sure. It would be. But that's not what my talk was about."

"But aren't all drugs bad?"

Dr. Lyle tried to explain. "Well, I would differentiate between hard drugs, which are very destructive, and milder drugs, which are purely recreational."

Lilly sounded puzzled. "But aren't they *all* illegal? Unless, like, you have a prescription from a doctor?"

Dr. Lyle was no longer smiling at Lilly when he replied, "Yes, true. And they are all *potentially* bad, even legal drugs such as alcohol, or, for that matter, aspirin."

Then he didn't say anything else.

After a long silence, Catherine Lyle spoke up. "All right! Thanks, Lilly, for that question. Are there any others?"

Ben raised his hand. "Dr. Lyle? What if you don't have the money to go to one of those substance-abuse facilities? Where can you go?"

Dr. Lyle suggested, "You could go to your church. They generally have programs."

"You mean like to an AA meeting?"

"Yes. Those meetings have helped people in the past. But they are amateur operations, where substance abusers try to help each other."

Ben followed up, "So . . . what if you don't have money *and* you don't belong to a church?"

Dr. Lyle answered, "Well, there *are* free social programs out there, but not everywhere. They are mostly in big cities."

"Yeah! I got diagnosed in Pittsburgh, by a social worker. I was eating stuff."

Catherine Lyle moved to cut Ben off. "Okay! Those were some good questions, and that was some great information about new options in substance-abuse treatment. I hope you have all benefited from this exchange. Now let's thank Dr. Lyle and let him get back to the university."

Most of us just stared at him. But Jenny, ever polite, muttered, "Thank you, Dr. Lyle," and a couple of other kids joined in.

He replied, "You are all very welcome. And good luck to you." Then he and his boys started toward the door.

Catherine and Wendy got up to walk them out.

That was when I overheard Wendy ask one of the boys a question. A very strange question. "Couldn't Joel make it?"

The boy shook his head no.

Arthur heard the question, too. He said to me, loud enough for everyone to hear, "Does she mean Joe? 'I don't have a website anymore' Joe? 'My mommy needs to buy me a new laptop' Joe?"

Wendy stopped and turned. She asked Arthur, "What are you talking about? How do you know Joel?"

Arthur assumed an innocent face. "I don't. I don't know any-body named Joel. I was thinking of a guy named Joe." He turned to me. "What was Joe's aura, Tom? Was it, like, ultraviolet? No, no, that's right—it was yellow. Total yellow."

Wendy snapped, "Shut up!"

Arthur snapped right back, "You shut up!"

Dr. Lyle stepped toward Arthur and warned him, "Don't you dare speak to my daughter like that."

Arthur met his gaze. "Okay. I'll speak to you, then. How much weed did you and the boys smoke on the way here?"

Dr. Lyle's eyes widened (and they were really bloodshot). He growled, "I beg your pardon."

"You beg my pardon? Why? Did you burp?"

"What?"

"Hey, come on, Doc. You didn't fart, did you?"

"What?"

"Are you having trouble hearing me? Is all that weed frying your brain?"

Dr. Lyle turned to his wife. "What is going on here, Cath-erine?"

Catherine Lyle had no idea, and her face showed it. She stam-mered, "I-I-I'm very sorry. Maybe you should just leave. Quickly. All of you."

Dr. Lyle spun around angrily. He stomped out through the office, with the boys on his heels. They weren't smirking anymore.

Catherine rounded on Arthur. "What was that about? Is that how you show respect to a guest? I am very disappointed in you, Arthur."

"Respect? We're an antidrug group, and they showed up stoned."

Catherine Lyle sputtered, "Arthur! That is not true!"

163

But Arthur knew what he was talking about, and he let her know. "That is true. I've seen those guys around Caldera."

Catherine clearly didn't believe him. "What? What on earth for? What would they be doing at—"

"They were trying to cop."

"What?"

"Trying to buy drugs."

"Drugs? What drugs?"

"Weed, I believe. That's what the frat boys prefer."

She sputtered, "I'm sure that is not so, but I will mention it to my husband."

"Yeah. You do that. Mention it to him. Mention that they were driving a white Saab convertible. That might help him remember. I can get the tag number for you next time, if you need it."

Mrs. Lyle backed away and started to gather her belongings. She looked like she might cry.

Wendy looked like she might punch Arthur. Instead, she grabbed her stuff and ran out of the room.

⊹

It had been a long day already, and I still had to go to the Food Giant. I was in no mood for sweeping floors or bagging groceries or rounding up shopping carts.

And I certainly was in no mood for Reg the Veg.

I opened the door of the anteroom, though, and found myself looking at the trio of Reg, Bobby, and John. And they were at it again.

Or at least Reg was at it again, trying to prank Bobby. I had long since given up on the Veg, but when was John going to grow up and stop this?

Reg recapped tonight's story, I suppose for my amusement. "So it's a Thanksgiving promotion, Bobby. Walnuts for three-ninety-nine a pound. Now, that's one heckuva price. All you gotta do is carry two walnuts like these"—he held out a pair of walnuts—"and put them in a Baggie like this." He dropped them into a sandwich-size Baggie. "Then you take it out and you ask customers, 'Aren't these beautiful nuts?'"

John started to laugh, but then he stole a glance at me and turned it into a wince. Still, he didn't speak up, not even when Bobby reached out to take the bag.

So I did. "No, Bobby! Don't do that. My father would not want you to do that."

Then John acted like he agreed with me, and like he was about to do the same thing. "That's right, Bobby. In fact, you should check with me before you do anything like this."

Bobby looked from John to me to Reg. His neck and ears turned bright red, like lava rising in a volcano. He slapped at Reg's hand, knocking the Baggie to the floor and causing the nuts to roll out by Reg's feet. Then he pushed past me, angrily, and exited the room.

John shook his head. He told Reg, "You need to stop bustin' his balls. I'm the one who catches hell about it, not you."

Reg bent and picked up the bag and the walnuts as John pulled on a slicker. Reg muttered, "Don't be so pusillanimous, Uno, my man."

John looked at him, puzzled—clearly not up on his PSAT vocabulary. He frowned and followed Bobby out.

Reg straightened up. He tossed the Baggie and the walnuts into the trash. Then he told me seriously, "There ain't much to do around here, Tom. Tom Terrific. Tom-Tom-the-piper's-son. I think you'll find that out someday. In the meantime, you have to get your laughs where you can."

Dad and I stayed after closing time to get some extra jobs done. We mostly stocked shelves—straightening, replenishing, removing misplaced items. After about an hour of working separately, we both ended up at the beer aisle, across from the frozen foods.

I could tell that Dad was upset about something. He had been all night. He finally came out and told me, "I had to fire Walter today."

I was dumbfounded. Walter had been one of Dad's favorites. I asked, "Why? What did he do?"

Dad shook his head back and forth. "I caught him with a carton of Sudafed in his trunk."

"No! Not Walter!"

"Yes. Inventory hasn't matched sales for weeks now. I suspected it was Walter, and I caught him today."

"God. Did he say anything?"

Dad shrugged. "He said he was sorry."

"Did you call the police?"

Dad looked toward the office. "No. I'm leaving that up to corporate. But from here on out, I'm locking all pseudoephedrine products up in the office. Every night."

Dad returned to straightening beer bottles, so I did, too.

I felt really bad for him. He hated firing people. After a few minutes, he told me something else. "I caught Bob Murphy shoplifting today."

"Oh yeah?"

"Yeah. Poor guy. He looked like hell—like a skeleton. I barely recognized him." Dad nodded thoughtfully. "Does his kid still go to Haven?"

"Mikemurphy? I think so. I haven't seen him in a while. He

was getting suspended a lot, so they might have sent him to the county school."

"That's too bad. He was a nice kid."

"What was Mr. Murphy stealing?"

"Beer. He had this big coat on, and he filled the pockets with cans of Yuengling Black and Tan. He couldn't even walk without clunking. I followed him outside with a cart and got it all back."

"What did he say?"

"He was mad! He said, 'I know you, Gene Coleman! You're a damn alcoholic. Who the hell are you to judge me?' I said, 'Whoa. I'm not judging anybody, Bob. But you can't come in here and steal stuff.'"

Dad got quiet for a moment. I asked him, "So . . . is it ever hard for you? Being around all this beer?"

He shrugged. "It used to be, but not anymore. That was a long time ago." Then, to my surprise, he went on: "I'm genetically disposed to be an alcoholic, Tom. My body converts alcohol into food and I just keep going, keep drinking, until I collapse. I'm not like other people." He directed a worried look at me. "And maybe, genetically, you are not, either."

"Genetically, from your side?"

"From both sides, I'm afraid. Your uncle Robby was worse than me." Dad stopped straightening. He turned and told me, "We used to drink together at the American Legion bar. He'd stop in after work at the Sears Auto. I'd stop in after the Food Giant."

"When was this?"

"Twelve years ago. Twelve years, two months, and seventeen days."

"Wow! You know it to the day?"

"Yep. I had your mother and you and Lilly at home; he had Robin and Arthur at home. But we'd drink every night, regular as clockwork, ten or twelve Rolling Rocks. We'd sit next to each other so it wouldn't look like we were drinking alone, but I guess we really were."

I shook my head. "I don't remember any of that. I don't remember you ever taking a drink."

"Well, I drank at bars," he explained. "I'd only drink at home on weekends—out back, usually, where you and Lilly couldn't see me. I got pretty good at it. I'd finish off my two six-packs a night sure as the sun would set."

"You didn't work on weekends?"

"No. Not back then. I was like Reg Malloy. I unloaded all the trucks, and they came Monday to Friday."

Dad looked down for a moment; then he went on quietly. "The beer was always enough for me, but not for Robby. He started taking Quaaludes. Did you ever hear of them?"

"No."

"That was the big drug back then, like crack was later, like meth is now. People called them 'ludes.' They were strong sedatives, like sleeping pills. Robby would wash them down with beer. They were a powerful combination, all right. A deadly combination."

I asked cautiously, "So, did he . . . OD?"

Dad nodded his head yes. "Robby left the bar a little early that night, twelve years, two months, and seventeen days ago— the last night of his life. It was raining, and he crashed into a telephone pole. I'm the one who found him, dead, with a broken neck."

Dad stopped talking for about thirty seconds, reliving the moment. He continued in a haunted voice: "All I could think of as I stared at Robby was the word *worthless*. A dead human being is worthless, no matter who you were just half an hour before. You can't ever do anything for anybody, ever again.

"I stood there in the rain and stared at him for so long that somebody else stopped, some other guy. He's the one who got the police.

"I was still standing there when they arrived. When they pried Robby out of the car, his eyes were wide open, like he was staring back, saying, *Do you want to end up like me?*

"The cops were going to take me away, too, for being drunk, but I made a deal with them: If they would drive me home, I would report to my first AA meeting the next night. Lucky for me, they gave me that chance.

"The next night, I was sitting at a folding table at a church in Minersville, listening to six guys and two women tell their stories about being drunks and fools and criminals. Then I stood up, and I told them my story."

Dad looked at me and smiled. "I guess you know how many years and months and days ago that was."

"Yeah." I asked, "And you never drank again?"

"I never drank again. But it's been hard. It has been, literally, one day at a time."

Dad clapped me on my shoulder and then went into the office. I stayed in the beer aisle, looking at all the colored bottles, trying to imagine my dad as being young and stupid.

It wasn't easy. And I knew it wasn't easy for him to talk to me about this. It was more than he had ever said to me about anything.

And I appreciated it.

Wednesday, November 21, 2001

I appreciated it. I really did. But not enough to stop my plan.

Today, I was going to betray Dad. And Mom. I was going to do the worst thing I have ever done, and nothing would stop me.

I got up before dawn, as focused (and as frightened) as I had been for the honor-vengeance trip up to Blackwater U.

I unzipped my backpack. I dumped out the contents and replaced them with underwear, socks, T-shirts, and a backup pair of pants. I zipped the bag up until it was nearly closed. Then I slipped down the hall to the bathroom. I wrapped my toothbrush in a tissue and stuck it through the hole at the top of the backpack. I did the same for my stick of Right Guard deodorant.

Then, just to be safe, I rooted under the sink, found a tube of Crest, and added it to my supplies. I couldn't trust Jimmy, Warren, or Arthur to have toothpaste. Beer, maybe, but not toothpaste.

I zipped the backpack completely closed, slid it over my shoulder, and walked down the stairs like it was a normal school day.

The plan was for Dad and me to arrive at the Food Giant at 6:00 a.m. to help Mitchell defrost and display fifty turkeys in his glass case. I told my parents that Arthur had to drive me to school because we were doing a project for Mr. Proctor's class. We had to act out a scene from *A Journal of the Plague Year*, but we hadn't rehearsed it. So Arthur was going to pick me up, and we were going to do that on the way.

I told them that big fat lie, and they believed me.

It was shocking for me, as someone who did not lie, to see how easy it was to get away with one. I must admit I was a little disappointed in them. I thought, *I could be lying to you all the time, and you would never know it.*

When we pulled into the Food Giant lot, two cars were already parked in the outer spaces—John's old Impala and Mitchell's Saturn SL. John and Mitchell were standing by the ATM, stamping their feet in the cold and waiting for us.

Dad and I walked briskly to the entrance, nodding hello to them. Dad unlocked the door and held it for us all to step inside.

That was when we got a nasty surprise.

There was a big mess over by the bakery aisle. Someone had been in here overnight and had tried to break down the office door. The doorjamb, the hinges, and the door itself all showed signs of violence.

While Dad dealt with that situation, the rest of us spread out and looked around. I'm the one who discovered how the thief had gotten in. He had sawed right through the storeroom's ceiling and climbed down the shelves. The Food Giant now had a gaping hole in its roof.

Dad called the police while John, Mitchell, and I cleaned up the office area and the storeroom.

By 7:00 a.m., things were almost back to normal. The police had come and gone, and the store-opening crew was hard at work. (I was hard at work alongside them, but I was not getting paid for it.)

Because of the break-in, and the mess, I felt even guiltier about my escape plan, but not guilty enough to change my mind. At 7:30, I was standing out front with my backpack. Only Bobby was out there with me, and he was preoccupied with the padlock on the propane cage.

Arthur pulled up right on schedule. I hopped in on the passenger side, the Geo Metro peeled out, and I never looked back.

I confirmed with Arthur, "Everybody at your house knows that I'm coming, right?"

"Right."

"And they're okay with it?"

"Yeah. I talked to Mom and Jimmy Giles this morning."

"What did they say?"

"Not much. I reminded Jimmy about you, and the three hundred bucks, and he said cool."

Now came the hard part.

I asked Arthur to pull over at Sheetz gas. I got out, put a quarter in a pay phone, and dialed the store number. Dad answered on one ring. "Good morning, Food Giant."

"Dad? It's Tom."

"Tom? Is everything okay?"

"Yes, sir. I just wanted to tell you that I'm on my way to Florida with Arthur, Jimmy, and Warren. I'm going to help them sell their Christmas trees."

After a long pause, Dad replied, "Tom? What are you talking about? Aren't you at school?"

"No, sir. It's the Wednesday before Thanksgiving. Nothing really happens at school." I restated, "I'm on the road, heading south to Florida. I'll be back on Sunday."

"Sunday! You can't do that. This is the busiest weekend of the year."

"Well, sorry, but I need a weekend off."

"You? *You* need a weekend off? What about me? What about the rest of us?"

"That's up to you."

He was silent for a moment. Then he tried, "Why does it have to be this weekend?"

"Because this is when they're driving to Orlando to sell their trees."

"Come on, Tom. You're needed here. What about the carts in the parking lot? Bobby can't handle them all."

"So put somebody else out there."

"Who?"

"Mitchell. Or Reg. Or Gert, for that matter. None of them work as hard as I do, but all of them get paid and I don't. I deserve some time off."

Dad exhaled slowly. He asked with resignation, "Does your mother know about this?"

"No. Of course not."

"She's not going to like it."

"She doesn't like anything."

"Tom!"

"Sorry, but it's true. I have to go. I'll be back home on Sunday. Goodbye, Dad."

I hung up. I felt bad for a few more seconds, but then I started to feel a great weight lifting off my shoulders. I was free, for the first time in my life. I walked back to the car feeling light as air.

We drove straight up to Aunt Robin's trailer. When we pulled in, I could see Jimmy's legs sticking out from under a flat-bed truck. The truck looked comfortable enough for a long ride. It had a large crew cab with two rows of seats.

Behind the crew cab was the flatbed, maybe twenty feet deep, with two wooden railings running along the side. The back area was open, except for an orange net hooked across it.

I commented, "No Christmas trees yet?"

Arthur explained, "No. Not yet. We pick them up on the way."

Aunt Robin came out with Cody in tow. She was lugging a cooler, so I took it from her and set it on the ground.

Jimmy rolled out from under the truck. He called out to her, "Any beer in that cooler?"

"No! Just ice and sodas. You can live without beer on the drive, especially since you got Tom along. You boys need to take care of him."

"Oh, we'll take care of him." Jimmy winked at me. "We'll take care to get him some beer."

Aunt Robin fussed, "Don't you say that, Jimmy Giles! Don't you even think that."

Jimmy laughed. "I'm just kiddin'."

Jimmy stowed the cooler in the truck cab. Then he climbed up onto the flatbed and told Arthur, "You guys start handing me wall stakes, about fifty of them."

I didn't know what that meant, but Arthur did. He hurried around the side of Aunt Robin's trailer, with me right behind him. We scooped up long wooden stakes from a pile that had probably been there since the previous year. The stakes were wet and dirty but still pretty straight. God knows what was living at the bottom of that pile. Fortunately, after three trips, we had our quota of fifty and didn't have to find out.

After that, all we could do was wait for Warren. I made the mistake of suggesting, "Should we go knock on his door?" and Arthur jumped all over me.

"No! We should not! We don't go in there. Ever. He'll come out when he comes out."

I stammered, "Okay. Okay." I even added, "Sorry."

Jimmy smiled kindly. "Warren's somebody who values his privacy."

So we just stood and stared at Warren's front door for five minutes.

I took the opportunity to ask Arthur, as casually as I could, "What's going on with the play? *The Roses of Eyam?*"

"What do you mean?"

"How are the actors doing with their parts?"

"I don't know. Okay, I guess. Chris Collier's pretty useless, and he's the main guy. He's married to the Grape."

"Uh-huh. Do Chris and Wendy have any romantic scenes? Kissing scenes?"

Arthur snorted. "No way, dude. If you kiss somebody in Eyam, they die. Slowly and painfully. You may as well blow their head off with a shotgun."

Okay. We left it at that.

Warren's door finally opened. He stepped out wearing his Haven High Football jacket and carrying a backpack. He locked up carefully and sauntered down to join us. "Cousin Tom! You made it."

"Yeah."

"You ready to sell some Christmas trees?"

"I am. I'm looking forward to it."

"Me, too. It beats the hell out of moving college boys in and out of Blackwater U." He asked Jimmy, "You ready, bubba?"

"Yup."

Warren thought for a moment. "Now, Tom, are you sure you're allowed to do this?"

"Yes, sir."

"Because we don't have any insurance if . . . if anything happens to you."

"That's okay. Nothing's going to happen to me."

175

"Are you old enough to drive?"

"No, sir."

"Too bad." He turned back to Jimmy. "You got all the stuff loaded?"

"Yeah. We got the stakes in the back; the chicken wire's underneath."

"Okay. Let's hitch up Arthur's car."

Arthur climbed into the Geo Metro. He pulled it up by the back of the truck and got out. Jimmy reached under the truck and slid out a cable. He knelt in front of the car and attached it to a pair of hooks. Then he reached under the truck again and started cranking a handle. The front of the Geo Metro rose up off the ground until the hood was even with the back bumper. Arthur then wedged a steel frame between the car and the truck, ensuring that the two couldn't collide.

Jimmy checked it and pronounced it "good enough for government work." Then we were ready to roll.

Warren pulled himself up into the driver's seat; Jimmy took shotgun. Arthur and I climbed in and sat on either side of the crew cab's bench.

Warren summarized, "I can drive, obviously. So can Arthur. If I am in no condition to drive, though, and if Arthur is tired, I guess brother Jimmy can fill in, suspended license and all." He looked into the rearview mirror. "And if all else fails, cousin Tom, it's up to you."

I smiled.

He winked and added, "And with us, cousin Tom, all else fails a lot."

We drove down from Caldera to Route 16 and started our long trek south, rumbling past a series of tree and shrubbery farms with names like Pioneer Evergreens, Rohrbachs Farm, and

Kilingers Nurseries. We soon pulled into the parking lot of a large barnlike building that had GROVIANA written across the top in weathered red paint.

We all followed Warren into a big square space filled with chicken wire, wooden stakes, and boxes. There was a desk over in the far corner, and a man in a blue work shirt was sitting behind it.

Warren called to him heartily, "Hey, my man! How's it going?"

The man eyed us suspiciously, like we might be there to rob the place.

Warren pointed to Jimmy. "My brother and me bought some trees here last year, right around this time. Sold them down in Florida. Remember?"

The man did remember. He said, "Yeah. Right. Did we ever settle that account?"

Warren looked to Jimmy and then back. "Yeah. We settled it up. We're good."

The man shook his head. "That's not the way I remember it."

"Well, if there's still any balance from last year, just add it to this year's tab. We're good for it. We got a sure thing going this year. We got a prime lot in Orlando on a main thoroughfare, right on Colonial Drive. That's the main drag. We'll be the only tree sellers in a five-mile radius. It's gonna be all gravy, bro!"

But the man was not buying it. He told Warren, "I talked to Mr. Levans about you guys, too. He said he never got paid from two years ago."

"No, that's a mistake."

The man picked up the phone. "Let's call him, then."

Warren backed down quickly. "No. No. Look, all we need is twenty-five Frasiers and twenty-five Douglases to start. Then we'll take fifty of whatever you got for the rest."

The man set the phone down hard, like a gavel. He thought for a moment, then told us, "No way. I'm not fronting you any Frasier or Douglas firs. I should just say a flat-out no, but I'm trying to do the Christian thing here. I'll tell you what I will do: For no money down, I got fifty Scotch pine you can have. They're already cut and ready to load, but the buyer never picked 'em up."

Warren sounded offended. "Scotch pine?"

"Sorry, but that's what I got. You can take them or leave them."

Warren raised up both hands as if to say, *Whoa*. He told the man, "We'll take them."

The man stood. "All right. Who's loading them up?"

Warren turned to us. "We all are."

So we trooped back outside. Jimmy and Arthur quickly unhooked the Geo Metro from the truck. We climbed back into our cab while the tree man got into a small white pickup.

He drove over a low ridge and out into the fields, so we followed. We passed many acres of small trees. Soon we were bumping past taller trees, though—very attractive, well-shaped trees that I figured were the Frasier firs and Douglas firs.

The white truck veered left and crawled carefully down a hill to a grove of pine trees. They were not as beautiful as the Frasier firs, but they weren't bad-looking, either. And they would certainly work as Christmas trees.

Nobody was saying anything. I guess Warren, Jimmy, and Arthur were disappointed at this turn of events, but I didn't know any better. I was excited.

A row of trees had already been felled—sliced off at the bottom with a chain saw—and were now lying on the ground. The tree man leaned out of his truck window and pointed at them. "There you go, cut and ready. You can take all fifty."

The four of us clambered out.

Warren shook his head. He muttered to Jimmy, "They're kinda puny." To prove his point, he picked one tree up off the ground and hoisted it high over his head. He carried it like that to our truck and tossed it casually over the railing. He came back and told us, "All right. Toss them in there any way you can. We'll straighten 'em up later."

So that's what we did. Jimmy and Arthur were able to do that tree-over-the-head, heaving-over-the-rail thing. I carried my trees waist-high to the back of the truck and slid them under the netting. Still, I was able to carry my share, and we soon had fifty trees on the truck. Warren and Jimmy climbed into the back and arranged them in neat rows. Then we took our places in the cab and followed the white truck back toward the highway.

Jimmy and Arthur hooked up the Geo Metro again while Warren and I sat in the cab. Warren told me, "We still have room, so we'll pick up some Frasier firs down in Pine Grove. I know where we can go." He looked in the rearview mirror. "I'm wearing my magic jacket today, Tom. All will be well."

We took Route 81 south for about fifteen minutes. Then we pulled off the highway into a similar-looking wooden barn. This one had a cement-block gas station and convenience store next to it.

Warren went into the barn and, not five minutes later, came out all angry and upset. And empty-handed.

He shouted, "Mr. Christian Thing To Do back there must have called ahead. He bad-mouthed us all over the county. Nobody will do business with us." Warren decided, "You take the wheel for a while, Arthur. Pull up to the pump there. We gotta gas up."

Warren fished something out from beneath the driver's seat.

Then he disappeared behind the block building. Jimmy and Arthur paid no notice, so neither did I.

He came back a few minutes later with a new attitude, smiling and flopping into the backseat next to me. As Arthur pulled out and we headed south, Warren started talking loudly. "These trees are total crap, man! Scotch pines? Well, hell, we'll just tell everybody they're Frasier firs and Douglas firs, and—I don't know—*Pennsylvania* firs. Those dumbasses down in Florida don't know the difference. They're just pretending it's Christmas down there anyway. It may as well be the damn Fourth of July!"

Warren poked Jimmy. "Put in the classic Christmas cassette, bubba. I need to hear that while we're still in cold country."

Jimmy snorted, "Those cassettes must be twenty years old. I'm surprised they're not eight-tracks."

"Every one of them is a classic," Warren insisted. "There is no need for anyone, ever, to put out another Christmas album. All the classic Christmas songs have been recorded. Mission accomplished.

"Check it out: The Christmas season runs from Christmas Eve until January sixth, technically, although most people have gotten sick of it by January first. But the stores start playing Christmas songs the day after friggin' Halloween. Why is that?"

Arthur interjected, "It's all supply and demand."

"There you go! There you go, Coach Malloy. I remember that lesson. Christmas *demand* is for two weeks. But the Christmas *supply* lasts for over two months. Go figure that one out."

He leaned forward. "Put on that Burl Ives cassette, Jimmy. Gimme some 'Frosty the Snowman.' Gimme some 'Holly Jolly Christmas' before we hit that Florida heat."

The music started, and Warren whooped his approval. "Yeah! Frosty. There's my man. Frosty!" But he soon turned philosophical. "Man, listen to that. Tell me: What did old Frosty get out of the deal? You know what I'm saying?"

He turned to me. "The kids let him dance and sing and tell jokes and . . . *amuse* them all day, and then he dies. He freaking melts, man! He's effing dead. And what did he get out of it?"

Jimmy drawled, "Why, the pure joy of amusing children."

"Screw that! What good is that? You can't take that to the bank. You can't make your car payment with that. Believe me, I have tried." Warren pointed forward again. "And Rudolph? Him, too. They were plain ugly to him his whole life. They treated him like a townie, bubba. A townie with a big red nose."

"I hear that."

"So what does he think is gonna happen after he . . . pulls their nuts out of the fire on Christmas Eve? After he friggin' saves Christmas? Does he think they won't make fun of his nose anymore? Does he think they're going to let him play their reindeer games?"

Jimmy and Arthur shouted out, as if they were at church, "Hell no!"

Warren continued: "For that matter, what does Santa Claus get out of the deal? He spends three hundred and sixty-four days making toys. He makes millions of toys, at his own expense. Then he travels by friggin' open-air sled! Does he have a heater in this sled? Does he?"

This time, I joined them. "Hell no!"

"He drives ten million miles. And then, does he sell these toys? Does he get a good price for his labors?"

"Hell no!"

"That's right. Hell no again. He friggin' gives them away! Then he starts all over again the next day. What kind of life is that? He may as well be a coal miner," Warren concluded. "He works like a devil, and he gets no money. He may as well be a damn coal miner."

Arthur contributed, "Santa gives bad kids lumps of coal."

Warren laughed. "What?"

"Kids who have not been good? Like me when I was six? They get coal instead of presents."

"Really? Are you serious? That happened to you?"

"It did. I kept my lump of coal to prove it. I got it under my bed."

"Man, that's hard. That's cold!" He hit his brother on the shoulder. "Jimmy Giles, how could you marry a woman who would do that?"

"That was before I met her," Jimmy explained. "She wouldn't do it now."

"Well, that's small consolation for little Arthur here."

Warren reached up and poked Arthur. "It's bad enough that he has to live over the fires of hell. Right, Arthur?"

"Amen."

"The flames that burn eternal."

"Amen."

"You're not gonna let them flames burn me, right, Arthur?"

"No, sir, Uncle Warren. No, sir."

"You're not gonna let me burn."

"No, sir. I am not."

Warren kept talking through Pennsylvania and most of Maryland. Then his voice started to drop, and so did his eyelids. After a long silent stretch, I reached into my backpack, pulled out my journal, and started to write about what had happened so far.

I was surprised when Warren's eyes popped back open and he asked me, "What are you writing there, Tom? Homework?"

"Sort of. It's a journal, for extra credit."

"What do you have to write about?"

"Anything I want. Now I'm writing about our trip."

"Yeah? This trip? Can I read it?"

"Uh, yeah. I guess."

"I'll wait till you're finished, if that's cool."

"All right."

Warren leaned over and looked down at a page. His eyes widened. "Hey! You wrote about Frosty!"

"Yeah."

He laughed with delight. "That is so cool."

Soon after, somewhere in Virginia, Warren fell asleep for good. By then, Arthur had been driving for ten hours. Jimmy said, "Pull off at the next exit, Arthur. We need a pit stop—gas, food, bathroom break. Then I'll take her for a while."

Arthur put on the right blinker and slowed our truck-car combination down. "A pit stop sounds good. I don't know about you driving, though, Jimmy. What about Warren taking over?"

"Warren? He's out. He's down for the count."

"I can keep driving for a while."

"No. Don't you worry about me. I'm a professional driver. You need some sleep. You can take her into Orlando in the morning."

So we left the interstate and rolled into a gigantic truck stop with a gas station, a picnic area, and a food court. Jimmy used a credit card to fill up the truck's large tank. Then Arthur drove us down to the extra-long spaces reserved for big rigs.

Jimmy said, "We'll leave Warren in the truck, for security."

Arthur snorted, "Fat lotta good he's gonna do."

"Ah, don't worry. None of these old boys're interested in Christmas trees. Or Geo Metros."

Jimmy, Arthur, and I walked together across the wide expanse of parking lot. It felt great to stretch my legs and breathe in the cold night air. Inside the food court, we all ordered hamburgers and fries. Jimmy ordered some for Warren, too.

When we got back to the truck, Arthur tried one more time to talk Jimmy out of driving, telling him, "I'm really fine, you know. Let me take it for a few hours more."

Jimmy was firm. "No. You need to sleep."

"But what if something happens?"

Jimmy thought about that. "Okay. You sit up front with me. If I see any flashing lights in the rearview mirror, I'll pull over, and we'll switch places real fast."

So we continued our ride south with Jimmy, suspended license and all, at the wheel. Arthur and I wolfed down our burgers and fries. This had an immediate and powerful effect on Arthur, as he was asleep within minutes.

I was tired, too, but I felt I could not go to sleep. Somebody had to stay awake with Jimmy to make sure that *he* was awake.

Jimmy was totally focused, though. Totally professional. He remained alert, driving the speed limit, getting the job done for as long as I was looking at him, which was not for long. I, too, conked out some time before midnight.

When I felt us slowing down and turning, I checked my watch; it showed 4:00 a.m. I asked Jimmy, "Where are we?"

"Georgia," he drawled. "The Peach State. Good place for a pit stop." He hopped out and filled the truck with gas again. By the time he drove us back to a space, Warren and Arthur were awake, too, and hungry.

Warren held up his bag from the night before like it was a dead rat. "What's this thing?"

Jimmy told him, "Dinner. You might want to toss that now."

"I just might. It's breakfast time, bubba."

The four of us walked stiffly across the lot. Arthur turned

back once to check on his car, but it was obviously safe. There was no one else in sight.

We all purchased the same thing—egg and bagel sandwiches. Warren and Jimmy got huge cups of coffee.

Arthur and I pulled out cans of soda from Aunt Robin's cooler. They were still cold, but the ice was all melted, so Arthur dumped the water out into the parking lot.

Then we set off again, with Arthur back behind the wheel.

Soon a bright red sun rose up on Thanksgiving Day. The holiday season had begun, like no holiday season I had ever known. Warren pushed in a Christmas cassette, and we completed the last leg of our journey in a happy mood. We exited the Florida Turnpike at Ocoee, turned right, and pulled into the parking lot of the Colony Plaza Hotel. That was to be my home, and Arthur's, for the next three nights. It was to be Warren's and Jimmy's home for the next ten nights, or until all the trees were sold.

Warren got out and walked into the hotel lobby to get us a room. While we waited, Jimmy lowered the front wheels of the Geo Metro to the ground and disengaged it from the truck. Arthur started the car up and pulled it into a parking space.

I stood there, wearing just a T-shirt, thinking, *I'm in Florida! I'm really in Florida.* I took a minute to duck into the truck and grab my notebook and pen. I'd be keeping them with me at all times. I didn't want to forget anything about this trip.

Warren came back out and announced, "Room two seventeen, boys, just like last year. Maybe that's an omen." He opened the driver's-side door of the truck. "Now let's go sell some Christmas trees."

We pulled around the back of the hotel and headed west. A divided highway named Maguire Road intersected the main road. Just as we turned onto Maguire, though, Warren slammed on the

185

brakes. He pounded the steering wheel and yelled, "No! No! This can't be!"

I leaned forward to see what was wrong.

Our lot was directly before us on the right. It was a rectangle of dirt about fifty feet long. Directly beyond it was a second lot, a lot that was supposed to be a Jiffy Lube. Instead, as its signs announced, it was once again a BOY SCOUT CHRISTMAS TREES lot.

Warren pounded and screamed some more. This time he went way beyond "No! No!"

I stared at the Boy Scout lot in the distance. It was lined on three sides by chicken wire. It had large, professionally printed signs. The lot also had a pair of green porta-potties sitting at the back.

Warren shouted, "That Peterson guy told me it was a Jiffy Lube. What the hell!"

Warren continued to curse and to pound the steering wheel, blocking traffic on Maguire Road, until Jimmy broke the spell. "Hey! Let me tell you what they don't have, bubba."

Warren stopped ranting long enough to ask, "What?"

"Christmas trees!"

That was true. There was not a Christmas tree to be seen down there. The Boy Scout lot was empty except for a lonely SUV parked at the south end. I looked closer and saw that there was a man sitting in it, watching us.

Warren was suddenly reenergized. "Yeah!" He stomped down on the gas pedal and our truck lurched forward. He executed a smooth right turn onto the sandy dirt of our lot.

That's when I noticed that someone, probably the much-cursed Mr. Peterson, had rigged out the lot with equipment. There was a red gas generator sitting on a sturdy piece of plywood near the back. The generator had wires running to the four corners of the lot. There were eight tall light poles, evenly spaced along the perimeter, for night selling. There was a canopy on the north edge for shelter.

Warren, Jimmy, and Arthur practically dove out of the truck. Arthur grabbed my arm and dragged me with him under the flat-bed. He pointed to a fat roll of chicken wire held in place by leather straps. "First thing to do is set up the tree pen."

I could hear Warren and Jimmy above us, hopping up onto the bed and wading through the trees until they reached the back. They started tossing the fifty wooden stakes to the ground on both sides of the truck.

Then the four of us worked like maniacs, planting the stakes and unrolling the chicken wire. Within fifteen minutes we had set up a three-sided pen to hold the trees. Then we started a bucket brigade to hand the trees down. Warren, up on the truck bed, handed one down to Jimmy, who passed it off to Arthur, who dragged it into the pen, where I set it up straight.

After the last tree was in place, Jimmy backed the truck to the north parking area. He emerged with a big plastic bag and handed it to Warren. The two of them set to work fashioning three signs, stapled onto pieces of plywood. The signs read CHRISTMAS TREES FROM PENNSYLVANIA; FRESH-CUT CHRISTMAS TREES; and FRASIER FIRS, DOUGLAS FIRS.

I whispered to Arthur, "But we don't have Frasier firs or Douglas firs."

"Hey, if anybody calls you on it, say we just sold the last one. And ask them if they'd be interested in a Pennsylvania fir."

"Is there such a thing?"

"Not really."

"Got it."

Just as we finished our work, the man in the SUV got out and stretched his arms high. He dumped out the remains of a cup of coffee. Then he walked along the side of Maguire Road toward us. He was a heavyset man, dressed in brown shorts. Although it was a hot day and we were all in T-shirts, he had on a long-sleeve shirt decorated with pins and badges, and a sewn-on patch that identified him as a Scout master.

He turned onto our lot and approached Warren, who smiled and called out, "Happy Memorial Day! Or is it the Fourth of July?"

The man did not acknowledge the greeting except to say, in a flat, lawyerly voice, "If you plan on conducting business in Orange County, Florida, you have to provide rest room facilities."

Warren smiled even wider. "What's that? You need to use the rest room?"

"No. *You* need to provide rest room facilities."

"Ah. Now, what are those exactly?"

The man pointed to the back of his lot. "Porta-potties."

Warren's smile slowly receded. He replied coolly, "Porta-potties? Just to sell Christmas trees? Is that really necessary?"

"I'm not here to argue about it. I'm here to tell you that you are currently in violation of the law."

Warren didn't reply, so the man turned and retraced his steps all the way to his SUV.

Two minutes later, a Sheriff's Department car pulled into our parking lot and a woman deputy got out. She was heavyset, too, but in a very muscular way. She and Warren had a conversation out near the road while the rest of us hung back. Warren was smiling and charming the whole time he spoke to her, and she was smiling, too, when she drove away.

Warren walked back to us and reported, "Okay. We'll probably get fined for not having porta-potties, but it's only two hundred and fifty dollars. We can absorb that. Let's start selling."

The Christmas tree sale started off well. Several cars pulled in. Couples and families got out, looked at our selection, and then either bought a tree or moved on. Warren handled all of the cash, making change from a wad of bills he kept in his pocket. Jimmy, Arthur, and I talked up the merchandise and tied the sold trees to the tops of cars and SUVs, or we slid them carefully into the beds of pickup trucks.

It was the first hot Thanksgiving Day I had ever known. I was liking it very much, and I was liking Florida. I was more determined than ever to move there for college.

Things continued this way for most of the afternoon, and we had probably grossed over a thousand dollars, but then our luck started to change.

First, a Ryder rental truck pulled up next to the Boy Scout lot. It made that reverse beeping noise and then backed in. We could see what its cargo was very clearly: Christmas trees—Frasier firs and Douglas firs included. Right after that, a stream of cars pulled into the south parking area, disgorging Boy Scouts and their parents.

Arthur muttered, "Enemy spotted, cuz." He spit on the ground. "Look at that. It's a damn jamboree down there."

The Scouts, all dressed in brown shirts, scrambled to unload their trees and set them up. A small group of Scout mothers took up positions along the chicken wire next to our lot. They started calling loudly to our customers, "Don't buy from them! They're outsiders! Support your local Scouts! Help your Scouts raise money," and so on.

The tactic worked. Some of our customers crossed over to the other lot to buy their trees. (It didn't help that the Scouts had a better selection.)

The sales battle continued, with us barely hanging in there, until about 9:00 p.m. That's when the street traffic stopped abruptly. The Boy Scout lot extinguished its lights first; then we shut ours down.

As we were cleaning up, Arthur got into an argument with a Scout mother. They were both standing where the fences met. I heard the mother say, "Why don't you go back where you came from and sell your trees?"

Arthur told her, with fake politeness, "We paid for this lot, ma'am, and we have the right to sell here."

"You come from Pennsylvania," she pointed out. "It says right there on your sign. You should go back there."

"Pennsylvania. That's right. Caldera, Pennsylvania. You ever heard of that?"

"No."

"It's kinda like hell. All fire and sulfur. Are you telling me to go to hell? Because that would not be a Christian thing to do, ma'am. That might, ironically, bring the wrath of God down on you."

I laughed at that, but Warren did not. He interrupted Arthur. "That's enough! Let's close up." He called over to his brother, "Jimmy, take the boys back to the hotel. You all get some sleep. I'll stay in the truck and watch the merchandise."

So the three of us trekked across the long asphalt parking lot, exhausted but mostly happy.

Jimmy bought a six-pack of beer and a two-liter bottle of Coke in the hotel store while Arthur called for a pizza delivery. We ate the pizza and watched holiday specials—including the cartoon version of *Frosty the Snowman*. (At the end, Frosty does *not* melt to death. He escapes to the North Pole and lives forever. I wondered what Warren would say about that.)

Jimmy fell asleep right after *Frosty*. As it turned out, that was exactly what Arthur had been waiting for. He gestured for me to follow him out of the room, so I did. He whispered, "Vengeance time, cuz. The Lord's vengeance. You down with it?"

"Uh, sure."

"Do what I do, then. And don't make a sound."

"Okay."

We slipped back through the parking lot like phantoms. Arthur led the way in a straight diagonal line, southeastward, toward Maguire Road. I saw our flatbed truck to the left, but I did not see any sign of Warren inside.

Soon, we were right behind the Boy Scout lot. When we reached the chicken wire, Arthur stretched it back so that there was enough room to squeeze through.

He did, and I followed.

He army-crawled on his elbows, with me copying him, to the back of the men's porta-potty. My nose twitched at the acrid smell of chemicals from inside it. (I hoped that was all I was smelling.)

Arthur turned and whispered, "Start digging."

He showed me what he meant. He dug into the sand with a cupped hand and pulled out as much of the sandy dirt as he could. I did the same thing on my side. We worked steadily for about five minutes, carving out a sizable hole beneath the back of the big green coffin-like box.

When Arthur was satisfied that we had dug enough, he slapped at my shoulder. He started back, army-crawling along the same path, so I did, too. We squeezed through the chicken wire and moved, quickly and stealthily, back to our hotel room door. Neither of us made a sound.

✤

The next morning at eight, I stuffed my notebook in my pocket and followed Jimmy and Arthur to the lot. Jimmy rapped on the window of the truck to wake Warren. He handed Warren a huge cup of coffee.

Arthur and I drifted over to the tree pen. I did a quick count and established that thirty-four trees remained, meaning we had sold sixteen. (It had seemed like more.)

The first sign of life at the Scouts' lot was the arrival of the Scout master's SUV. He got out and entered their tree pen. He was holding a huge cup of coffee, too. Arthur and I watched him on and off for about ten minutes. Suddenly Arthur emitted a short, sharp *psst*. He snapped his head in the direction of the Scouts' lot. I looked and saw that the Scout master was walking rapidly toward the men's porta-potty.

My eyes focused in on him like binoculars. My heart started to pound. I whispered to myself, "Please. Please do it. Do it."

And he did.

The big man opened the door of the green box and stepped inside. Just a few seconds later, just long enough for him to pull down his shorts and sit, the green box started to move. It was a slight tipping move at first. We heard a muffled cry, and then the whole thing tilted back crazily.

The cry turned into a yell as the big green box crashed backward down the hill, making a cracking and then a sloshing sound.

Arthur and I both doubled over, laughing hysterically, until we couldn't breathe. It took a full minute for us to recover enough to look up again. By then the Scout master, his shorts pulled most of the way back up, had pushed up the coffin lid of the porta-potty. He struggled to climb over one side, turning enough to show us a very wet, very suspicious-looking stain on the back of his decorated shirt.

He half crawled up the sandy hill to our side. His face was bright red. He looked right past us and screamed at Warren, "You'll pay for this!"

Then he turned and stomped away. That stain on his back was suspicious, all right.

Warren watched him go, looking very confused. He motioned for Arthur to come over to the truck, so I followed. "What's going on? Why's he yelling?"

Arthur smiled at me. He told Warren, "Uh, I think he had a problem using the rest room facilities."

"What?"

"I'm thinking it was all those medals on his shirt. You know? Weighing him down?"

"Arthur? What the hell are you talking about?"

Arthur's smile faded. He tried to explain. "We did the porta-potty."

Warren's voice was all business. "What does that mean?"

"We rigged it so the next guy in it would fall over."

Warren and Jimmy looked over at the toppled green box. Arthur added, "It was payback for last year. For the air horn. We got them back good!"

Arthur tried smiling again, but they were definitely not smiling back.

Warren snapped at him, "Damn it, Arthur! Why did you do that?"

"Like I said—payback, that's all."

"That's all?" Warren looked around like he was frightened. He turned toward the hotel room and then toward the truck.

Arthur's face fell. He whispered in an agonized voice, "Oh no, Warren. You're holdin'?"

"Shut up."

Warren turned away. He was soon huddled with Jimmy, whispering.

I asked Arthur, "What? What's going on?"

"Damn. We should not have done that, cuz. Things are different this year. Warren's holdin'."

"What does that mean?"

"He's got drugs on him."

"What? Where?"

"In the truck. In the room. Both? I don't know."

A sheriff's car arrived before Warren and Jimmy could even formulate a plan. A skinny young guy got out and approached quickly, freezing us all in our places. He stopped when a squawking noise came out of the speaker on his shoulder. He responded to the voice and then just stood still, surveying the scene. The woman deputy from the day before pulled in a minute later.

She walked right up to Warren and informed him, "If what I just heard is right, Mr. Giles, you are looking at a charge of criminal mischief."

Warren said, "I don't know what you heard."

"I thought we had an understanding yesterday. I guess I was wrong."

"I don't know what you're talking about."

The woman deputy scrutinized Warren carefully, especially his eyes. She nodded briefly. Then she pointed back toward the parking area. "Do you mind if I look in your truck?"

"Yes, I do."

"Why?"

Warren replied politely but firmly, "There's no *why* about it. It's my truck, and I say you can't look in it. That's my right as an American."

"I got a police dog. He won't have to go into that truck. He'll know from out here what's in it. Do I call for him or not?"

Warren shrugged. "Go ahead and call. I like dogs."

I could see that the deputy didn't really want to. She tried again. "I'm just doing my job here, sir. How about some cooperation."

"I'm doing my job, too, Officer, which is selling Christmas trees, on this lot that I paid good money for. I've done nothing wrong, so let me get to work."

"That's your final word?"

Warren answered, "That's my final word." He walked back and stood with us.

Arthur hung his head and turned away. I think he was crying. The deputy got on her shoulder speaker, and soon a third patrol car pulled in. An officer got out, along with a big German shepherd.

By now about a dozen Scouts and their parents had arrived and were hanging out along the wire fence.

Then something so bizarre, so totally impossible, happened, that I just stood there with my mouth open, failing to comprehend it.

A car pulled into our lot and sat there next to the three police cars.

It was Mom's Ford Taurus. And Mom got out of it.

She walked, somewhat stiffly, right toward me, her eyes locked onto mine like a laser beam. She got within two feet and stopped. "Get in the car, Tom. Now," she ordered.

I started to protest. "I . . . I can't. I have my stuff in the—"

She cut me off angrily. "Now! I don't care what you have here. Get in the car."

I felt scared, like a little kid. I turned to look at the others.

Warren was trying to talk to the policewoman, but she was no longer listening. Jimmy was standing there looking down, just shaking his head. Arthur had fallen to his knees in the dirt; he was definitely crying.

So I just walked to the car and got in without another word.

Mom peeled out of the lot much too fast. (Hadn't she seen the three police cars?) She made an illegal U-turn on Maguire Road. Then she took a quick left and a right, and we were on the Florida Turnpike, heading north.

She did not speak for quite a while, but when she did, she really let loose. "They were all getting arrested, right? For drugs, right? This is who you want to spend Thanksgiving with? This is who you want to ride around the country with?"

"The cops just want to talk to Warren."

"About drugs?"

"No," I lied. "About criminal mischief."

"What?"

"Warren, Jimmy, Arthur—they're not bad people, Mom. You should give them a chance."

That shut her up for a while. A short while. Soon she was back to haranguing me about the Food Giant, and personal responsibility, and the evil of lying, and the corrupting influence of Aunt Robin's side of the family.

When I could finally speak again, which was near the Georgia border, I asked her a question that had been on my mind for many miles. "How can you drive like this without stopping?"

She blinked rapidly. Then she said, "What do you mean? I did stop. I stopped last night."

"Where?"

"I don't know. Never mind where. We're talking about you now, not me."

And we did talk about me, off and on, for twelve more hours, over three more states, until we finally pulled into the carport behind our house.

It was mind-numbing. And horrible. And I felt so bad for the guys I had left behind.

Things had been going so well. Then everything fell apart.

Damn Boy Scouts.

December

Monday, December 3, 2001

Mom and Dad grounded me for two weeks. That made very little difference in my life, since I hardly do anything but go to school and work, and I was still allowed to do those things. I was not, however, allowed to call Arthur or to contact him in any way. Questions about the Florida trip were eating me up, but I couldn't get any answers. Arthur had not shown up for school on Monday. He had not shown up on Tuesday, Wednesday, Thursday, or Friday, either. So all I could do was wait.

Mom and Dad were barely speaking to me, but it seemed like Lilly was going out of her way to. She never came right out and said it, but I think she actually respected what I'd done. (Or did she just appreciate someone else getting in trouble for a change?)

Before school, while I was messing with the N64, she came into the parlor and stood behind me. She asked, "Can you help me find something on the computer?"

"Sure," I replied, figuring it was another weird sex website she'd heard about, but I was wrong. As I slid over to the Gateway, she said, "Is there a job you can do that helps drug addicts?"

I nodded. "Yeah. I think that's what social workers do. Ben's always saying he got diagnosed by a social worker."

I searched the Internet for "social work careers." That pulled up several sites, and I clicked on three of them. Lilly read the information over my shoulder. Each time she asked, somewhat disappointed, "Is there another one?"

By the end of the third site, she sounded totally discouraged. "They all say 'bachelor's degree.' What does that mean?"

"Four years of college."

Lilly shook her head. "No. No way. I'm not doing that."

She started to leave, but I said, "Wait a minute. Let me type in 'drug counselor.' A site titled "Substance-Abuse Counselor" popped up, so I clicked on it. Lilly leaned over my shoulder and read along with me. The very first line, under "Education," said "high school degree."

I slid out of the chair. "Here. I'll let you read this."

Lilly took my place in front of the Gateway. When Mom called her for the ride to school, she was still reading.

⚓

I waited outside Mr. Proctor's class, like I had for five days, watching for Arthur's approach. When I finally saw him, I waved happily, but he walked right past me without a word. I turned and followed him inside, slipping into the next desk. I hadn't gotten one syllable out before he growled at me, "I'm not ready to talk about it yet!"

Mrs. Cantwell hurried into the room, causing everyone to quiet down and face forward. She announced, "Mr. Proctor has called in sick today. I am in the process of getting a sub to cover this class. Until then, is there some work you could do?"

She swiveled and looked at the whiteboard. It had the word *Vocabulary* written at the upper right. She said, "Jenny Weaver, is there a vocabulary assignment you could all be doing?"

"Yes, ma'am."

"What page would that start on?"

Jenny thumbed through her vocab book. She replied, "Forty-two."

Mrs. Cantwell picked up a marker from the desk and printed *Page 42* under *Vocabulary*. She told us, "All right. You all have your assignment; now get to work." And she hurried back out.

Most kids put their heads down.

Arthur slapped my arm with the back of his hand. He pointed to two desks near the window and commanded, "Over there."

I followed him to the more secluded area. I guess he was ready to talk about it, because he plunged right in. "This is for your ears only. Understand?"

"Yeah."

"Okay. Here's what happened after you pulled away." He took a deep breath and exhaled. Then he started talking, as if reading from a play script: "You pulled away. The police dog started going nuts around the truck, barking and scratching at the door like he'd found something. The sheriff lady told Warren, 'You can open up the truck right now, or I can send for a search warrant. It'll be here inside of an hour.'

"Warren told her, 'Go ahead. Send for a search warrant, because I'm not letting you look in my truck.'

"So all three cops and the cop dog stayed right where they were, glaring at us. The sheriff lady walked over and asked me about you. She said, 'Where's that other boy?'

"I didn't know what to say, so I played dumb. I said, 'Who?'

"Warren jumped in. He told her, 'That other boy wasn't with us. I think he was a Boy Scout.'"

I laughed in spite of myself, though none of this was funny.

Arthur frowned and continued. "So for the next hour, we had three cop cars on our lot with their lights flashing, and three cops, and a freaked-out German shepherd. How many people do you figure bought Christmas trees from us?"

"None?"

"That's exactly right. So this fourth car finally pulled up, an unmarked car, and this Detective Sergeant something got out waving a piece of paper. By now the cops were pissed off at

Warren because he'd made 'em do all that. They surrounded the truck. The detective sergeant showed him the paper. Warren read it. Then he said, 'I'm still not giving permission, but I guess you're gonna look in my truck now. It's not locked.'

"The lady sheriff and the K-9 team pulled open the doors and climbed in. About ten seconds later, the lady reached under the driver's seat and pulled up a metal pipe and a Baggie with some rocks in it."

I had to interrupt because I didn't understand. "Rocks?"

"Yeah. Crystal meth. Or crack. I don't know. Could have been either one. Doesn't matter, really—they're both illegal. So the lady sheriff called out to Warren, 'Do these belong to you, Mr. Giles?'

"Warren said, 'Nope.'

"Then she looked at Jimmy and me, but she was still talking to Warren. 'I must assume they could belong to anyone who had access to this truck. In which case, you will all need to come down to the county courthouse for processing.'"

Arthur stopped talking. He swallowed hard. Then he continued: "Warren knew it was over then. He told her, 'No. Those two don't know anything about it. The stuff is mine.'

"And that was that. They cuffed Warren's hands behind his back. They leaned him against the truck and searched him. Then they stuck him into the back of the lady's police cruiser. She handed us a card showing where they were taking Warren, and they drove away.

"I looked over at the Boy Scouts. They were all staring at us. I swear, if one of them had said anything, or blasted a boat horn, I'd have ripped his freakin' head off."

An angry flush crossed Arthur's neck and face. "Me and Jimmy didn't know what to do. People started pulling into our lot again. Me and Jimmy started selling off the Christmas trees for forty, twenty-five, even ten bucks each. Whatever the customer said, we said, 'Yeah, whatever. Take it.'

"About four o'clock, a lady from the hotel came walking over. She handed Jimmy a paper with a phone message on it. Warren had gotten himself out on bail already. He wanted to get picked up outside the courthouse."

Arthur shook his head in admiration. "He had appeared before a judge, who had set his bail at five thousand dollars. Warren told the judge, 'I'll get you the five thousand dollars if you let me go back and sell my Christmas trees. That's what I'm down here for.'

"The judge said no. He asked Warren what else he had as collateral. To make a long story short, Warren met with a bail bondsman and signed over the truck. The bail bondsman paid five thousand dollars to the court, and the judge let Warren go.

"Anyway, I took off in my car as soon as we got the note. I drove straight down Colonial Drive until I got to the courthouse. I was expecting Warren to be mad as hell at me, but he wasn't. He was just standing outside there like it wasn't any big deal. I rolled down the window and started to apologize, but he waved it off. He told me to slide over because he wanted to drive."

Arthur stopped and swallowed hard again. "He said that he forgave me. He understood why I did it. He knew I meant well. All that kind of stuff. He made me promise to save him from hellfire, like he always does. Then we drove back out to the lot. Warren rolled down the window and said, 'Get in the damn car, Jimmy Giles.'

"We pulled around to the hotel. That took no time, you know? We had never really unpacked. So we were right back on the road, Warren behind the wheel, heading for home.

"After a minute, Jimmy asked Warren, 'What about the trees?'

"Warren said, 'Eff the trees, man. We're out of the tree business.'

"Jimmy asked, 'What about the truck?'

"'The bail bondsman can keep the truck. He can keep the trees, too. I ain't never coming back to Florida. What do I care?'"

Arthur paused.

I commented, "It must have been a long drive back."

"Yeah. It was kind of quiet. After Warren told us what went down in the courthouse, he didn't have much else to say. And he had left all his Christmas cassettes in the truck.

"He drove until South Carolina. Then him and Jimmy bought a whole case of Pabst Blue Ribbon and proceeded to drink it. So I drove the rest of the way up."

What could I say except "Arthur, I am so sorry"?

"Yeah. I know. So am I." He added, almost imperceptibly, "Damn Boy Scouts."

✛

When I entered the office conference room, the unlikely team of Arthur and Mikeszabo were sitting together, working on a poster.

I asked Arthur, "What's that?"

He flipped the poster over so I couldn't see it. He answered impatiently, "Nothin'. I had an idea, that's all."

When he didn't go on, I prodded him. "What was the idea?"

"I talked to Mrs. Lyle about a new slogan. Maybe something stronger than 'NEO.' She hooked me up with Mike here."

"And?"

"And nothing. You'll have to wait for the rest."

"Okay."

As kids filed in, they looked curiously at the poster, too, but no one else asked about it.

Wendy Lyle has not been back. I guess that scene with her father and Arthur was the last straw. Chris Collier doesn't come anymore, either. Maybe they're too busy with play rehearsal, being the two leads and all.

But otherwise, the group is growing. And the plague is growing. We might not have known much about meth in September, but we sure do now. There has been a major increase in car robberies, in panhandling, and in zombie sightings on the streets. There has been a major increase in corpses down at the hospital, too.

At least two kids per week join our group. Some are court-ordered; some come on their own. Folding chairs now ring the table two deep.

When everybody was seated, Catherine Lyle opened the meeting by laying out a topic. She touched her notebook with a long fingernail and said, "I'd like to talk today about living with someone who has a drug or alcohol problem."

She looked at Jenny. "Jenny brought up this topic two weeks ago, and I noticed that a lot of you responded to it."

Not surprisingly, Ben responded to it again. His hand shot up. "Yeah. Jenny talked about having to be the perfect kid so people won't know your parents are using." He asked Jenny, "But what if you can't be the perfect kid?"

Jenny replied, "Well, you can't. Nobody can."

"What if you keep screwing up, and they send a social worker out to your house? And everybody gets mad? And you get a lot of tests, and then you get diagnosed?"

Ben looked at Catherine Lyle, who smiled at him kindly.

Mikeszabo held up his hand. He said, "I lived with parents who were using drugs, but I don't anymore."

Catherine squirmed slightly. "Why is that, Mike?"

"Because they got arrested. They're in jail."

"Oh?" Her eyes darted to her notebook. "Mike? Did this happen *after* you joined the group?"

"Yeah. A month ago."

"Okay. So . . . where do you live now?"

"With the Weavers." He smiled at Jenny. "Now I gotta be perfect all the time, too."

A few kids chuckled—at the irony, I guess.

Some high school kids started telling stories about living with alcoholics and drug addicts. The stories were different, but they had points in common—missed birthdays, angry Christmases, public embarrassments.

Arthur really got my attention when he contributed this: "I have a . . . a relative who lives near me. I used to go over to his place all the time and play Nintendo. I guess he used to get high, but I didn't know what was happening.

"Once, when I was about ten, he started a fire in his kitchen." Arthur shook his head. "He totally freaked out. He just stood there screaming at me, 'I don't want to burn! Don't let me burn!'

"My mom came running in the back door. She beat the fire out with a dish towel. She was real mad, because he wasn't thinking about *me* at all. He was just thinking about himself."

I looked at Lilly. Did she know he was talking about Warren? She didn't act like it. I pictured the two white trailers in Caldera as Arthur continued. "She never let me go back there to play. To this day, I can't go inside his house."

Catherine Lyle responded, "That's so true, Arthur. Addicts don't think about anyone but themselves."

Once everyone who wanted to speak on the topic had, Catherine Lyle summarized the discussion. "Thank you all for sharing those stories. Obviously, you do not have to be a drinker or a drug addict to be the victim of drinking or drugs. You can just be trying to live your life, minding your own business, and drugs can ruin everything."

I had a sudden strong feeling that Catherine Lyle was talking about herself. Arthur apparently thought so, too. He asked, "Do you live with someone who has a drug problem, Mrs. Lyle?"

"Pardon me?"

"Do you live with someone who has a drug problem? Or did you when you were our age?"

Catherine Lyle looked down. I could see the wheels turning in her head. She finally said, "The point is, Arthur, that I understand people who have these issues. That's part of my job." She measured her words carefully. "That sort of . . . empathy helps me to help others."

She ended the discussion by pointing a manicured finger down the table at the overturned poster. She announced, "Now Arthur and Mike have a presentation to make. Arthur has come up with a suggestion for a new slogan. Let's give them our full attention."

Mikeszabo took that as his cue to flip the poster over and show us. The poster had a bright green background with blood-red lettering that said in no uncertain terms I HATE DRUGS.

Arthur leaned forward. He pointed to the words and began, "This slogan, 'I Hate Drugs,' is very direct."

Arthur looked at Mikeszabo, who nodded with conviction. He continued, "It's a simple message. No more pussyfooting around. No more 'Just Say No.' No more 'NEO,' although that was a righteous slogan. It's more serious now. It's war now, and it's to the death."

Catherine Lyle smiled nervously. "Well, that certainly is a direct, clear message, Arthur."

"Thank you."

"Now, how do the rest of you feel?"

Mikeszabo spoke first. "I know how I feel. My parents are in prison. My sisters and me are living on charity. I've had enough. It's war for me."

A high school stoner went next. "Meth killed my dad. My mom and me watched him die. Then we had to pay for his funeral with the last money we had. We lived in our car for six months. Then we started to freeze to death, so we live in a homeless shelter now. You'd have to kill me before I'd smoke meth."

Arthur asked, "Are we gonna let meth destroy everything we have? Everyone we know? Look outside. It's a war out there, and we have to fight back."

Jenny agreed. "It's like *Night of the Living Dead*. The people fought for their lives in that movie. Has everybody seen it?"

The kids who were not in Mr. Proctor's class shook their heads or said no. Jenny explained to them, "People in a little town like ours were attacked by zombies. So they fought back with anything they had—bats, axes, fire.

"The zombies were spreading a plague. They were turning their friends, their family members, and everybody else into more zombies. The only way to stop them was to kill them."

Catherine Lyle looked nervous. She interjected, "Well, there are always other options."

Lilly agreed. "That's right. You *can* help people. I mean, what do we have around here? We have coal, and we have drug addicts." Some kids laughed, but quietly. "So if you want to work around here, you can dig coal, or you can help drug addicts."

Mrs. Lyle nodded vigorously.

Arthur muttered, "Righteous." Then he told the group, "All right. Let's take a vote. Who is in favor of the new slogan?"

Every kid's hand shot up. It was unanimous. Catherine Lyle gulped. "All right, then. This will be our new . . . direction. Thank you, Arthur and Mike."

Arthur asked her, "So, are you gonna pay for shirts, like last time, and will the Student Council sell them?"

"I'll speak to Mrs. Cantwell this week."

Arthur looked her in the eye. He had wanted to hear a simple yes. Instead, he had heard ambivalence (PSAT word). I could tell that it bothered him, but he let it slide. For now.

Two separate zombie couples were wandering through the store today, looking suspicious, looking to shoplift.

Dad was already shadowing one couple when the second one entered. He waved to me, pointed two fingers at his own eyes and then at them.

I fell in behind my pair, a thirty-something husband and wife. Both wore really old black leather jackets. She had long, matted hair, torn jeans, and flip-flops, despite the freezing temperatures outside. He had on weird rust-colored pants, a plaid work shirt, and sneakers. I took to straightening boxes on random shelves nearby, keeping my distance, keeping an eye on them.

Gradually, I became aware of a noise, a commotion, near the front of the store. It wasn't a bad noise, though, like a busted shoplifter screaming at Dad. It was a good noise—laughing, congratulating, oohing and aahing.

I left my zombie couple to investigate. Here's what was going on, in a nutshell:

John had delivered Lilly's cash drawer to her register, which was unusual. It turned out he had a secret plan—a plan that was romantic in a Food Giant sort of way. He waited for Lilly to count the money in the drawer. But when she looked inside, instead of seeing the usual coin rolls and small bills, she found a square jewelry box. She opened it and saw a diamond engagement ring.

John then got down on one knee between registers two and three and said, "I love you, Lilly. Will you marry me?"

Lilly screamed, jumped up and down, and answered, "Yes! Yes, I will!"

The customers from the next register, and new people coming in, and people shopping near the front all got caught up in the excitement.

It was a very happy scene, with kissing and hugging and congratulating. I got in there and gave my future brother-in-law a high five and my sister a brotherly hug.

Dad finally abandoned his zombie couple, too, and joined us. Lilly held up her ring finger and showed it to him. She gushed, "John just asked me to marry him, Dad! And I said yes. Isn't that wonderful?"

Dad assured her, "Yes. Yes, it is wonderful." He shook hands manfully with John and gave Lilly a big kiss on the cheek.

While all this was going on, I saw Dad's zombie couple slip out the front door with their faces turned away. I wondered what they had stolen.

My zombie couple, though, was standing on the edge of the crowd. They had an equally good chance to escape with merchandise, but they didn't. Instead, they stayed to look at Lilly and John and the diamond ring. The woman in the flip-flops had tears running down both cheeks. The man was smiling sadly in approval.

I thought, *The hell with it. They can steal whatever they want tonight.*

After about ten minutes, things settled back down. Lilly got her real cash drawer, and everybody went back to their business.

Dad ducked into the office, apparently to call Mom and tell her the news.

I started rounding up carts in the parking lot. There were fewer of them every night. I figured they were getting recycled as hibachis, dollies, and firewood baskets. Maybe people were selling them for drugs, too.

I had just pushed a train of seven carts into the store (two over the Food Giant guidelines) when I saw Mom through the window. She was running from her car toward the entrance. (The last time I saw Mom run was on Memorial Day, when Dad had dropped a propane tank in our backyard and it started to fizz.) She ran right past me, all the way up to register two, where she screeched to a halt.

Mercifully, Lilly had no customers in line as Mom started in on her. "What do you think you are doing? You never said a word to me about this . . . this choice you are making! This choice that could ruin your life!"

Lilly stopped smiling in an instant. And she gave it right back to Mom. "Ruin my life? What life? My life can only get better, believe me."

Dad hurried out of the office. He grasped Mom's elbow and started moving her back outside, like a bouncer removing a loud drunk.

Lilly watched for a moment, but then she locked her register and took off after them. There was no way I was going to miss this, so I took off, too.

We all converged near Mom's car. Lilly leveled a finger at Mom and shouted, "I got a call this morning from the Kroger Pharmacy, Mom. Do you know anything about that? They told me they couldn't refill my Adderall prescription again because it was all used up. That prescription was for two refills, at thirty pills each, and it was all used up. Do you know anything about that?"

I expected Mom to say no, or some variation of it, but she didn't. She just stared back at Lilly, her face suddenly white.

Lilly went on, "That's ninety pills, Mom! I took *one* of them, because you made me, and I felt sick. So tell me: What happened to the other eighty-nine pills? Who's been calling for those refills?"

Dad's jaw was hanging open by now, and I guess mine was, too.

Mom looked at us all and replied quietly, with some dignity, "Am I supposed to be the only one who never has a problem?" She told Dad, "You had yours. For years." She told Lilly, "And you had yours. So this is mine. All I am trying to do is . . . keep up. I'm trying to keep up with two children and a house and a stack of bills. And the pills helped. At first."

A strange silence seemed to fall over the parking lot. No one could think of a thing to say. This was just too weird, almost incomprehensible. Mom was taking Adderall? Of course. How else could she have driven for twelve hours straight?

Dad finally said to Lilly, "Go get your coat and drive your mother home. Tom and I can handle things here. You two can talk about . . . Well, you can talk."

Lilly and Mom stared at each other like two schoolchildren who had been fighting and who now had to make up. They both silently agreed to the plan, though, and they were soon driving away.

I watched them go, wondering, *What are they talking about? About why Mom took the pills? About why none of us even noticed? About what to do next? Or are they talking about wedding plans? About bridesmaids' dresses and stuff?*

This was just too weird to comprehend.

Dad took over register two and ran it until closing. Near the end of the night, I did a last shopping cart run. I spotted Arthur's Geo Metro pulling up by the propane cage, so I headed over there. But I was surprised when the door opened and someone else emerged—someone wearing a green satin Haven High Football jacket.

I called out, "Warren! You're driving the Geo?"

He looked at me and smiled. "Don't tell anybody, okay, Tom? I got a reputation to maintain."

"Okay. Uh, did you want some propane?"

"Yeah, give me three tanks. Robin says she's running low. And we gotta eat, right?"

"Right." I fished out the key and unlocked the cage. I could barely look at him when I said, "Look, Warren, I am really sorry about what happened down in Florida."

He made a dismissive gesture with his hand. "Forget about it. Things like that happen. You just have to deal with them."

I said, "You really told that sheriff lady some stuff. You sounded like a lawyer."

He smiled. "Did I? Hey, you have to know your rights in this country. And you have to use them."

"Yeah. Well, I'm really sorry about that . . . that prank thing. If there's anything I can do to make up for it, please let me know."

He nodded thoughtfully. "Tell you what: Buy me the propane and we're even."

I was happy to oblige, to pay him back in any way. "Okay! Sure."

"That way, I can save my money for the Drunken Monkey."

I pulled out three white tanks, set them on the ground, and relocked the cage.

Warren continued: "Arthur was real upset about what happened down there. He thinks it was all his fault, but it wasn't. It was my fault." He thought for a long moment. "Arthur doesn't have any role models in his life. Never has. His biological father was an alcoholic. Did you know that?"

"Yeah. He was my uncle Robby."

"Oh, right. Well, his stepdad has some drug issues. And you don't want to know about the guy who lives in the trailer behind him. It's a race to the bottom with those guys. They're all facing hellfire."

I laughed awkwardly.

So did Warren. He was totally serious, though, when he said, "You seem to have a plan, though. Is that right?"

I shrugged. "Yeah. I guess."

"Can you help Arthur make a plan for himself? He can be all talk and no action sometimes."

What could I say except "Sure. Yeah. I'll try"?

Warren looked out toward Route 16. "I don't want him hanging around here, talking trash that he could have been this or could have been that but he isn't. You know what I mean?"

"I think so."

"Help him make a real plan and stick to it. Something solid: the military, college, whatever."

We stood still for a moment. I finally had to ask him, "Do you have a plan, Warren?"

"Me? You mean aside from going to the Drunken Monkey tonight?"

"Yes."

Warren shrugged. "Well, I've always wanted to use my degree."

"Yeah? What was that in?"

216

"Chemistry."

"Oh."

Warren walked around to the hatchback and opened it. He pointed at my back pocket. "Hey, is that what I think it is? Is that the story you were writing? About the trip?"

"Uh, yeah."

"Did you ever finish it?"

"I finished the trip part."

"Cool. Can I read it?"

"Sure." I felt a sudden stab of guilt. "I . . . uh, I put the bad stuff in it, too."

"The bad stuff?"

I pulled the notebook out of my pocket and handed it to him. "I wrote about the cops and the arrest and all. I hope you don't mind."

"Oh. *That* stuff." He leafed through it. "Hey, if it weren't for bad luck, we'd have no luck around here at all. Am I right?"

"Yeah. I guess so."

Warren held the notebook up. "You sure I can have this?"

"Oh yeah. That one's just about full. I need to start a new one."

"I'll get it back to you. I will. I'll send it with Arthur."

I said, "Sure." And I knew he meant it. But the fact is, I never saw that notebook again.

As I headed inside, Warren called out, "Hey, thanks for the 'pane, Tom."

"The what?"

He hoisted up a tank. "The propane."

"Oh. Yeah."

Monday, December 10, 2001

I was staring through the window of Dad's van as we drove to the Food Giant. There were no abandoned shopping carts at the intersections this time. I guess they had gotten too valuable. There were, however, abandoned human bodies.

Zombies. Meth addicts.

Zombies stood on two of the four corners at Sunbury and Lower Falls Road. Each had a small cardboard sign with words scrawled in ink. It didn't matter what they said; the message was clear enough to me: *I am dead now. I have lost my life to methamphetamine.*

Lost people like these haunt the main intersections in Blackwater, the parking lots, and anywhere else where people congregate. It was shocking at first, but now they are just part of the scenery.

When we arrived at the Food Giant, Dad parked the van in his outer space and we started in.

That's when we saw her. A woman emerged from the shadows near the ATM. She came toward us, almost floating, like a gray ghost.

The woman moved steadily, purposefully, with one hand held out in front of her. I realized with a shock that I knew her. She was the woman I had followed just one week ago, the one who had cried for Lilly and her engagement. She was back here now, and alone.

She didn't say anything, just extended a red, cracked hand. When she got close to us, Dad took out his wallet, extracted a ten-dollar bill, and placed it in that hand. The woman then turned and, without a word, wandered off across the lot, back toward the shadows.

I watched her go, thinking, *This is normal now. This is what I see every day.* So I want to set down what I have observed about zombies. It seems to me that there are three stages of them. Stage-one zombies can go to a store and shoplift, successfully or unsuccessfully. Stage-two zombies can stand on a street corner with a handmade sign and beg. Stage-three zombies can only wander, like this woman. I guess you could add another stage: death. Stage-four zombies are dead.

Anyway, I asked Dad, "Shouldn't we call the police?"

He shook his head. "What can the police do? Arrest her?"

"No! Not at all! They could take her to a hospital."

"There aren't enough resources in the county, not for all these people. We've run out of hospital beds, and we've run out of jail cells."

I turned sarcastic on him. "How about graves? We haven't run out of them, have we?"

Dad looked offended. "I don't make the rules, Tom. You know how it goes by now, or you should: You make your choices, and you deal with the consequences." He pointed toward the receding woman. "She chose to try meth."

"I know." I muttered, mostly to myself, "Not even once."

A green Mustang pulled into the slot next to Dad's. Del got out on the driver's side; Mitchell got out on the passenger side. I watched them as Dad unlocked the front door.

Mitchell has always been a slow, simple guy. He has been at the Food Giant for twenty years, but he has never had an outside life, as far as anyone knew. He has certainly never had a girlfriend. Suddenly here he was carpooling with Del. Lilly thinks it's a romance, but I'm not so sure. I think it might be more sinister. I think it might be meth. Suddenly Mitchell is working three times faster than he used to. When his last assistant quit, Dad didn't even hire a replacement. He didn't need to.

Del has changed, too, but in the opposite direction. She used to be a bundle of energy. She used to talk so much at the register that Dad had to reprimand her. Now she only speaks to Mitchell, and she has no energy, and her hair is falling out. (She stops by the meat department every morning and gets a hairnet to wear up front.)

Dad held the door for me. He whispered, "I have to speak to Mitchell and Del this morning, first thing. So I'll need you to open up the meat counter. Okay? Just for ten minutes. Then I'll drive you to school."

"Why can't Reg do it?"

"Because he's not here yet."

I rolled my eyes. "Will it really be ten minutes?"

"Just help me out here, Tom."

"Do I have to wear a hairnet?"

"Of course. Anyone touching food has to."

I sighed mightily, followed Dad inside, pulled on a hairnet, and got to work setting out the trays of meats. I prayed no one would place an order in the next ten minutes.

Some early-morning customers filed in. I watched them as best I could. How many people were in the store to buy, and how many were there to steal? People I had seen for years, normal-looking people, slightly overweight people, now looked like they were wearing somebody else's clothes. Their jackets hung limply from their shoulders, like they were several sizes too big.

These honest, hardworking people had become thieves, really inept thieves. They stuffed bunches of grapes into pockets with holes in them; the grapes fell out and rolled away as they walked. They stuffed frozen food items into their jeans; the ice melted, and they stood in the checkout lines looking like they had peed themselves.

It was all so pathetic.

Dad was as nice to them as he could be. He just took the items back and told them not to return to the store. He never called the police.

Of course, my prayer did not come true. I looked up and saw the close-cropped hair and round head of Mrs. Smalls, Bobby's mother. She was wearing a blue raincoat, opened to reveal her white uniform beneath. I said, "Good morning, Mrs. Smalls."

"Good morning, Tom. They got you in a hairnet today?"

"Yes, ma'am."

"You can't really tell. It's black, like your hair."

"Thanks."

"Let me have a pound of Lebanon baloney and a pound of American cheese."

"Yes, ma'am." I pulled out the long cylinder of lunch meat and plopped it onto the slicer.

Mrs. Smalls pointed to the zombie couple in the produce section. "Do you see those two people?"

"Of course."

"They're shoplifting, you know."

"Yes, I know."

She shook her head. "You'd be surprised how many people don't see them. Or who claim they don't see them. Professional people, with excellent eyesight, who claim they don't see them anywhere."

I wrapped up the Lebanon baloney and pulled out the cheese as Mrs. Smalls continued. "Well, I see them every day in the emergency room. That's where this all ends, Tom. In the morgue. On a slab. They come into the ER, and they die. Or they come in DOA. All from methamphetamine."

I was surprised to hear her actually say the word—*methamphetamine*. Hardly anyone outside of our group ever said it. She went on: "Seventeen people so far this month, more than all other causes of death combined. But nobody will admit it—not the hospital administrators, not the police, not the politicians. Nobody wants to admit that this little town has a gigantic problem."

Her voice rose as I finished up her order. "So the problem will only get worse! Am I right?"

I told her sincerely, "You are right. Everything you're saying is right."

"I know I'm right. And if *we* don't do something about it"—she stopped to point at herself and then me—"you and me, Tom, it's not going to get done."

I gulped.

"Do you think I *ever* ignored my Bobby's problems?"

"No, ma'am."

"'No, ma'am' is right. I faced those problems, and I got him an education, and a job, and now he earns his own way." I handed her the order.

She said, "Thank you," then paused. "You don't know anything about Bobby buying Gold Bond talcum powder, do you?"

"No, ma'am."

She cast an angry glance toward the produce department on her way out.

Reg appeared right after Mrs. Smalls left. I wondered if he'd been hiding from her in the storeroom. He smacked the top of the counter and told me, "You are relieved, Thomas! Your dad says you can stop beating the meat."

I pulled off the hairnet and tossed it in the trash. I advised him wearily, "You really need to get some new material, Reg."

"What? Not precocious enough? Too invidious? Was I being puerile?"

"Yeah. All of the above."

In class, Coach Malloy attempted to read us a summary of the Dred Scott decision, and free states versus slave states, but that was not to be. He kept getting interrupted by dissatisfied customers.

Angela raised up her hand and then a glass jar of strawberries. "My mom said I have to return this. It didn't whoosh when she opened it."

Coach looked puzzled. "It didn't what?"

"Whoosh. She said if it doesn't whoosh when you open it, it wasn't sealed right."

The coach laughed. I think he wanted the rest of us to laugh, too, but we didn't. "Well, we're not selling whooshes here, honey. We're selling strawberry preserves."

Ben raised his hand. "I had the runs all day Saturday."

Several people groaned, but his point was made.

A girl named Mia spoke up. "We gave some to my grandmother, and she had to go to the hospital."

Coach sputtered, "Aw, come on now! That's not fair. Maybe your grandmother was sick anyway. She's an old lady, right? Old ladies get sick."

"It happened right after she ate the strawberries."

Ben followed up. "My dad says you have to give us our money back."

Coach held up one hand and spread out his fingers. "Well, on that deal there, I can only tell you what Reg told me. He takes your money, and he uses it to pay for the fruit, the jars, and the pectin. So that money is gone."

Ben was ready with a reply. "Then my dad says we can sue you."

Coach shook his head. He answered tightly, "Well, I guess what your dad chooses to do within the United States legal system is up to him."

Then he went back to the Dred Scott decision.

⚜

The door to my second-period classroom was closed. That was unusual, so I stopped and peeked through the window. Mr. Proctor was pushing desks toward the back of the room, one row at a time, like he was pushing a train of supermarket carts.

Arthur came up behind me and looked in; then Jenny did, too. Neither seemed surprised.

Jenny said, "It's for play rehearsal. Mr. Proctor told us that we need more rehearsal. He's going to use our class time for it today."

Arthur added, "I guess we suck. I know I do."

Jenny objected to that. "We do not!" She took a quick look left and right and then whispered excitedly, "Did you guys hear that a teacher got arrested?"

From the looks on our faces, we clearly hadn't. It was Arthur who replied, "No way."

"Yeah. Arrested in the parking lot, after school on Friday."

"For what?"

"Selling drugs." Jenny reconsidered that. "No, wait. It wasn't selling. It was possession of drugs."

I asked, "Who was it?"

224

"Mr. Byrnes, from the high school. He carpools with Mr. Proctor."

"How'd they catch him?"

"One of his own students turned him in."

Arthur said, "No way! A kid was a narc?"

"Sort of. See, the kid got busted himself, right outside the auditorium, for selling weed." Jenny went on with total authority. "The kid made a deal with the police. If they would charge him with possession instead of selling, he'd give them the name of a teacher who had weed."

Arthur nodded knowingly. "He traded up." Seeing that I was confused, he explained. "They offered Jimmy Giles a deal like that. If he'd trade up, if he'd give the name of his dealer, they'd go easy on him. Jimmy wouldn't do it, though. Jimmy's no narc."

Mr. Proctor, red-faced and panting, finally opened the door. He pointed me and the other nonactors to the back of the room. He pointed the actors—including Jenny, Arthur, Wendy, Ben, and Mikeszabo—to the front. They stood by the whiteboard, where they were soon joined by a half dozen high schoolers from the Drama Club, including Chris Collier.

Mr. Proctor told the nonactors in the back, "We'll be having play practice today. You're welcome to watch us, or you can do other work." Most of the kids put their heads down and fell asleep.

I watched.

Mr. Proctor told the actors, "We'll start with the blocking."

Arthur commented, "That's what we do in football, Mr. P. We start with the blocking."

Arthur was clearly joking, but Mr. Proctor didn't get it. "No, no, Arthur. Blocking in Drama Club means placing actors where they need to be onstage."

Arthur rolled his eyes.

Mr. Proctor positioned the lead actors, Chris and Wendy, first. Chris had his Bible cheat sheet in hand; Wendy did not. She had memorized her part.

Wendy delivered her lines like a real actress, with emotion (and empathy). Chris, however, was awful. He may as well have been delivering his "Vote for me for Student Council" speech. He sure didn't sound like the priest in a plague village four hundred years ago.

Anyway, after the priest and his wife had been blocked, Mr. Proctor took other actors by the elbow and positioned them. Then they read their lines.

Ben's character had a long argument with Jenny's character. Ben was actually pretty good, and Jenny was very moving as a doomed teenage girl.

Mr. Proctor took Arthur's elbow and moved him in and out among the others. Arthur had a few lines, and they were pretty crazy, like a village idiot's should be. I had to admit he wasn't bad, either.

After class was over, I walked out with Arthur. I asked him, "So, do you mind playing an idiot?"

He looked at me quizzically. "I've done some hard things, cuz, but this ain't one of them. All I have to do is show up, wander around, and read my lines. For that, Proctor gives me an A in English. Even if I don't do anything else, which I probably won't. I can just sit in front of him and sleep for the rest of the year. So tell me: Who's the idiot?"

Arthur suddenly grabbed my elbow and turned me toward the wall. "Listen, I gotta tell you something. Something not good." He checked around for eavesdroppers. "Jimmy Giles started using again."

"Oh no!"

"Oh yeah." Arthur shook his head, disappointed. "He bought himself some crack and smoked it up."

"No!"

"Yeah. It's what Catherine Lyle would call a 'relapse.'"

"Right. Is he okay now? Has he stopped?"

"I don't know. I doubt that *he* knows."

I used my counseling-group experience to ask, "What was the trigger for him?"

"United flight ninety-three."

"Really?"

"Yeah. He saw something on TV about how they're identifying the dead people at the crash site. They're finding all these little bits of human bodies, you know? Like bone fragments and teeth. They're asking their families to bring in people's combs, toothbrushes, and stuff for DNA samples. It flipped poor Jimmy out."

"That is some creepy stuff."

"He just got up from the TV, climbed into his Ranger, and took off. To his old dealer, I'm thinking. My mom heard the truck leaving and thought somebody was stealing it, or it was damn repo. Then she saw that Jimmy was gone. By the time she woke me up, it was too late."

A large group of students swirled past us. Arthur lowered his voice. "Guess where he wound up?"

"Where?"

"The crash site in Somerset County, down those dark country lanes. He drove off that gravel road and broke the back axle of the truck. The county sheriff called us at five a.m. to come get him. As far as I know, the Ranger's still out there, or they towed it to that big scrapyard."

He finished by saying, "Don't tell anybody."

I assured him, "No. I won't."

When I showed up for the counseling group, I saw kids huddled in front of the conference room door. I joined them, leaning my face over Jenny's shoulder to see what they were looking at. (I couldn't help noticing how good her hair smelled.)

A note was taped to the door, written in a feminine cursive hand. It read: *Due to a recent family emergency, the group will have to be canceled this week.* The note was signed *Wendy Lyle*.

I whispered to Jenny, "What's the family emergency?"

Jenny looked at Mrs. Cantwell's office before answering, "Her father got busted."

"What?"

"The state police raided a bunch of houses up at Blackwater University—frats mostly, but Dr. Lyle's house, too."

Arthur demanded to know, "Where do you hear all this stuff?"

Jenny's hands fanned out to encompass the whole office. "Right here. Officer O'Dell was talking about it today."

I asked her, "Did they find anything?"

"They did. They found weed at his house."

Suddenly the stoners all started talking at once about police raids, and search warrants, and narcs. They really knew their stuff.

Mrs. Cantwell stepped out of her office, frowning at the level of noise coming from our group. She pointed at the door. "Jenny Weaver, what does that note say?"

Jenny read the note aloud to her. Mrs. Cantwell shook her head. "No. That's not right. Mrs. Lyle called me an hour ago. She said they're moving away, so the group is canceled permanently."

Ben Gibbons's face drained white. "Permanently! She can't do that. I still have pica disorder."

"You have what?"

"Pica disorder. I eat things that aren't food. Compulsively."

Mrs. Cantwell just stared at him. He added, "I eat chalk. I eat wood. I eat rocks."

Mrs. Cantwell finally found her voice. "Please, that's enough! You need to stop doing those things."

Lilly turned the conversation back to the note. "But Mrs. Lyle can't just end the group like this. Can she?"

Mrs. Cantwell said, "I'm afraid she can. Mrs. Lyle is a parent volunteer. This group was her idea. If she leaves, then it's over."

A ringing telephone pulled Mrs. Cantwell back into her office.

Arthur commented bitterly, "She said she was gonna talk to Mrs. Cantwell about the new shirts. Yeah, my ass."

Mikeszabo pulled out a red marker. "Listen, that's no problem. I will turn any T-shirt into an 'I Hate Drugs' shirt. Just bring it to me and I'll do a custom-made design for you."

Arthur nodded. "Righteous. That'll do it. Everybody bring your shirts to Mike."

After that, though, the group members started moving toward the exit, heads down, feet shuffling, looking totally defeated.

Jenny raised her voice. "Wait! We can't just leave like this. We can't just give up. We're in a war here. Remember?"

She waited until she had everybody's attention. "All right. My parents ran an Alcoholics Anonymous meeting every Monday night until a few months ago. People stopped showing up because, well, because alcohol is not the problem anymore. We could meet where the AA did and do our small sessions, just like here. We don't need a leader."

Lilly asked, "Where was the meeting?"

"The Hungarian church on Sunbury Street."

"I know where that is."

"Everybody does."

Ben asked, "What will we talk about? Should we think of topics?"

Jenny replied solemnly, sincerely, "There's only one topic now: the meth plague. We need to talk about that. Bring whoever wants to come. The people in our town are dying. We need to save as many of them as we can."

When I told Mom about the meeting at the Hungarian church, she got all excited. She started talking about it like it was the homecoming dance. "I can drive you! And I'll stay if they need adults. And I'll get your father to donate some food."

Lilly's face contorted. "Geez, Mom. Do you want to hang up balloons, too? It's a frigging drug-counseling group."

"Lilly! Don't talk like that."

"Like what?"

Mom persisted, "That f-word. And there is nothing wrong with me volunteering to help your group."

Lilly tried reason. "We can't have a parent sitting in our group, listening to us talk about how messed up our parents are."

"Is that what you do?"

"Yes."

I interjected, "No. We do more than that."

Mom said, "Well, how about if I just set up a table, away from you, and serve the food?"

I decided. "Yes. That would be fine."

Lilly just shook her head.

The Hungarian church has a real name, St. Stephen's Catholic Church. We learned that from Mom on our drive to the Food Giant. Mom then went on in great detail.

"Most of the coal miners around here were Catholics. Some

came from Eastern Europe, like the Hungarians and the Poles; some came from Western Europe, like the Irish, Italians, and Germans. They all had their own little churches. But now all the Eastern Europeans go to St. Stephen's, and all the Western Europeans go to St. Michael's."

Lilly muttered, "I wonder where the Puerto Ricans go. I'll have to ask John."

She was trying to be funny, but Mom answered seriously, "They go to St. Michael's."

When we arrived at the Food Giant, Dad was in a frazzled state. He told us, "I've got nobody to run the register. I've got nobody to bring back shopping carts. I'm getting robbed blind here."

I figured that meant I would have to stay, but Lilly volunteered. "I'll take a register, Dad, until closing if you like. And I'm sure John will help with the carts. That way, Tom can go to group."

I really did want to go. "Are you sure?" I asked her.

"Yeah. But tell me what happens. I want to know everything."

"I will. Thanks."

So Mom and I filled a bin with lunch meats, cheeses, and bread products that had reached their sell-by dates. Then we loaded it into the car.

Once we started driving again, Mom hinted at why she wanted to attend the meeting. She said, "Tom, I just had a scare with drugs, too. I hope and pray that it's over. I understand now that it can happen to anybody."

"Yeah, it can."

"That 'Not Even Once' slogan is true."

"It definitely is. And you'll hear stuff like that at the meeting." I added, "But you'll have to stay away from the small groups. The kids won't want you listening. It's all confidential."

"I wouldn't repeat anything."

"You might. You might not be able to stop yourself from telling a parent what his or her kid said."

"Well, if I thought the child was in danger—"

"There you go! This is why you need to stay far away."

"Okay. I said I would. I'll set up the food and serve it; that's all."

We didn't say anything else for the rest of the ride. Instead, I found myself staring at the full moon rising over the mountains and thinking how beautiful it was. Then I found myself thinking about that beautiful moon and a beautiful girl.

But the girl was not Wendy Lyle.

It was Jenny Weaver. Jenny, with her nice-smelling hair and her pretty eyes and her . . . righteousness, as Arthur, or Jimmy, or Warren might say.

When we arrived at St. Stephen's, I had to shake my head to get back to reality. We turned into the driveway and continued back to a narrow parking lot. Mom pulled into a space next to the Weavers' Explorer. A bright light was pouring out of the basement level of the church. I grabbed our big plastic bin and followed Mom down a wide flight of stone steps, right into that light.

The basement was huge. The right side of it seemed to be for storage. It had neat stacks of wooden chairs and folding tables. The left side had a long cork bulletin board attached to a wall that was, to my surprise, totally blank. I looked around and saw that all the white block walls were blank, too—no crucifixes, no holy icons, no church announcements.

I saw two old refrigerators in the far left corner, so I headed that way. Mr. and Mrs. Weaver, Jenny, and Mikeszabo were arranging rows of wooden chairs, but they stopped when they saw us.

Jenny gave me a shy, waist-high, limited-movement wave,

which I found really cute. I thought about her again—with me, in the moonlight.

She and Mikeszabo went back to arranging chairs, but Mrs. Weaver hurried over to help Mom sort out the Food Giant donations. Mr. Weaver and I dragged over two wooden tables. Ten minutes later, those tables held plastic trays of ham-and-cheese and turkey sandwiches; small vats of coleslaw and potato salad; and pint-size containers of regular milk, chocolate milk, and orange juice.

Mrs. Weaver was delighted. "Look at this bounty! This is so generous of you."

"It was all going into a Dumpster if we didn't take it," Mom explained.

The high school kids started to arrive, either solo or in groups. Some had driven themselves, and some had carpooled together. (Only the junior high kids, like me, still depended on their parents for rides.)

Ben Gibbons walked in with his father. I had expected his dad would be a big guy with amazingly strong teeth, but he wasn't. He looked kind of scrawny, and his teeth were discolored and broken. He had red splotches on his face, too. So of course I thought, *Oh no. Is he a user?*

Suddenly other people started walking in, too, but they weren't parents or students. They were not like anybody in our group. They were meth zombies from the streets of Blackwater.

One man asked me through a broken smile, "Is this the AA meeting?"

"Alcoholics Anonymous? No, sir. This is a school counseling group."

His pockmarked face dropped. "Is it open to the public?"

"No. Not really."

His arm rose toward the table. "We can't eat any of that?"

I didn't know what to say. I wasn't the leader; no one was. I said, "Why don't you take a seat. We'll start the meeting, and we'll talk about it."

I watched the man as he sat down. He was, to say the least, underdressed for the weather. He had on a pair of filthy white sneakers with no laces, thin blue jeans that were ripped and stained, and a Blackwater U sweatshirt so worn that the letters were barely visible. It was about thirty degrees outside, and that's all he had on. Bizarrely, he would be one of the better-dressed zombies in the room.

Dozens of desperate-looking people appeared at the door and walked timidly inside.

Jenny whispered to me, "Where did they all come from?"

"I guess they saw the light and figured it was the AA meeting."

"We have to let them in."

"Sure. I think we should give them food, but I want to put it to a vote."

Jenny said, "Okay, good plan." Then she squeezed my arm. I loved how that felt.

Arthur was the last of the Haven students to arrive. He stopped inside the door and stared at all the zombies. There must have been forty of them at that point. He spotted me, smiled, and raised his eyebrows.

Every wooden chair was now full. I stepped forward with Jenny. She whispered to me, "What should we do?"

I heard myself say with total confidence, "I am going to speak to them."

Jenny looked surprised. But then she lifted up her hand, touched my shoulder, and gave me a light push. "Go for it."

I have to admit, I was terrified. All the moisture was sucked right out of my mouth. I started to stammer, "I'd . . . I'd like to welcome you here tonight. This . . . this is a meeting of a student group that was formed in September. Our purpose was to talk about different drug issues. Well, maybe back in September, there were different drug issues. Now there is only one, and that is the meth issue, the meth plague that is destroying our town."

I looked at the lost, ravaged faces before me. "Those of you who wandered in here tonight are welcome. You are welcome to talk to our group members about meth. Maybe we have learned something about it that will help you. Maybe you can help us to understand some things, too."

I cast my eyes over toward the food table. "I realize that you came here for something more than talk." I looked at the first zombie guy I had met. "We don't have a leader in this group, so . . . well . . . the passengers on flight ninety-three took a vote before they acted."

The zombie guy nodded at me. He said quietly, "They were brave people."

"Yes. So let's do what they did. I'd like to ask the group members to vote about the food. If you think we should offer the food to everybody here, raise your hand."

Every group member raised his or her hand. Some, like Ben and Mikeszabo, raised two hands. It was immediate and unanimous. Out of the corner of my eye, I saw Mr. and Mrs. Weaver and Mom raise their hands, too.

I put mine up last, joining the sea of hands that remained upraised. We were going to help the meth zombies. We were going to feed them, at least.

As the hands slowly dropped, I said, "Okay. We'll pass out the sandwiches in a minute. I just want to say a few words first about the meth plague.

"You know . . . people can live with a drinking problem, and join Alcoholics Anonymous, and maybe get over it. My dad is an example of that, and maybe some of your loved ones are, too. But meth isn't like that. There is no meeting place for Meth Addicts Anonymous." I paused to look out. They were all listening to me. "No, actually, there *is* a place where meth addicts meet. It's down at Good Samaritan Hospital, on the slabs in the morgue."

I felt myself channeling the voice of Mrs. Smalls. "We have a gigantic problem here. We need to do something to solve it. If we don't, nobody else will, and it will destroy our town. We need to fight back. We need to counterattack. And I think it could start right here, in this place. It could start right now."

Unfortunately, I had no ending to this speech, so I just stopped talking—right in the middle like that.

Everyone continued to stare at me.

I stared back.

Ben Gibbons's father looked so intense that I thought he might pitch forward off his seat and fall. I finally asked, "Does anyone else want to speak?"

Mikeszabo hopped right up. He addressed the audience from the back row. "I do! I had this idea. I was thinking that we could bring winter clothes next week. But now I'm thinking that next week might be too late. Some people here might freeze to death before next week. So I'd like to come back tomorrow with a bunch of coats and sweaters and blankets. If the church is locked, maybe Mr. Weaver would let me hand them out from his truck."

Mr. Weaver assured him, "It won't be locked. I'll see to that. We can distribute the clothes from here in the basement."

Mikeszabo unzipped his lined windbreaker and pulled it off. "For now, who needs a coat? I don't really get cold. Let me give this to somebody."

None of the zombies moved, so Mike draped his coat over a woman in front of him. It hung down over her frail shoulders.

Arthur pulled off his black hoodie. "I know what you mean, bro. I don't get cold, either. Never. Not Arthur Stokes. Somebody else can use this."

Other Haven kids stood up.

Soon a dozen more had pulled off jackets and hoodies and sweatshirts and had pressed them into the hands of the zombies.

I took off my own down coat and placed it in the lap of a man in the front row. His hands clutched it, but otherwise he didn't move.

Mom was now crying her eyes out. She spoke up. "We'll bring more food back tomorrow, too. The Food Giant throws food out every day. We should bring it here."

I spoke directly to the zombies. "So, there will be food and clothing here tomorrow night. Tell anyone who needs those things to come here." I looked over at Mom. "Okay, so, I guess we're ready to eat."

Several of the zombies were unable to deal with a food line, so group members shuttled food and drink to them in their chairs. In one case, Jenny actually fed a shaky, toothless lady. I don't think any of the Haven kids ate or drank, but soon all the food was gone. The zombies got up shortly after that and walked back out. Those who could talk said thank you.

Ben Gibbons's dad came up to me. I expected him to sound gruff, but he was soft-spoken, humble even, when he said, "Thank you for doing this." Then he hurried out so fast that Ben had to run to catch up to him.

We never did form our Catherine Lyle discussion groups. Everyone got involved in breaking the room back down— returning the chairs and tables to their storage spots. Mom,

Mrs. Weaver, and Jenny did some cleaning up in a small kitchen off the refrigerator area.

I grabbed the Food Giant bin and lugged it back outside. I popped open the trunk of Mom's car, slid it in there, and turned around with a start.

Jenny was standing in front of me, very close. She said, "That was a great speech, Tom. Really moving."

"Thank you."

"You're a good speaker. I really wish you were in the play."

"Yeah. Me, too."

Then she just stood there, and so did I. Though neither of us had on a coat, and it was freezing.

I decided to seize that moment. I blurted out, "I was thinking of you on the drive here tonight."

She cocked her head, still dangerously close. "Oh yeah?"

"I had a vision, I guess you'd call it, of a great thing that I wanted to do."

"The speech?"

"No. The speech just kind of happened. This was something private. Personal." I looked up at the moon. "I saw myself with a beautiful girl, and that girl was you."

She blinked once. I could see her trying to process my words. She looked surprised, but not totally so. And, more importantly, she did not move away. She did not slap my face; she did not knee me in the groin.

If anything, she tilted her face slightly upward.

So I did it. I kissed Jenny Weaver, and I kept kissing her for a long time, in that cold parking lot under the full moon.

And it was beautiful.

Wednesday, December 12, 2001

Coach Malloy began class today by addressing his growing problem, the Haven Family Preserves scandal. He said, "Okay. I talked to Reg about your complaints. He explained some things to me, and I think those things fit in pretty good with our social studies curriculum."

He consulted an index card. "One thing is . . . the small farms we used to have in Pennsylvania just don't exist anymore. They've been taken over by big agribusinesses that kick the small farmers out and dump pesticides in the water and exhaust the soil. It used to be, you would buy your strawberries right here in town, on the side of the road, from the local farmers. I can remember those days.

"Now you got to buy your strawberries at the Food Giant or Kroger, and those strawberries probably come all the way from Mexico.

"Well, I don't need to tell you, they don't have our standards of cleanliness down in Mexico, so the strawberries Reg bought probably had"—he checked his index card again—"E. coli or some other bacteria on them that would not come off during the normal rinsing process. Reg said not to worry, though. He has a special double-rinsing process for next year that will take care of all these Mexican bacterias and make Haven Family Preserves an even better holiday gift choice."

The coach looked around hopefully.

I looked around, too. If Coach saw what I saw, he realized that it was all over. Haven Family Preserves would not be having a next year.

A kid named Joey Sanchez raised his hand. "My aunt lives in

Mexico City. She sends us food all the time, and we don't get sick eating it." He pointed to a mason jar on the desk. "Not like that stuff."

Coach squirmed. "Well, I'm just telling you what Reg told me. And I'm trying to tie it in to the social studies curriculum for Haven County. I can't speak for everybody's aunt that ever sent anybody anything. I can only speak for myself."

After that, Coach retreated to his chair. We read a chapter about the interstate highway system and answered questions about it for the rest of the period.

As Arthur and I approached Mr. Proctor's room, we could see Jenny ahead. She was practically hopping up and down, just bursting to tell us something. When we got within whispering distance, she began, "Are you guys ready for today's news?"

I whispered back, "Yeah. What's going on?"

"Dr. Lyle came in the office to withdraw Wendy."

That got Arthur's attention. "What? The Grape's leaving?"

"Yes."

"When?"

"She's done with classes as of *now*."

"Is she still in the play?"

"She is. She asked if she could be, and Mrs. Cantwell said yes." Arthur looked relieved to hear it.

Jenny continued: "But before Dr. Lyle left, he asked to speak to Officer O'Dell."

Arthur asked, "Who's that again?"

"The junior high resource officer. The real big guy?"

"Right."

"I drifted over by the door to listen, and I couldn't believe it! Dr. Lyle totally ratted out Mr. Proctor. He said Mr. Proctor was at a Halloween party at the college, with Haven High students, and he was doing drugs."

I said, "Wait a minute. *We* were at that Halloween party."

Jenny looked shocked. "What?"

I explained, "Wendy invited us." Jenny's face fell, so I added, "It was a really awful party."

Arthur agreed. "The worst."

"I saw Mr. Proctor for one second, at the most. He wouldn't even talk to me. He sure wasn't doing drugs with me." I turned to Arthur. "Or with anyone else. Not that I saw."

Arthur looked pained. "Sorry, cuz. That's not what I saw."

"What?"

"I saw him smoking with some frat boys, and it wasn't Marlboros."

"No! Where?"

"Across the street. On a frat house porch." He looked at me strangely. Sympathetically? "I know you look up to him, cuz. But in the end, I think you understand he's one of them."

I didn't reply. We all just stared at each other until Arthur shouted, "Still! Why would 'the doctor' rat him out?"

I suggested, "Just to be a jerk?"

Arthur shook his head knowingly. "No. He's too smart, too creepy smart. Something else is going down." Then he figured it out. He smacked his head. "Man! He made a deal!"

Jenny said, "What?"

"The doctor. He made a deal with the cops. He gave up Mr. Proctor, and they gave him a lesser charge, or they dropped his charge."

"Why? Why would the cops do that?"

Arthur thought for a moment. "Because the cops don't like to waste their time. They know Dr. Lyle's creepy smart. If they come down too hard on him, he'll just skip town. Hell, he doesn't want to be here anyway. But Mr. Proctor's stuck. He's got his job; he's got his grad school thing."

My head was reeling. Mr. Proctor? I felt so confused. Then I looked through the door, and I got even more confused.

Mr. Proctor was in there!

He was standing in front of the whiteboard, just staring at it. He was holding a black marker in his right hand, with the cap off, but his hand was not moving. No part of him was moving.

It was an awkward situation, to say the least. We all filed into the room silently and took our seats. We got ready to do vocabulary, as usual. But there was no vocabulary to do.

Ben finally broke a long silence. "What's wrong, Mr. Proctor? Can't you think of a sentence today?"

No reply. No movement.

Ben suggested, "How about if we help you?" Mr. Proctor's head rose up slowly. That led Ben to ask, "What's today's word?"

Mr. Proctor did not turn around, but he did say, loud enough for all of us to hear, "*Apologize*."

Ben said enthusiastically, "*Apologize!* That's an easy one. Okay. How about 'Guys apologize'?"

Mr. Proctor's right arm moved forward. He wrote, in his large, cursive hand, *Guys apologize*.

Ben looked over at Jenny and me. He shrugged. "That's all I can think of."

But Mr. Proctor could think of more. He kept writing, adding *for their lies*. Then he stepped back.

Ben read the sentence aloud. "'Guys apologize for their lies.' Okay. Should we write that?"

Mr. Proctor tossed the marker into his trash can. He pressed a button, and the vertical arm of the whiteboard lit up and started to crawl across the face, copying what was written there. When it reached the end, he pressed another button, and a page popped out from the bottom right side.

Mr. Proctor tore it off, folded it, and stuck it in his shirt pocket. Then he told us quietly, "No. You don't need to copy this. You will have a substitute today. She will be working in the regular vocabulary book with you."

He picked up the vocab book and set it on the corner of the desk. Then he muttered, "I was trying to do some things outside of the county curriculum. . . ."

His voice trailed off. When he spoke again, it was more businesslike. "I would like to get in one final pitch for *The Roses of Eyam*. It will take place at the school auditorium on Sunday evening, December thirtieth, at seven p.m. Please come out and support your classmates. They have worked very hard."

He glanced nervously toward the door. "It is a good play. It has some things to say to people who are living through an annus horribilis, a year of horrors, a plague year."

He held his arms out wide. "One of those things is this: Your little town is the center of the whole world. What you do here affects the whole world." He looked at me. "So don't put this place down. Don't put yourselves down."

He looked at everybody. "This year *will* pass, you know. Yin and yang. A good year will follow this one. Just hang in there."

The large figure of Officer O'Dell appeared in the doorway, signaling for Mr. Proctor to step outside. Mr. Proctor took one more moment to stretch his neck and straighten his shoulders. Then he walked out of the room.

He was gone. Just like that. We would never see him again.

The doorframe remained empty for a few seconds, but then an old woman entered.

And I knew her.

It was Mrs. Kerpinski, my fourth-grade teacher. She was our sub. She briskly took charge, as always, assigning a page from the vocabulary book. I doubt if anyone actually did it, but they opened their books and pretended to work. No one went to sleep in Mrs. Kerpinski's class.

I started writing, of course, and she soon walked over to me. "Aren't you Thomas Coleman?"

"Yes."

"You have the same face." I didn't like hearing that, but then she added, "And you still do all your work."

This was true, and I realized that I was proud of it. Geeky as it was, I lifted up my vocabulary book and showed her my PSAT prep book hidden beneath it.

"Oh! Are you making plans for college so soon?"

"Yes, ma'am."

"Penn State?"

"No. Well, I don't know. I had been thinking about Florida."

"Florida?" She said it like it was some unsavory place, like Las Vegas. Mrs. Kerpinski arched an eyebrow. "Surely there is no reason to go all the way down there, not with all the fine universities around here. You could go a little ways away—to Pittsburgh, or to Philadelphia. That way, you could enjoy some independence. That's a good thing."

I gulped. "Yes. Well, I haven't really made up my mind yet."

She said, "No. You shouldn't. Not yet. You have plenty of time."

My last class of the day is chemistry. It's taught by Miss Mancino, who went to Haven High just five years ago. She's short and baby-faced and looks like she's still a student. I don't think she ever intended to be a teacher; she seems to have no aptitude for it at all. She just leads us through the textbook, chapter by chapter.

Anyway, I am writing about her class because Miss Mancino did not show up today. Neither did her sub. Neither did an administrator to cover.

We just sat there, unsupervised, doing mostly nothing. A few kids went to sleep. I reviewed some PSAT math problems, but then even I had had enough. After a few minutes of staring at my watch, I decided to leave.

What the hell, right?

I got up and walked out. I wandered down the hall, down another hall, past the office, and out the front door. Normally, an administrator, or a school secretary, or Officer O'Dell would have stopped me. But this wasn't "normally." Not anymore. Not in a plague year.

I stood outside next to the Battlin' Coal Miner and gazed out at the mountains. They looked beautiful, as always.

A few cars were already idling in the riders' area. I recognized one of them and started toward it. It was Arthur's midnight-blue Geo Metro.

As I got closer, I could see that Arthur was not at the wheel. In fact, no one was. I peered into the back and saw baby Cody asleep in his car seat. Then I saw Jimmy Giles asleep up front, on the passenger side, with his head against the window. (I later learned that Aunt Robin was the driver. She was in the office, applying for a job, although there was no one to apply to.)

I decided not to disturb Jimmy. I was turning to go, when

his eyes popped open. He cranked down the window and said in a "Don't wake the baby" voice, "Hey, Tom. I've been wanting to talk to you."

I asked, "Are you okay now, Jimmy?" and immediately regretted it. That was none of my business. But Jimmy acknowledged the problem. "Yeah. I'm okay. I had a bad day or two, but I'm clean now."

"Good. Glad to hear it."

"Look, I'm real sorry you didn't get paid."

"Oh, forget that. I'm real sorry, too, about what happened."

He raised his shoulders up and down.

I went on: "I'm still glad I went, though. I liked it until, you know, that stuff at the end."

"I guess you heard we lost the big truck. No more moving business."

"No more Christmas-tree business, either?"

Jimmy smiled sadly. "Nah, I think we were out of that business anyway. No way they're giving us credit three years in a row, no matter how Christian they are. No. I'm back with WorkForce now. One day at a time."

Arthur came walking up. He got into the driver's seat and called through the window to me, "Can you believe these people are driving *my* car?"

Jimmy muttered, "It's all we got left."

We hung out for a minute, listening to Cody's heavy breathing in the back. Finally, Arthur pointed toward the school and asked me, "Did you know that Warren played football here?"

"I saw that on his jacket."

Arthur nodded. "Yeah. He was a star. He was the quarterback."

"Really?" I asked. "What about you, Jimmy?"

"What?"

"Did you play?"

"Nah. I was a stoner back then, too."

I asked, "What's Warren doing now?" Both Arthur and Jimmy clammed up. "I mean for work."

Jimmy mumbled, "He's got a plan. Warren always has a plan. He's buying materials now."

Arthur snapped, "Jimmy!"

Jimmy looked puzzled. "What? We can talk in front of Tom."

"No, we can't. This is none of Tom's business."

My heart was suddenly up near my throat. "What kind of materials are you talking about?"

Arthur pounded the steering wheel. "Dammit, Jimmy! You see? You can't talk in front of Tom."

Jimmy muttered, "Forget what I said, Tom. He's got a plan to pay off some bills. That's all I know."

I stood there for a full minute, letting Arthur simmer down. I remembered my promise to Warren. Since Arthur was already angry, I figured it was as good a time as any to ask, "What about you, Arthur? Do you have a plan?"

Arthur didn't move for several seconds. Then he spit out the window. He replied coldly, "You never mind about me. You go study your college prep book. Get ready to go to Florida, or wherever the hell you think you're going."

"I don't know where I'm going. I know I'm going to college, but I don't know where."

"Well, I know I am *not*, so I guess that's the plan." Arthur turned his face away. I knew our conversation was over.

Jimmy, though, looked up at me. He said quietly, like I should have known this already, "Arthur's signing up with the marines."

247

I said, "Okay. Yeah. That's a solid plan. I'll see you guys later," and headed back over to the Battlin' Coal Miner.

I stood there for fifteen minutes, waiting for everyone else to come out. I tried looking at the mountains again, but they didn't interest me. I felt a cold wind whipping up all around, and I watched a dark cloud cover the sun.

I found myself thinking about Warren, and what his plan was, and why he might need three tanks of propane.

Friday, December 21, 2001

When I started down the stairs this morning, I saw Lilly leaning out of the front door. Apparently, someone was on the other side, because I heard her say, "Sure I know you. You're in the counseling group."

A boy's voice said, "Right."

I came up behind Lilly and looked out. It was Mikeszabo. When he saw me he explained, probably for the second time, "I'm collecting clothes and blankets for the homeless."

Lilly turned and squeezed past me. I heard her run back up the stairs.

"Do you want to come in?" I asked him.

He shook his head. "No. No time. I'm only halfway through your block." He looked to his left, away from the sun. "I try to hit one block every morning—before school, or church, or whatever."

I saw a Hefty trash bag behind him. It was the thirty-gallon drawstring size, and it was almost tipping over. I asked, "Did you collect a lot today?"

Mikeszabo looked surprised. "Yeah. I collect a lot every day." He leaned toward me, lowering his voice. "Hey. Did you hear about Mike Murphy?"

"No. What?"

He lowered it even more. "It's bad, man. He was found dead yesterday."

"No! No way!"

"Yeah. The Weavers used to stop over there sometimes, you know, to see if anybody needed help. Well, Mr. Weaver couldn't get nobody to answer the door yesterday, so he called the cops.

They found the whole family laid out on the floor—all three of them."

I was having a hard time processing this. I shook my head and tried to paraphrase, "Mikemurphy, and his dad, and his mom are all dead?"

"Yup."

"Dead of what?"

His surprised look returned. "Of smoking meth! I guess that's *all* they've been doin' at their house for a long time."

"Man! That's horrible."

"I know. And it really makes you think. My dad and mom are in jail, but at least they're alive. Maybe they were the lucky ones. They got busted in time."

"Poor Mikemurphy."

Mikeszabo looked away again, down the street. He whispered, "Yeah. Poor Mike Murphy. Poor Dad and Mom. Poor everybody."

Lilly came back down behind me. She had taken the wool blanket off of her bed. Mikeszabo stepped back and opened the Hefty bag for her. Lilly folded the blanket into squares in midair. Then she leaned out and stuffed it into the bag.

Mikeszabo said, "Thank you," then added, "I'll see you guys at the church."

I asked, "Aren't you going to school?"

"Nah. There's no reason to." He set off for next door, hoisting the black bag over his shoulder like Santa Claus.

✛

Mikeszabo was right about school. This was the Friday before Christmas break. That meant that all the tests at school had been taken; all the grades had been recorded. There was no reason in the world to be at Haven Junior/Senior High. It was obvious the moment Mom dropped us off. No one but the Battlin' Coal Miner was standing outside.

Lilly threw up her hands. "This is ridiculous! There is nobody here. I could be sleeping."

Mom answered automatically, "It's a school day. That means you go to school."

"But there's nobody here!"

"Of course people are here."

"Where? Do you see anybody?"

"They are all inside."

I thought, *Mikemurphy sure isn't here*.

Lilly held up an angry index finger. "I will go to one class. One. If nobody is there, I am calling you, and you are coming back to pick me up."

Mom, to my surprise, conceded. "All right. But you'll see—people are here. It's a normal school day."

I thought, *A normal day? Not in a plague year*. As it turned out, though, Mom was partially right. There *were* teachers and students inside, just not very many.

I entered my first-period class, sat down next to Ben Gibbons, and looked around. Mikeszabo (I guess I can just call him Mike now) was not there, of course. He was collecting clothes for the needy. Jenny was not there, either. (I would later learn that the Weavers were making Christmas baskets for the needy. I thought, *Damn! I could be doing that, too*.)

Coach Malloy was there, in body at least. He was seated behind his desk, with his nose stuck in a *Sports Illustrated* magazine. (Maybe he should have been reading *Strawberry Preserves* magazine.) When the bell rang, he announced, "It's a free period. You can all do homework."

Ben raised his hand. "It's the last day of the semester, Coach. Nobody has any homework."

The coach lowered the magazine and looked at him. He growled, "Okay, so it's just a free period, then."

The TV blipped to life. Mrs. Cantwell addressed us as if it were a regular day. She made a very solid pitch for Mike's clothing project. "The Student Council is collecting warm clothes for the homeless and the needy. That is becoming a big problem here in our community.

"I know that, historically, when the town of Blackwater has faced a problem, the people have come together and solved it. I remember my grandmother telling me about the Great Depression, back in the 1930s. People with only two blankets to their name gave one to people with no blanket at all. That's how we do things here. We all pull together, and we all get by, so please give generously."

Mrs. Cantwell would normally have been followed by Wendy Lyle reading the news, but there was no Wendy Lyle because her father had withdrawn her, and there was no news because it was the last day of the semester.

The Pledge of Allegiance came on, so the coach rose out of his seat. We did, too. We remained standing for the national anthem. Then we all sat down, and most of the kids went to sleep.

Ben and I did not, though. We stared at each other for a moment. I finally said, "How's the play going?"

"Good." He added, "That Chris guy sucks, though."

"Does he?"

"Yeah."

"Maybe he doesn't have the time, you know? Between the play and work."

Ben looked surprised. "Chris doesn't work."

"Yes, he does. At the bowling alley."

"Not anymore. He got fired."

It was my turn to be surprised. "Why?"

"For stealing the shoe money! People would pay two bucks for shoe rental, and he'd put it in his pocket."

"How do you know that?"

"He *told* us about it. It's like he didn't care who knew it."

"Huh. Well, how's Wendy Lyle? She's good, right?"

Ben's eyes lit up. "She's great. She's a great actress."

"Yeah. I know."

Then Ben lowered his voice. "I like what we're doing with the counseling group. You know? At the new place."

"The church basement?"

"Yeah."

"Yeah. Me, too. It's better away from school."

"Definitely. That way, parents can come. And siblings. And anybody who is, you know, messed up. I'm trying to get my mom to come. And my sister."

"You have a sister?"

"Yeah."

"Does she go to Haven?"

"No. She's older. She went to high school in Pittsburgh. Then she joined the army. Then she got kicked out."

"Whoa. For what?"

Ben shrugged and said, "I don't know," in such a way that I believed him.

"What's she doing now?"

"She's at home." He added, "My dad was in the army. He joined up when he was eighteen, and he retired when he was thirty-six."

"That's a sweet deal."

"Yeah. I know."

"What's he doing now?"

Ben looked puzzled. "I just told you. He's retired."

"Oh. Okay. How about your mom?"

"She's at home. They're all at home."

"Really? So, you're the only one who gets up and goes out in the morning?"

He thought for a moment. "Yeah. I guess I am."

I remembered what Wendy had told me, that Ben was a "designated patient." Then I remembered Catherine Lyle's ethical rules. But I decided to ask him anyway. "Do any of them have problems?"

"What do you mean?"

"Well, you have that pica disorder, right?"

"Right. I eat—"

"Yeah, yeah. How do you know about that?"

"Uh, I got diagnosed at school, back in Pittsburgh, by a social worker."

"Are you the only one in your family with a disorder?"

Ben looked offended. "Yeah. Like I said, I got diagnosed. Nobody else in my family got diagnosed."

"Okay. Sorry. Well, I hope they do come to the meetings."

Ben eyed me suspiciously. Had I crossed a line? If so, I decided to keep going. I told him, "My mom will be coming. She's hoping to get some help from the group."

"Help for what?"

"She had a problem with prescription pills."

His eyes widened. "Really? Your mom?"

"Yeah. I hope my dad will come, too. He used to go to AA meetings all the time. Do you know what those are?"

"Sure."

"And my sister had a problem with pot last summer. I hope she'll keep coming, too."

Ben leaned back and exhaled. "Wow, Tom. I had no idea."

"Nobody does. You heard Jenny talk about her father's problem. And hell, Mike's parents are both in jail."

"Right."

"Everybody acts like everything is okay at home, Ben. But that's not true. You know?"

Ben looked really grateful. He answered huskily, "Yeah."

Mrs. Cantwell appeared in the doorway. She spotted the coach behind *Sports Illustrated* and snapped, "Coach Malloy!"

He dropped the magazine and jumped to his feet.

Mrs. Cantwell directed a withering stare at him. I noticed a group of kids clustered behind her in the hall. She said, "We have numerous teachers calling in sick today. I will be placing some students in your classroom for supervision." She added, "I fully expect you to supervise them."

Coach Malloy gulped and nodded. Mrs. Cantwell stepped aside, and ten kids shuffled into the classroom. They all took seats, put their heads down, and slept.

I continued to chat with Ben for the rest of first period. He wasn't as strange as I had thought. I believe he *is* being used as a designated patient. (Of course, that's just my uneducated opinion. I am not a mental-health professional. Or a famous professor. In a field.)

The bell finally rang. I don't know where those extra kids went for second period. I don't know where Ben went, either. Home, most likely. I entered Mr. Proctor's room by myself and stopped in my tracks. Bizarrely, a sub was sitting at his desk, a sub who I knew.

Aunt Robin!

How weird was that? She looked incredibly out of place. She had on a pair of black pants and a very tight white blouse, like something she might wear for karaoke night at the Drunken Monkey. She had teased her hair up for the occasion.

She certainly looked relieved to see me. "Tom! Are you in this class?"

"Yes."

"What class is it?"

I said, "English. Language arts." Then I asked her the obvious question: "Aunt Robin, what are you doing here?"

Her hands shot upward, like she was signaling a touchdown. "Damned if I know! I got a call from some lady this morning at six a.m. Woke me up. And she asked me to come in here."

"Some lady?"

"The principal lady."

"Mrs. Cantwell?"

"Yeah. That's her." She explained, "I came in here a couple of days ago to apply for a job—secretary, cafeteria worker, anything, really. That's how she got my number. She called me this morning and asked if I would come in as a parent volunteer.

"I asked her, 'Do I get paid?' She said, 'No, I can't pay you. But if a paying job opens up, I'll remember that you did me this favor.' So here I am."

"Wow."

"Arthur don't even know I'm here. He's sleeping in today."

"Yeah. Good plan."

She pointed to the sleeping kids in the back. "It's just like babysitting. I don't mind."

I took a seat in front of her. A few seconds later, Lilly appeared at the door. She cupped her hands around her mouth and whispered loudly, "Tom! I called Mom. She's on her way here."

Lilly had not looked at the sub. But even if she had, I don't think she would have recognized her. The context was just too wacky. I pointed to the desk and whispered back, "Look! It's Aunt Robin! She's the sub!"

Lilly's head, followed by the rest of her body, bent backward in disbelief. She managed a friendly smile and a wave. Aunt Robin motioned for her to come in, which she did.

Aunt Robin followed our lead and continued the loud whispering. "Congratulations, Lilly! I hear you got engaged."

Lilly instinctively held up her left ring finger. "Yes!"

"That's great, honey! I hear he's a nice guy, too."

Lilly actually blushed. "Yeah." She held the ring out for Aunt Robin to ooh and aah over.

"Beautiful. That's real nice. I got married twice, but I never got a diamond ring."

"No?"

"I got wedding rings, two of them, but I never got an engagement ring."

Lilly told her sincerely, "I hope you will come to our wedding. We'll send you an invitation."

Aunt Robin seemed surprised, and touched. "Oh, thank you, honey. That'd be an honor. Did you set a date?"

"Not yet."

"June, maybe? I was a June bride. The first time, anyway."

"Is that when you married Uncle Robby?"

"Yeah." She thought for a moment. Then she laughed, a little embarrassed, "I can't remember the exact date now. June the third? The fourth? It was a Saturday, the Saturday after Robby graduated from here."

Lilly observed, as if for the first time, "You were Robin and Robby! That's so cute."

"Yeah. That's what everybody said."

"Did you guys get married in a church?"

"Nah. The county courthouse. No muss, no fuss. Then we went back to Robby's mom's house. That's where we were livin' anyway." She recalled, "Your mom and dad came over! Yeah. Your dad brought a case of Rolling Rock with a white bow around it. That became the big joke of the wedding—that my colors were green and white, like on the Rolling Rock beer bottle."

Lilly laughed. Then she stole a look at her watch. "I'm sorry, Aunt Robin, but I'm pretty sure my mom's parked outside."

Aunt Robin pointed at the door. "You go! Both of you."

As we started out, Lilly assured her, "I'll be sending you that invitation."

"All right. And I'll start saving up beer bottles for you."

We laughed. But I did whisper to Lilly, "Does she know you're too young to drink?"

"She's real nice. Don't put her down."

"I'm not."

"And do not tell Mom that she was here."

"Okay."

So the ride home featured no talk about Aunt Robin, or her surprise career as a substitute teacher, or her beer-bottle wedding colors, or anything else, for that matter.

As it turned out, Mom was saving all of her talking for lunch. Over bowls of Campbell's tomato soup (the same company that owns Pepperidge Farm, V8, and Swanson) and grilled cheese sandwiches, Mom opened with a blockbuster announcement: "I was talking to your father. I am going to start working at the Food Giant on Sunday, on the cash register."

Lilly practically spit out her grilled cheese. "Why? I thought you had to be here for us, like a traditional housewife, so you could keep the household together, or whatever."

"Well, you're both older now. And you're both working at the store now. The best thing *I* can do is help your father hold on to it."

I was alarmed. "Hold on to it? Is he going to lose the store?"

"He could. The corporation could decide to close it. The corporation only cares about profits, Tom. Your father can't show profits if people aren't buying."

Lilly seemed stunned. "Close the Food Giant?"

"Quite a thought, isn't it? What would people do? Where would they go for food?"

"Did Dad tell you this?" I asked.

"Yes. He said that if he was paying all his employees, the store would already be in the red, and the corporation would close it."

Mom pointed to us in turn. "He has you, Tom, and you, Lilly, and now he'll have me, all working for nothing. And John is working eighty hours a week, but he's only getting paid for forty. That's how your father is keeping the store open—with people working for nothing."

Lunch ended on that note, with fearful glances all around.

John was outside chasing down shopping carts when Mom dropped us off. He blew a kiss at Lilly as she hurried inside to get out of the cold. He waved me over, saying, "Bobby went home for a few hours. He's coming back later to clean the storeroom. You, Bobby, and your dad."

"Sounds like another late night."

"Yeah." John scanned the parking lot nervously. He added,

"Hey, you gotta keep a close eye on these carts, bro. People are stealing them. It's unreal."

"Yeah. I know."

When I saw Dad inside, he told me what I already knew. "We'll be cleaning out the storeroom tonight. You, me, and Bobby."

"John told me."

He shook his head. "Reg has been putting off cleaning that place since before Thanksgiving. And he called in sick today, probably because he knows we're doing it tonight. Still, it can't wait any longer."

The storeroom had been in complete disarray for a month. The hole the robbers made in the roof hadn't been properly repaired. The Food Giant Corporation had to approve all payments, and Dad had used up his repair budget for the year. He could not even submit a request until 2002. In the meantime, Dad had climbed up on the roof with a piece of plywood, a few trash bags, and a roll of duct tape. So far, the repair job had held.

After completing the closing checklist, Dad and I stacked up the day's pallets and waited for Bobby. Dad seemed to be struggling with something. He finally said, "Mitchell came into the office today. To talk."

"Yeah?"

"Yeah." Dad's face turned pale. "He told me that Del is gone."

"Gone?"

"Yes."

"Do you mean . . . dead?"

Dad said softly, "No. She's not dead."

"But she's gone?"

Dad nodded, and I knew what he meant. She was a zombie

now. He added, "Mitchell won't say anything else about her. He seems to be okay, though. He's focusing on work."

"That's good. We need him."

"We sure do. And I just talked to Walter. He's coming back on Monday."

"Really?"

"Yeah. I'm putting him in the bakery, on the early shift. Gert can use the help. She's having some trouble with her arthritis. She's been calling in sick." (I wondered if it was really arthritis. I'm suspicious of everybody nowadays.)

Dad continued: "Walter knows he can't go anywhere near customer service, or anywhere near the pseudoephedrine, and I think he'll honor that."

He set the last pallet against the wall and looked at me. "This store is Walter's life. It's Mitchell's life, too. And Gert's. Where else are they going to go? We have to keep this store open."

Bobby appeared in the doorway. He was far enough away for Dad to whisper, "This store is Bobby's life, too. He's not"—Dad stopped and searched for the word—"inferior here. He's as good as anybody else."

I agreed. "He's better than some." I amended that to, "He's better than most."

Bobby walked over to us, shaking out his arms, getting ready for some hard labor. Dad gave us our assignments, and we set to work. With three people doing it, and with no interruptions, the cleanup went very smoothly. The storeroom was back in shape (except for the hole in the roof) in a little over an hour.

Bobby announced, "My mom's coming at eleven!" He asked me, "What time is it?"

"Ten after ten."

"I gotta call her, then. She said to call if we were going to be early. Or late."

Bobby and I walked up front and stood by the carts. He punched in his home number, then practically shouted into the phone, "Mom! We're done early! Come get me."

He listened for a moment, then replied, "I'm at the front window, with Tom. That's where I'll be. That's where I am." He turned the phone off.

I said, "She's coming now?"

"Yeah. She's coming." Bobby looked outside and frowned. He pointed through the glass. "Hey! That wasn't there before. I came in that way, and it wasn't there."

I looked out into the parking lot. A lone cart was sitting in a space about twenty yards from the entrance. Bobby said, "Somebody must've stole that. Then they felt bad and brought it back."

Dad stuck his head out of the office. "What's going on?"

"There's a cart outside," I explained.

He nodded. "You better get it, Tom. We're losing too many."

"Yeah. All right."

He pointed to the entrance. "The keys are in the door. Be careful." Then he waved at Bobby. "Come here, Bobby, I need you to sign your pay card."

"Okay," Bobby replied, and walked into the office while I headed toward the entrance. I turned the key in the inside lock, opened the door, and stepped outside.

But I guess I wasn't being careful. Or careful enough.

My eyes, and my attention, were on the cart in the distance. I didn't hear the low thrumming of the engine, or the running feet, until it was too late.

I turned toward the sounds.

A black tow truck with a silver hook was idling just past the propane tanks. Two men in black ski masks were running toward me. The one on the left had a hunting rifle. The one on the right reached me first and grabbed my arm.

Then I felt the cold steel of the rifle jab into my neck. I braced for the sound of a shot, and the end of my life, but that didn't happen. Instead, they quick-marched me back into the store, turned me, and headed right toward the office.

Bobby was standing in front of the bakery counter. As soon as he saw us, he started yelling, "No! We're closed! You can't come in here!"

The rifle bore pulled out of my neck. The robber, still walking, aimed it at Bobby. Suddenly I heard a painful blast in my ear.

Bobby spun around 180 degrees and fell to the ground.

Dad came running out of the office, but he froze when he saw us. The rifleman aimed at him but did not shoot. Instead, he pushed me toward Dad, hard, causing us both to fall backward. Dad and I landed together on the floor. My head was on his chest. I could feel his heart pounding.

The rifleman stood over us, sweating and twitching, breathing like a crazed bear. He jammed the rifle into my neck again, under my ear, and held it there.

The other robber ran into the office. We could hear him pulling out drawers and ransacking the place. Looking for money? Drugs? Both? This went on for at least five minutes, five unbearably long minutes. I could hear Dad's voice in my ear, whispering, "Shhh."

My face was turned toward the back of the store. Just by focusing my eyes, I could see Bobby. He was lying on the floor, ten feet away. A round red spot was visible on the right side of his back. He had been shot at close range. Was he dead?

No! I could see his hand moving. It was punching buttons on his phone. I thought, *No, Bobby, please. Do not make a sound.*

The robber in the office continued to break things and crash around. The rifleman grunted at him impatiently, angrily, desperately. Finally, the robber emerged with a trash bag bulging with small boxes. I knew what they were by their size and shape—boxes of cold capsules.

The rifleman pulled the bore away from my neck. He pivoted and, without looking at us again, took off running for the door. The robber with the bag followed him.

I took a few seconds to get my breathing under control—in and out, in and out.

Dad eased me off of him slowly, whispering, "Stay here, Tom." He army-crawled over to Bobby; then he called back to me, "He's alive."

I whispered back, "I know. I saw him dialing his phone."

Suddenly a blinding flash of light filled the entranceway. I rose up as high as I dared and looked. I could see a police car. It was facing the store dead-on, just ten yards out, with its search beam aimed at the entrance. As my eyes adjusted, I could see two officers crouched behind the opened car doors. Each was aiming a pistol at a robber.

The officer on my right screamed, "Drop it! Both of you! Drop what you are carrying!"

The robber with the black bag dropped it and raised his hands up in surrender.

The other one, though, made another decision, a fatal one. He let loose a rifle blast that shattered the police car's searchlight. Then he took off running for the tow truck.

Both officers leveled their weapons, sighted, and opened fire at him. Their first shots missed the robber, but they hit the propane cage. I could hear their bullets strike the outside wall of the store. Then I heard two loud *booms*, one right after the other, as two tanks of propane exploded and started to burn.

The officers sighted again, aiming lower. This time, they found their mark. Bullets ripped into the body of the rifleman. He fell to the ground, immobile, just beneath that silver hook.

The officer on my right raised his pistol and stood. He approached the remaining robber, shouting, "Get on your knees! Keep your hands where I can see them!"

The robber obeyed.

The other officer stood and approached his man, too, with his pistol still trained on him, but that officer didn't say anything.

There was nothing to say. Because the other robber was dead. The officer stared down at the body for a long moment. As he did, the outside wall suddenly shook with another loud *boom*, and then another, and then a whole series of explosions. The propane tanks, at least fifty of them, burst open and flamed upward into the sky.

I dared to stand all the way up. To my left, I saw Dad kneeling next to Bobby, putting pressure on his bullet wound. To my right, I saw a Ford Explorer screech to a halt near the entrance. Mrs. Smalls, dressed in her white uniform, jumped out of the car and ran in. She looked at me and shouted, "Bobby! Where's Bobby?"

I pointed at Dad. "Over there!"

"Is he alive?"

Dad himself answered, "Yes! Yes, he is." As Mrs. Smalls hurried past me, Dad added, "He's the one who called nine one one."

Mrs. Smalls bent over Bobby and set to work checking his vital signs.

I turned back to watch as three more police cars, two ambulances, and a fire truck raced into the parking lot.

The propane tanks were still burning wildly, scorching the outside wall of the store, casting an unholy light on it all—on the police, on the paramedics, and on the two robbers—the one still kneeling near the entranceway, and the one lying dead near the truck.

No one told me to stay where I was, so I walked to the door and stepped outside. I saw two paramedics reach the rifleman's body, check for a pulse, and find none. I was just a few feet away when one of them grabbed the ski mask and pulled it back, revealing his face.

I knew him.

I think I knew him from the very beginning—when he was sweating and grunting and pushing me around.

It was Rick Dorfman.

He had stuck a rifle bore in my neck. He had shot Bobby for no reason. Now he was dead.

I turned back to the second robber. The police officer had just pulled his ski mask up and off. And I knew him, too. There, kneeling on the asphalt, blinking in the firelight, with a half-amused expression on his face, was Reg the Veg.

Reg Malloy. And I was surprised. Despite everything, I was surprised.

I stood there for a long time, looking between Dorfman and Reg, as the awful, bloody scene ran its course. I watched Bobby and his mom leave in the first ambulance. Then I watched the body of Rick Dorfman leave in the second. Then Reg Malloy left in the back of a police car. He was staring straight ahead.

The firefighters were still training their hoses on the propane cage when Dad walked out. He and I spent about an hour answering questions for the police.

Finally, after all the fires were extinguished and all the police cars had left, Dad and I were free to go home. Before we did, though, Dad motioned to me to wait. He muttered, "Give me one minute, Tom." He walked back inside and soon emerged with a small sheet of butcher paper. He had made a sign, by hand, and now he taped it to the front door. It said CLOSED—DECEMBER 22 AND 23.

On our weary trek out to the van, all he said was, "I need a weekend off. We all do. Believe me, life will go on."

Monday, December 24, 2001

Life went on.

I thought Mom would be freaked out by the news of what had happened, but she was not. Neither was Lilly. Even though Dad and I had nearly been killed, and Rick Dorfman *had* been killed, and Bobby had been wounded. I think we're all just numb to disaster now, in all its forms, in the dark days of a plague year.

The store reopened on Christmas Eve. Things looked pretty normal except for the ugly black burns behind the propane cage. Some employees were angry because they had arrived on Saturday, read the sign, and then had to go home. But they got over that fast when they heard the facts about Bobby, and the break-in, and Reg, and the dead robber. Some customers were angry, too. I guess they had to go across town to Kroger, or to the 7-Eleven. Too bad for them.

Our family had taken a weekend off for the first time in recent memory. Here's what we did:

On Saturday morning, Dad and I drove out to Good Samaritan Hospital. We met John in the lobby. The first thing he said to Dad was, "We're *really* closed all weekend? Corporate gave us permission to close?"

"They did," Dad assured him.

"On the weekend before Christmas? The whole weekend?"

"Yes." Dad surprised me by explaining further, though I am not sure what he said was true. "We had no choice. Our store is a crime scene now. The police will let us know when we can reopen."

That sounded good, and John bought it completely. I guess Dad's bosses at corporate had, too.

We took an elevator up to the fifth floor and walked around

until we found Bobby's room. His mother was the only other person in there. She was sitting in a chair, doing a crossword puzzle.

Bobby was propped up in bed, staring at a high-mounted TV set. Bobby's right shoulder was heavily bandaged and bulged out from under his blue gown. When Mrs. Smalls saw us, she closed her book, stood up, and turned off the TV, using a button on the side of the bed. She said, "Mr. Coleman! Thank you so much for coming. Hello, Tom. Hello, Uno."

Bobby corrected her. "He doesn't want to be called that anymore, Mom! He wants to be called John."

"Oh. I am sorry. Hello, John."

John muttered, "No problem."

Dad asked, "How are you feeling, Bobby?"

"How am I feeling? I'm feeling hungry."

"You're not eating?"

Bobby made a face. "The food here is horrible."

His mother interrupted. "You're in a hospital, Bobby. They're giving you hospital food. Nobody likes hospital food."

"I sure don't. It's horrible."

Dad tried again. "How is your wound feeling, though? Your shoulder?"

Mrs. Smalls answered for Bobby. "The bullet passed right through, under the shoulder blade. It severed veins and arteries, and it damaged muscle tissue, but it didn't break any bones." She shook her head. "Bobby has low muscle tone to begin with; that's part of Down's syndrome. He has a very delicate system. It's not like yours and mine." She added bitterly, "You can't go shooting holes in him."

Dad asked, "Is he going to be okay, though?"

She replied, "Yes, of course," but she did not sound totally convinced.

Bobby suddenly shouted, "The guy who shot me is dead!"

Dad nodded. "Yes. Yes, that's true."

"I'm glad he's dead!" No one replied to that, so Bobby asked, "Who was he?"

Dad raised his shoulders. "I didn't know him." He turned and looked at me.

I told Bobby, "His name was Rick Dorfman. He went to Haven High. He played on the football team." Everybody was looking at me like they wanted more, so I added, "I only saw him in the store once. I know he had some legal problems, and some drug problems."

Mrs. Smalls expanded on that. "Some meth problems."

"Yeah, I think so, the way he was behaving."

Bobby shouted again, "And what about Reg the Veg?"

"Well, he's in jail, and he's going to stay in jail."

"No! I mean what's his problem?"

"Oh. I don't know, Bobby. Maybe he has a drug problem, too. I know he has money problems."

Bobby mulled that over. "Drug problems. They all have drug problems, all the ones who shoplift. They're all stupid thieves. They steal cold pills and make meth. They cook it up at home; then they smoke it, right?"

I was surprised at how much he knew. "Yeah. That's right."

He went on: "It makes them feel good for one week. Then it makes them feel bad for the rest of their lives. They're stupid."

"They sure are."

"I hope they shoot Reg the Veg!"

Mrs. Smalls intervened. "Come on, Bobby. That wouldn't be right."

"Yes, it would."

Mrs. Smalls stared at him until he looked away. Then he clammed up.

Dad, John, and I shuffled in place for a few more minutes after that, looking around uncomfortably. Dad finally turned to Mrs. Smalls and said, "Well, I'm glad to see that Bobby is up and talking and everything. Is there anything we can do for him, Mrs. Smalls?"

She leaned over the bed and stared at Bobby again, forcing him to make eye contact with her. Then she looked back at Dad. "Bobby thinks he is ready for a little more responsibility at work, Mr. Coleman. He thinks he could be the one who unloads the produce trucks, now that . . . that . . . Reg person won't be."

Dad agreed right away. "Sure. Sure, Bobby. That's a good idea. The job is yours."

Bobby managed a shy smile.

"And that new job would come with a raise."

Bobby's eyes bulged and his smile widened.

"The job will be waiting for you when you come back," Dad assured him. "For now, you take your time and get better."

We then muttered our goodbyes to Bobby and Mrs. Smalls.

John and I were actually out the doorway when Dad turned back to say one more thing. "And, Bobby, thank you. You're the one who called the police, in spite of your injury. You knew just what to do. That was a smart and a brave thing to do. You're the reason why those criminals didn't get away, and why they're not out shooting someone else right now. You are a hero, Bobby, and I am proud to have you as an employee."

Bobby stared at Dad curiously, as if none of that had ever occurred to him.

Dad walked past me. He had tears in his eyes. I took a last look back at Mrs. Smalls. Big tears were running down her face, too.

✢

After an early dinner, we drove to Pottsville to see a movie, *The Lord of the Rings: The Fellowship of the Ring*. It was pretty cool. It was the forces of good against the forces of evil, and we could all relate to that. The evil Orcs really creeped me out. They had rotten teeth, and they wore filthy rags, and they moved like the living dead. After the movie, nobody mentioned them by name, but I bet we were all thinking the same thing: They were the Blackwater zombies, the meth addicts.

When we got back home, we played a short game of Parcheesi and then a long game of Monopoly. It was a busy, unusual, totally enjoyable family day.

And so was Sunday, but that was more of a day of rest. Rest for everyone except Mom, that is. She cooked and served up roast beef, mashed potatoes, green bean casserole, and apple pie.

I slept in. I awoke at nine, staring directly at my Florida colleges collage. I sat up in bed, slid down to the bottom, and set to work dismantling it. I peeled off all the beautiful pictures of sunny campuses, lush greenery, and tanned, smiling people. For me, that was now Wendy Lyle land, and Christmas tree–drug bust land. I was no longer interested. Like Warren, like Jimmy, like Arthur, I was never going back to Florida.

John knocked at the front door around noon. Lilly let him in and kissed him right in front of Mom. But then Mom walked over and kissed him, too, on the cheek. She led him by the elbow into the dining room. "Welcome, John. You're just in time."

Dad sat at the head of the table, with his back toward the kitchen. John and Lilly sat on the window side; Mom and I were on the inside. Once everyone had a full plate, Dad said, "This is our family. There are five of us now, with the addition of a new son. Welcome to you, John."

John was clearly moved. He muttered, "Thank you, sir."

Lilly laughed. "'Sir'? You don't call him that at work. You call him Gene."

Dad said, "He can still call me that. But I hope, in family matters, you'll feel comfortable calling me Dad."

John replied, "Yes, sir. Yes, Dad."

Lilly and I both looked at Mom. She quickly added, "And Mom." She told him, "I look forward to meeting your parents, John, and your siblings. Do you have siblings?"

He said, "I do. I have one older sister."

"Ah! What does she do?"

"She works in a dentist's office. She's a hygienist."

That killed the conversation, but only for a moment.

Dad reached out his hands, one to Mom and one to John. Lilly and I joined in, so that we were all holding hands. Then Dad threw me for a loop by saying, "Okay, Tom? Will you say grace for us?"

I blanked for a moment. My mind started racing. I found myself thinking, *What do we have to thank God for? We are in the middle of a plague year, an annus horribilis. Are we supposed to be thankful that things aren't even worse? I guess so.*

I finally said this: "We've seen other families lose a lot this year. They've lost family members to death, and to jail, and to just . . . zombieland."

Mom and Dad looked uncomfortable, like they were wondering where this prayer was going. So was I. I continued: "But our family has hung in there. We're all healthy, and we're all still here, and we're not in jail, and we have even added a family member in John, so that's all good."

Mom and Dad quickly said, "Amen!" Lilly and John followed. Then we started to eat.

Sunday, December 30, 2001

The show went on, too. *The Roses of Eyam*.

Arthur had offered to drive me to it, and I was happy to accept. He picked me up outside the house on Sunday evening, immediately handing me one of Mr. Proctor's Bibles with dialogue inside. We drove to the school, with me reading lines from the play and Arthur trying to remember his responses to them.

We parked in the row nearest to the auditorium. The Weavers' Explorer was next to us. The Lyles' red Suburban was in the row behind, three spaces over.

I followed Arthur through the main doors. We then veered left down a side corridor that led to the back of the stage. Arthur joined Jenny and Mike at a table, where they were going over their lines. I started to sit with them, when a hand reached out and grabbed me.

It was Wendy Lyle's. She had not spoken to me in over two weeks. She had not bothered to tell me that she was leaving school and that she was moving away forever. But now she was pleading with me, like we were best friends, "Tom! You have to help. This play is a total disaster!"

I said calmly, "Hello, Wendy. How are you?"

She replied with controlled fury, "There is no director! We haven't rehearsed in forever. Ben is in the bathroom, throwing up. And Chris Collier has bailed on us!"

"What?"

"He's the freaking male lead, and he's not here!"

I looked at the side door. "Well, there's still time."

But she was adamant. She practically babbled, "No, he has

bailed on us! I knew he would, the jerk. He was only doing it for a grade from Mr. Proctor, and now Mr. Proctor has bailed, too!"

I couldn't let that go. I repeated, "Mr. Proctor has *bailed?*"

She looked at me, puzzled. "Uh, yeah. Do you see him any-where?"

"You think he just . . . quit because he felt like it?"

She answered simply, even convincingly, "Yes. He got the hell out of this place."

I thought, *Maybe she doesn't know the truth. She's been out of school. Maybe no one has told her.*

Wendy looked at the door. She spoke bitterly. "Chris sucked anyway." Then she added, to my shock, "It's because he's a freak-ing druggie."

"No way!"

"Yes."

"How do you know?"

She looked at me like I was deaf, dumb, and blind. "Please! He couldn't memorize his character's *name*, never mind his lines. He was still reading every word from the book."

I was dumbfounded. "Chris Collier is using? Using what?"

"Who cares? Something that makes you stupid; that's all I know." Suddenly Wendy put both hands on my shoulders and begged me. "Tom! *You* have to do it. You have to play the lead!"

"Me?"

"Yes! You were Mr. Proctor's first choice. He wrote the part for you." She spun around and grabbed a black book off a table. She opened it and thrust it in my face. "Look! All you have to do is find the name Mompesson and read his lines. I'll move you around where you need to be onstage. Please. Please!"

Arthur appeared beside me, bent double. He had obviously been listening, because he said in an idiotic voice, "Do it, Mr. Tom! Do it! The show must go on. Arthur needs to get his A."

I stared at his hunched figure. "Are you serious?"

Arthur stood erect and spoke normally. "Dead serious, cuz. Come on, it's no big deal. You just stand out there and read the lines. Nobody expects you to be any good."

Jenny called from the table, "Yeah! Come on, Tom. We need you."

I looked at all of their faces (well, mostly at Jenny's face). I heard myself say, "Okay, then. All right."

Fifteen minutes later, I was on the stage. I was appearing in *The Roses of Eyam*, by Don Taylor, as adapted by Mr. Proctor. I was the star of the show, in fact, performing before a small crowd consisting of mostly the actors' parents.

I could see the Weavers in the first row. I could see Catherine Lyle in the second row. She was sitting with her creepy husband and a line of three frat boys, including, of all people, Joel. It was bizarre to see his curly head again. He didn't seem uncomfortable to be there, either. He was just chatting with Dr. Lyle and the boys, acting like nothing was wrong. I thought, *Why did they come tonight? Just to make fun of us?*

I put them all out of my mind, though, and concentrated on my character. I stood where the Reverend Mompesson was supposed to stand, and I read all his lines the best I could. The Reverend had to convince the villagers of Eyam to stay where they were; to fight the plague to the death; to save the rest of England.

I liked the part. And I liked the character. Mr. Proctor had given the Reverend Mompesson some stirring speeches about honor, and responsibility, and shared humanity.

Mr. Proctor had condensed the play down to one long act, a

little over an hour's running time. Halfway through, Dr. Lyle's frat boys got up and left. They returned ten minutes later, and suddenly everything was funny to them. They laughed particularly long and hard at anything Arthur did as the Bedlam, the village idiot.

But I must say, from where I was standing, that Arthur performed his part very well. He really threw himself into it. So did Wendy and Jenny and Mike; so did Ben, despite his earlier bout with stage fright. We managed to deliver Mr. Proctor's version of *The Roses of Eyam* competently. Maybe even with some conviction. Maybe even with some passion.

There was a nice round of applause when it was over. There was also some silly hooting from the frat boys, causing Catherine Lyle to look uncomfortable. We took a group bow, with me in the middle, and made our exit. It was really an exhilarating feeling.

Backstage, Arthur was hopping around and slapping five with everybody, still in his stooped village-idiot posture. Wendy had her head down, muttering, "Thank God that's over." But Jenny, Ben, Mike, Arthur, and I were all up and giddy and elated.

I felt elated for Mr. Proctor, too. This had been his vision, and we had made it real. It wasn't great; it wasn't Broadway. But it was good, and it was Blackwater.

Our group walked together, going back down that side corridor and out into the night. As soon as we pushed open the auditorium doors, we were greeted by a swirl of blowing white snowflakes.

Ben stuck out his tongue and shouted sloppily, "I love eating snow!"

Arthur slapped him on the back. "Eat all you want, dude. It's only water."

We moved along in a laughing, chattering bunch to the first

row of cars. Mrs. Weaver rolled down the driver's window of her SUV. She called out, "You kids were great!"

"I know!" Ben replied.

"We want to take you to Friendly's, the whole cast."

Ben clenched his fist. "Yes! Real food!"

Jenny looked at me, so I looked at Arthur. He raised his shoulders up and down and said, "Sure. Sounds good. We'll meet you there."

Jenny, Mike, and Ben piled into the SUV, and the Weavers took off. As they backed out, Arthur and I got a clearer view of the Geo Metro.

Something was wrong. It was slumping to one side, like a man leaning on a crutch.

"Damn!" Arthur spat out. "Flat tire. We don't need that now."

"Can I help?" I asked him.

"You ever changed a tire before?"

"No."

"Then how can you help?"

I was going to press the issue, but I heard the sound of people emerging from the auditorium, heading toward us. It was the Lyles—Dr., Mrs., and Wendy—and the college guys.

I could hear Joel teasing Wendy. "That was the worst play in history, like in ancient Greek history, like in three thousand years of history."

Wendy said flatly, "Shut up. You were sleeping."

"Only in the first half. We got it up for the second half."

"Yeah. I bet you did."

As they got closer to the Suburban, Wendy noticed me. She raised a gloved hand to silence Joel. She called over, "You did a nice job tonight, Tom. You were the best actor out there."

Joel disagreed. "Next to you," he said.

She ignored him.

I replied humbly, "Well, maybe the others shouldn't have rehearsed, either."

"Yeah. Maybe."

I didn't say anything else, and neither did she.

Dr. Lyle then joined the boys in mocking our production of *The Roses of Eyam*. They all started repeating lines of dialogue and guffawing, amusing themselves.

As I listened to them carry on, I thought, *What the hell do they know?* Mr. Proctor had chosen the play for its message, and they had missed it completely.

Dumbasses.

Catherine Lyle turned away. Did she think she still had to ignore me? Was this confidentiality again? Or was she just plain ignoring me?

I looked back at Arthur. He had changed the tire very quickly, very expertly, like a NASCAR pit-crew guy. He was now hefting the old tire into the trunk and spinning it around slowly, looking for the puncture.

Wendy stepped closer and spoke to me. "We're leaving tomorrow."

I said, "Yeah? To where?"

"Florida. My dad is going back to his old position at FIT."

"Yeah? Is that a college?"

Her lip curled. "Yes, it's a college. What do you think it is?"

I curled my lip right back at her. "I don't know. It sounds like a gym, maybe, or a ladies' spa."

To my surprise, Dr. Lyle stopped goofing around with the frat boys, stepped forward, and snapped at me, "For your information, young man, the Florida Institute of Technology has one of the top Psy.D. programs in the nation."

I nodded. "Oh? Psy.D.? Is that some new kind of workout? Like yoga, maybe?"

Spit flew from his lips. "It's a doctor of psychology degree!"

Just as I was pondering a reply, Arthur came shuffling up next to me. He was bent slightly and slurring his words, like he was still playing the Bedlam. "A doctor? There's a doctor here? Can you fix a crooked back? Are you that kind of doctor?"

Dr. Lyle rolled his eyes. He pointed to the Suburban and told his group, "All right, that's enough. Let's go."

"I was taught, at Haven High, that doctors cure things like that."

Dr. Lyle muttered, "I'll bet you were." He pointed at the school doors. With contempt in his voice, he told his wife, "I *said* this school was a mistake. Wendy never learned a thing here."

I couldn't let that go. I asked him, "No? She didn't learn about supply and demand?" I raised my voice and addressed his group. "Well, here it is, then, in a nutshell: If *demand* is high, like if frat boys and old professors with ponytails demand to have illegal drugs, then *supply* will be high, too."

Dr. Lyle and his boys froze in place.

I went on: "If demand is low, or if demand disappears, then supply disappears. And there is no more drug problem." I asked them, "Everybody understand?"

No one replied. No one even moved.

Arthur stepped in front of me and pointed at Joel. "Hey, Joe? It's snowing, and I got ice building up on my windshield. You don't have an ice pick on you, do you?"

Joel's eyes shifted toward the Suburban.

Arthur waited a moment and then continued. "No? You

don't?" Arthur looked at the Suburban, too. "Becaus[e]
swear somebody put an ice pick in my tire. I thought [it]
have been you."

Joel stepped behind the other two guys.

Arthur turned his attention to Catherine. "Exc[use]
Mrs. Lyle? Did you get a chance to speak to the doct[or about]
that"—he lowered his voice—"that sensitive matter?"

She seemed genuinely puzzled. "What do you mean?"

"If you recall, I suggested that some of Wendy's comp[any,]
these boys right here, in fact, were seen in a very unsavory [neigh-]
borhood. And I should know, since it's my neighborhoo[d. And]
they were perhaps involved in some illegal activity?"

Catherine Lyle swallowed hard. Clearly, she had not s[poken]
to her husband about it.

Arthur continued: "Because, if I am not mistaken, th[ere is]
once again a strange smell coming from these boys." He wh[acked]
me in the chest with the back of his hand. "Tom? Did you n[otice]
a strange smell?"

I had not, but I said, "Yeah. I did."

Arthur held up his head and sniffed the air like a ten-p[oint]
buck. He walked back toward the Geo Metro. He pulled a [tire]
iron out of his trunk, turned, and retraced his steps toward us.

The Lyles all exchanged frightened looks, but they were [not]
Arthur's target. Not his direct target, anyway. Arthur crossed o[ver]
to the red Suburban. He cranked back his right arm and delive[red]
a mighty blow to the back window. The wide pane of glass sh[at-]
tered, splitting into long horizontal lines. But the glass did n[ot]
fall.

Arthur then pulled back and struck again at the center [of]
the window, and again, and again, pounding away until he ha[d]
opened up a hole about two feet in diameter. He poked his hea[d]

in, then pulled it out quickly. "This is it, Mrs. Lyle! The source of the smell. It's coming from inside this very vehicle."

Everyone in the Lyles' group remained frozen except Wendy. She held out her hands to them all, demanding to know, "Aren't we going to do something about this? We need to call the police. We need to have this psycho village-idiot jerk arrested!"

I told her, "Your family doesn't call the police."

"What?"

"Isn't that right, Dr. Lyle? No talking to the police? Oh, wait. Wait!" I slapped my own head, as Arthur likes to do. "You *did* talk to the police, though—to Officer O'Dell. You talked to him last week. You ratted out Mr. Proctor to save yourself, right? So you probably don't want to talk to them again so soon, not with your vehicle having a suspicious smell and all."

I walked over to the Suburban and stood next to Arthur. I leaned my head into the hole he had just made. There was no question about it; Joel and his boys had smoked weed here during the play.

I was pulling my head back out, carefully, when I noticed a toolbox. Some pieces of the windshield had fallen down onto an open metal toolbox, but I could still see what was sitting right on top—a wood-handled ice pick. I reached in, brushed the glass shards away, and pulled it out.

Arthur's eyes narrowed. But before he could do anything, I did it for him. I gripped the wooden handle tightly and stepped around to the left side of the Suburban. I pulled the ice pick back and plunged it, hard, into the left rear tire. I heard a quick hissing sound; then I smelled stale air rushing past my nostrils.

Arthur just stared at me, amazed. He finally proclaimed, "Righteous, cuz," and clapped me on the shoulder.

We turned and walked back to the Geo Metro, leaving the ice pick, still hissing, in the sidewall of that very big, very expensive-looking tire. Arthur tossed the tire iron into his trunk and slammed it shut. Then we got in the car and drove off.

And we didn't look back.

Arthur gunned it down the long entrance, laughing all the way. "I can't believe you, cuz! I can't believe that act of blatant vandalism. And with an ice pick! That was *righteously* blatant."

"Well, they deserved it."

He held up a hand to slap, which I did. He slowed down to negotiate the right turn onto Route 16. "Hey! Forget them, right?"

"Right."

"Forget all of them. Forever."

"Right again."

"I have already forgotten them."

"Me, too."

"Now tell me: Where are we going?"

"The Friendly's downtown. It's across from Kroger."

"Got it." Arthur shook his head, bemused. "Those losers are too stoned to change a tire."

I added, "And too pusillanimous."

"Yeah. Whatever. Hey! Do you think they belong to triple A?"

"Yeah. Probably."

"Check it out: We belong to double A; they belong to triple A."

We slapped five again.

The car kept skidding at every stop sign and traffic light, so Arthur dropped the transmission to a lower gear. Still, we managed to arrive at Friendly's right after the Weavers.

As soon as we walked inside, I saw Jenny wave to me from a

vinyl-backed booth. I cut in front of Arthur and slipped in next to her. The lineup was this: Ben, Jenny, me, and Arthur on the red vinyl side: Mike, Mrs. Weaver, and Mr. Weaver in chairs on the other side.

Ben ordered a sundae with a cherry and nuts on top. He picked up the cherry, held it out to Arthur, and asked, "Can I eat this?"

Arthur assured him, "Yeah. That'd be okay."

"What about the stem?"

"Ah, no. No stems."

"Oh, man!"

We all laughed. The Weavers seemed puzzled, but they smiled along with us.

The Weavers started talking about the play and its themes, Mr. Proctor's themes. They understood that it was all about Blackwater, and that the plague was meth. We talked about meth and what it had done to us, and how we could continue to fight against it.

Mrs. Weaver said, "Your parents have been terrific, Tom. Your father has been so generous with supplies from his store. Your mother has been so generous with her time."

Mr. Weaver added, "We're getting more people at the church basement—desperate, desperate people. We're going to expand our services to food, clothing, and medical care. We'll need more volunteers."

Everybody raised a hand, nodded, or spoke up. We would all volunteer. We would have it covered.

I asked, "Medical care? How are we doing that?"

Mrs. Weaver said, "Nurses from Good Samaritan."

"Is Mrs. Smalls one of them?"

"Oh yes. She's organizing it."

"I'm not surprised. She really knows what's going on. She's been calling it 'the meth plague' for a long time."

Mrs. Weaver nodded. "We all need to do that. We all need to call it what it is."

We continued to talk, and eat sundaes, and plan our counterattack against the meth plague for over an hour. When we finally trooped out into the parking lot, I saw that the snow had stopped falling. The sky was now clear and dark, with twinkling stars. The temperature had dropped, though; it had dropped a lot—so much that a runoff from the roof had crystallized, leaving foot-long icicles hanging over our heads, like swords.

Arthur jumped up and snapped one off. He handed it to Ben. "Here. Take this in case you get hungry later."

Ben took it and stuck it between his back teeth. "Great. I'll eat this before it melts."

We all laughed; Mr. and Mrs. Weaver looked puzzled again. Then Jenny gave me a beautiful smile, and they took off.

It was a perfect moment, I thought. On a perfect night.

But if I had known where to look, to the north and west, I might have thought differently. I might have seen a faint red glow in the dark sky.

⁜

Yin and yang.

Heaven and hell.

Paradise Lost.

All the things Mr. Proctor had talked about.

If I was thinking that this plague year would end on a happy note, or on a positive note, or even on a not-horrible note, I was mistaken.

Arthur saw the glow in the sky before I did, but he misinterpreted it. "Looks like a fire up in Primrose. Maybe a forest fire."

"A forest fire? In the snow?"

"No, you're right. Maybe a grease fire. Or maybe somebody was cooking with propane and the damn thing blew up."

But as we drove on, Arthur got less sure of that, and less talkative. Something bad was happening, but it wasn't in Primrose.

It was in Caldera.

He finally said, "Sorry, cuz. I gotta know where that fire is. You okay with getting home late?"

"Yeah. Sure."

Neither of us spoke again as we rose higher into the mountains. The first sign of the tragedy was, oddly enough, something comical. The heat of the fire was melting the snow and ice above us, creating a river of running water. As we slowed to turn onto Arthur's road, I saw an orange duck—a small plastic one—floating by.

As we accelerated up the road, I saw orange plastic rings floating in the runoff, too, followed by black Transformer parts.

By then, we could see the red flashing lights of a Haven County ambulance up ahead. We could see the blaze by then, too, through the sparse winter trees.

It wasn't Aunt Robin's trailer, but it was right behind it.

It was Warren's.

Arthur slammed to a halt in the middle of the road. He turned off the ignition and bolted out of the car. I got out and followed him as best I could, scrambling up the short hillside, slipping in the river of icy water that was running down.

Jimmy Giles, wearing nothing but jeans and a T-shirt, was standing halfway between his trailer and Warren's. He looked devastated, broken, shaken to the core.

The ambulance was parked on a spot well away from the blaze. Aunt Robin, Cody, and a paramedic were sitting in the front cab. The paramedic was speaking into a black microphone.

A second paramedic, a stocky guy in an orange coat, was standing between Jimmy and the burning trailer.

Arthur ran up to Jimmy. He had to shout to be heard. "Where's Warren?"

Jimmy opened his mouth slowly, reluctantly. Then he spoke through gulping sobs. "He was the doomed one. Not me."

"What?"

Jimmy's voice rose. "Warren's dead, Arthur! He got killed in there. By an explosion."

Arthur shook his head from left to right. "What are you talking about?"

"He's got chemicals in there. You know that. Bad stuff . . ." Jimmy's voice trailed away.

The paramedic took a step toward Arthur and yelled, "The man inside the trailer is dead from an explosion. It blew a hole in his chest."

Arthur pressed both hands against his ears. Then he yelled back above the roar of the blaze, "Where is he now?"

"In the kitchen area."

"Why isn't he out here? Why aren't you working on him out here? Why aren't you trying to save him?"

The paramedic took another step and explained. "I looked inside. I saw the man very clearly. He is dead. He is surrounded by volatile chemicals, though. We can't remove him until the firefighters get here, put out the fire, and tell us it's safe to remove him."

The paramedic half turned at the sight of flashing lights. His right arm shot up and pointed. "Okay! Here they are! They're turning up the road."

Arthur looked confused. He finally asked, "You're not leaving him in there?"

"No. I just explained to you—"

"No, I'm explaining to you! We gotta get him out of there!"

The paramedic opened his mouth, but he stopped speaking at the blast of a horn from the fire truck. A voice called out from the passenger-side window, "Move this car! We can't get the engine in!"

My head was whirling around—from the blaze, and the smoke, and the noise, and the rush of the icy water. Here was something I could do. I yelled, "I'll get it!" and took off back down the hill.

Almost immediately, my feet flew out from under me and I slid to the bottom, my back caked with ice and mud. I hurried to the driver's side, jerked the door open, and jumped in. I cranked the car key, dropped the transmission into gear, and lurched forward about twenty yards up the road. Then I turned the car off and ran back, as best I could, to the blazing trailer.

I couldn't see Arthur anywhere.

The paramedic was gesturing angrily to his partner, and to the firefighters. Suddenly I heard an explosion inside the trailer, like the propane tanks at the Food Giant. The fire surged even higher into the night, bursting through a hole in the trailer's roof.

I looked at Jimmy. He was staring, stunned, at the trailer's front door. Then I knew where Arthur was.

I took off running toward that door. The paramedic made a move to block me, but he was too slow, and I slipped around him.

The heat got stronger, like a wall of energy pushing against me. I reached the trailer just as Arthur's back appeared inside. His hood was up over his head. The top peak of it was on fire, like a small candle. His sleeves were on fire, too, at the elbow. He backed out rapidly, so fast that I had to scramble out of his way.

He was dragging a body after him.

Warren's body.

Warren's face was gray with death. He was wearing the remnants of that Haven High Football jacket. His chest had a large bloody indentation in it, the size and shape of a bowling ball.

Arthur kept moving, kept dragging, seemingly unaware that his own clothes were on fire. I sprang forward and drove my shoulder into Arthur's, hitting him a solid blow, like a football block. He released his grip on Warren and fell backward. I could hear the flames on his head and arms hiss out on the watery ground.

Arthur's face contorted in pain. His mouth opened, and he screamed. Then he flipped himself over spastically, rising up on his elbows. He started coughing rapidly, deeply, uncontrollably.

Somewhere behind me, the firefighters unleashed two streams of water onto the roof of the trailer. One of them barked at us, "Get back! Both of you! There are chemical vats in there!"

The paramedic grabbed hold of Warren's body, just as Arthur had done. His partner joined him, and they soon had Warren away from the trailer. They fastened him to a stretcher and hoisted him into the back of the ambulance.

Jimmy and I helped Arthur rise to his feet. We led him, step by step, to a spot in front of the ambulance. Arthur dropped to one knee and stared at the ground, panting and coughing miserably.

Jimmy spoke in that haunted voice. "It was Warren. He was the one. He was doomed."

The first paramedic returned to take a look at Arthur. He said, "You are injured, son. We need to treat these burns. We might need to take you to the ER to check out your lungs."

Arthur hacked up some foul liquid and spit it on the ground.

He managed to say, "Treat the burns. But I ain't going to no ER. I'm staying here."

The paramedic applied salve to Arthur's ears, arms, and hands; then he wrapped both hands with gauze and tape. He lectured him, "I told you he was dead already. Didn't you believe me?"

Arthur answered softly, almost to himself, "He didn't burn."

The paramedic asked, "What?"

But Arthur didn't answer him. He spoke to Jimmy and me, his voice rising in intensity. "He didn't burn, goddammit! He may be dead, but I didn't let him burn."

I nodded rapidly; then Jimmy did, too.

"He didn't burn."

The paramedic stared at Arthur for a moment, confused. Then he went back to wrapping the bandages.

From somewhere behind me, I heard Cody start to cry. Aunt Robin crossed in front of us, bearing him up in her left arm. She paused for just a moment to stretch out her right arm and touch the top of Arthur's head, keeping her hand away from the burns. Then she stepped carefully through the mess and continued on into her trailer.

Jimmy trudged in after them. His feet were bare. His bony shoulders showed through his T-shirt. He had to be freezing.

I stayed outside with Arthur. He remained kneeling in the slop, his head bowed. The runoff water continued to flow around him. He was holding up a bandaged hand at a ninety-degree angle, like he wanted to ask a question. His lips were moving.

I leaned forward until I could understand. He was repeating three words in a low and barely audible voice, over and over, through choking sobs. The words were "I hate drugs."

A minute later, a big vat exploded inside Warren's trailer. It took out the entire kitchen area. The flames continued to lick higher, filling the dark sky with a hellish light.

It was all life and death, and water and ice, and fire and cold. When I finally took a look at my watch, I saw that it was ten minutes past midnight.

It was December 31.

The last day of the year.

Spring

Thursday, March 21, 2002

The day after the fire, New Year's Day, I sat down and started writing a new journal, this one. Because the old one, like everything else in Warren's trailer, had gone up in the conflagration.

At first, I was in a panic, thinking that I couldn't do it; that I had forgotten too much. But that was not true. I remembered everything very clearly. I wrote nonstop all day, and the next day, and for many days after, trying to get down what had happened to me, to us, to Blackwater over the last year.

In the three months since the fire, things have gotten a lot worse. But nobody has run away. We have stayed here, and we have fought.

January and February were especially bad times for the town. There was a big demand for food at the church. There was a big demand for warm clothing there, too. And there was a big demand for slabs at the morgue.

But, looking back from today, it seems like that was the worst period. It seems like things have bottomed out; like things might be slowly getting better.

Today is the first day of spring. That means that we, the people of Blackwater, have survived the long, dark winter. We have done everything we could do. Every day, every night, we have provided the zombies with food, or clothes, or shelter, or medical care, or a decent burial.

The circle of helpers has widened: The county has opened up trailers on the north spur of Caldera for homeless families. More churches have opened their basements. Kroger has joined the Food Giant in contributing its expired foods to the needy. Everybody has pulled together, like they did back in Mrs. Cantwell's grandmother's day, back in the Great Depression.

Because that's what we do in Blackwater.

I also want to update some things.

Bobby Smalls recovered from his gunshot wound without any complications. When he returned to work, Dad did make him the produce manager. It was Reg's old job. It was also Dad's old job.

Reg Malloy was charged with armed robbery and assault. He is being held in the Haven County Correctional Institution. Coach Malloy doesn't talk about it. Jenny says that Coach is not returning to Haven Junior/Senior High next year.

Lilly and John have set a marriage date. It is Thursday, October 31, 2002. Halloween. They plan to send out orange-and-black invitations.

Arthur will graduate with his class, thanks to two A's in ninth-grade English—one from Mr. Proctor and one from Mrs. Kerpinski. He has a plan. He will report for Marine Corps basic training in September. (He also has a tattoo, on his right bicep— a poker hand with four deuces and a joker, and *Deuces Wild* underneath.)

Mom still runs the food table at our zombie-support group at the church. She never misses a night. Dad still donates the food, and he still declines to prosecute shoplifters at the Food Giant.

Aunt Robin now works at Haven Junior/Senior High in the cafeteria. (Mrs. Cantwell called and offered her the job.) Jimmy is still signed up with WorkForce, doing whatever comes up.

Last but not least, Jenny is my girlfriend now. (I love to write that.)

So, finally, is the plague over?

I think it is.

Why?

In the end, it may simply have come down to this: Everybody who was going to try meth has tried it. And they have either survived the experience or they have not. (Most have not.)

The rest of the people in Blackwater have responded to the NEO and the I Hate Drugs campaigns and have kept far away from meth. And they always will stay away from meth, and crack, and weed, and whatever comes along next.

Because the people in Blackwater *truly* hate drugs.

Because the people in Blackwater have been through a plague year.

Epilogue

Sunday, July 28, 2002

I had thought that the first day of spring was a good place to end this journal, but now something else has happened here, and I want to write about it.

It's another national news story. It began on Wednesday night, and it continued until today. Here's a brief summary:

Nine miners at Quecreek broke through a wall, only to discover that it was holding back an underground river. They should have drowned right then, but they were somehow able to scramble to higher ground. Still, they were trapped, and were almost certainly going to die down there. That was Wednesday. The Quecreek Mine is in Somerset County, just a few miles from where United flight 93 crashed in September.

It's incredible. Two national stories within a year, within a few miles of each other, and within a short distance from Blackwater, where nothing ever used to happen.

The Quecreek Mine disaster began five days ago. I have been watching it on and off all that time on the news.

I took a break yesterday, though, to help Jimmy, Aunt Robin, Arthur, and Cody move. Jimmy has now been drug-free for seven months, but Arthur says he has been struggling. Memories of Warren are a definite trigger for him, so it's good for him to move away from that place.

Jimmy rented a truck and transported the entire trailer to a lot on the north spur, about five miles away. The underground fire has been extinguished there, and families are allowed to move back in.

A crew that included Mom, Lilly, and Jenny came up to move

the small stuff. It all went smoothly. By midafternoon we had the trailer in its new location and water and electricity running into it.

By dinnertime the job was finished, and Aunt Robin went to pick up four boxes of Domino's pizzas. We chowed down on those and drank various Coca-Cola products.

While we were eating, Lilly filled us in on a job she was hoping to get. She explained, to everybody's surprise but mine, "A new federal program is starting up in Haven County to help teenage drug users. They're looking for counselors, and all you need is a high school degree. So I applied."

Mom looked puzzled, but in a good way.

Lilly continued: "I've had two interviews. I think they really like me."

Mom said, "Of course they like you!"

Other people said the same. And I realized that, after all these years, I now like her, too.

Jenny, Lilly, and Mom went back home soon after that, but I stayed. Arthur and I got the TV running in the living room. The Quecreek Mine disaster was the big story, 24/7, on the local station. We were determined to stick with it, along with thousands of other people. If those miners were going to die, they would not do it alone.

Aunt Robin put Cody to bed at nine o'clock. She and Jimmy watched the news with us until eleven, when she said good night.

Jimmy stayed with us for another hour, staring straight ahead but not speaking. When he finally wandered off to bed at midnight, things looked pretty grim for the miners. They had been trapped underground, freezing and wet, with no food or water, for five days.

But then suddenly, miraculously even, the news started to change. Special equipment had arrived. Contact had been made. And within one hour, the tragic story had turned 180 degrees.

The TV screen showed a narrow yellow cylinder being lowered into a shaft. It was thin enough to fit into a drilled hole but wide enough to hold a human body.

Arthur and I sat forward on the couch. Arthur started praying, I think, in a language that only he could understand. Then, over the next two hours, his prayers were answered.

The yellow cylinder returned to the surface and was opened by the rescue crew. A coal miner, covered completely in black soot, soaked to the skin, was pulled out of it. And he was alive.

The cylinder went down again, back into the bowels of the earth. It came up again fifteen minutes later. Another shivering black body was extracted from it. Another miner was still alive.

Here are the names of the miners and their rescue times: Randy L. Fogle—1:00 a.m.; Blaine Mayhugh—1:15 a.m.; Tom Foy—1:30 a.m.; John Unger—1:40 a.m.; John Phillippi—1:55 a.m.; Ron Hileman—2:10 a.m.; Dennis Hall—2:23 a.m.; Robert Pugh—2:30 a.m.; Mark Popernack—2:45 a.m.

All nine miners emerged from that cylinder alive and well. Arthur and I kept watching, mesmerized, as the TV station kept rerunning the tape.

Jimmy Giles came back out of the bedroom at 5:00 a.m., dressed in a white shirt and tie. He stood next to us and stared at the TV. He looked like he was having a rough morning. His face was flushed and his eyes were watery. He was facing some major triggers.

Arthur took immediate action. He pointed at the screen and

exhorted Jimmy like a preacher. "Do you know what happened here, Jimmy Giles?"

Jimmy gulped, his Adam's apple rising and falling. He replied weakly, "What? What happened? Did they all die?"

"Hell no! They did not die! They all got out! Every one of them. Nine for nine!"

Jimmy seemed to change with that news. His eyes came into focus. His shoulders pulled back.

Arthur continued: "Miners went in and got them, goddammit. Coal miners went in and got their own out. Because nobody else would, because nobody else could! Now, what do you think of that?"

Jimmy's eyes filled with tears. "That's good."

Arthur pointed at the screen. "That's great stuff! Right there!"

Jimmy added quietly, "That's what you did for Warren. You went in and got him out."

Arthur answered humbly, "Yeah. I guess so." Then he returned to that preacher way, his voice rising. "The devil's after us, Jimmy Giles. Right here, right where we are living. He's after us something fierce, huh? He came at us from above on 9/11 and took forty souls. You know about those souls, don't you?"

"Oh yeah."

"He came at us from all sides with the meth plague, and all the zombies walking around here, and he killed a lot of us. Didn't he? He killed Warren that way. Didn't he?"

"He did."

Jimmy's tears spilled over onto his lined cheeks, running down in rivulets.

Arthur concluded by saying, "And now he came at us from below, in the Quecreek Mine. He trapped nine miners, and there was no way for them to escape. But they *did* escape, didn't they? We got nine souls back today, didn't we? We got nine back."

Jimmy responded, "Amen," and Arthur's work was done. He didn't need to say anything else; Jimmy was completely transformed. He straightened his back. Then he pulled up the knot on his tie (not all the way, but close enough for government work).

I got up and joined Jimmy and Arthur near the door. When Jimmy opened it, I saw a faint red glow in the east lighting the tops of the mountains.

I watched Jimmy's lips carefully, trying to read them. Then I figured out what he was saying. He kept whispering over and over, "Amen. Amen to that. Amen."

He was going to be all right.

We all were.

One day at a time.

Arthur and I stood out on the roadway, on either side of Jimmy, as he waited for the WorkForce van. The air smelled fresh and the birds were singing. It was a beautiful Pennsylvania morning.

It was like a morning in the Garden of Eden.

Like a morning in paradise.

About the Author

Edward Bloor is the critically acclaimed author of the novels *Taken, London Calling, Story Time, Crusader,* and *Tangerine.*

He grew up in Trenton, New Jersey, and currently lives in Winter Garden, Florida.

Praise for *Taken*

"Charity Meyers is thirteen when she is kidnapped in the year 2036. Her father remained wealthy even after the World Credit Crash, and since child-snatching has become 'a major growth industry,' she is trained in what to expect. According to the rules, her parents will turn over the contents of their home vault within twenty-four hours. But this isn't a 'normal' kidnapping. As the hours pass and tension heightens, we learn Charity's back story. Taut and disturbing, the ending is a gobsmack."   —*Daily News*

Praise for *London Calling*

"Seventh-grader Martin Conway gets to time-travel in this beautifully written story of an unusual friendship that grows between Martin, an unhappy boy in modern-day New Jersey, and Jimmy Harker, a British boy living through the bombing of London by German airplanes in World War II. There's a little bit of history and a little bit of fantasy in this book. And there's a lot to think about as Martin struggles with his sometimes rocky relationship with his father, and Jimmy struggles with life in a war zone. Read the first three pages and then see if you can put this book down."
—*The Washington Post*